# HOW FULL OF BRIARS

## ORDINARY SORCERY
### BOOK FOUR

## ALEA HENLE

eISBN: 978-1-952735-12-7

ISBN: 978-1-952735-25-7 (print, as by Alea Henle) 978-1-952735-13-4 (inactive print, as by A.R. Henle)

Published by Crabgrass Publishing

Editing by Rare Bird Editing

Cover design by Augusta Scarlett



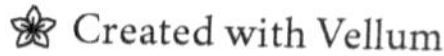 Created with Vellum

# ACKNOWLEDGMENTS

*With gratitude for Ronkwahrhakónha D ("Lune") and others who provided helpful advice.*

*This book is dedicated to the memory of my mother.*

*O, how full of briers is this working day world!*

William Shakespeare

# CONTENT WARNING

Includes references to instances of female violence, abortion, suicide, racism, homophobia, and abusive domestic and parental relationships.

# PART I
# MARTA

Thursday 13 September –
Thursday 20 September 1951

## BLACKMAIL

$\mathscr{P}$ossession of magic never changes a person's nature. A slob with magic remains a slob. Sadly, Marta Floding's children took after their father no matter how hard she tried.

Marta's once-starched white linen nurse's uniform had lost any remaining crispness but bore only minor stains along the calf-length skirt. Her feet hurt from hours of standing on hard floors in thin-soled shoes.

As she opened the kitchen door, she swept shaky fingers through her light brown hair, dislodging hairpins and her nurse's cap. A fleck of pink polish flaked off a fingernail as she caught the pins. She dropped them into a blue-and-white ceramic pot on the countertop, laying the peaked cap over— then came to a complete stop as the room's condition registered.

Dust bunnies gathered along the base of the enameled cabinets. Spots of dried food adorned the blue-and-white tiled counter. The room always appeared smaller when dirty: cabinet fronts narrower, tiles dingier, and the old-fashioned overhead light grayer. An autumnal breeze blew through the open window over the kitchen sink, fluttering through the yellow-and-green voile curtains and bringing the smells of peanut butter and souring orange juice rather than fresh-cut grass blowing over from the neighbors.

Two school bags rested on the floor in the far corner, the edge of a textbook rising above the ties of one and crumpled papers bearing mathematical scrawls half-stuffed into another.

A bright yellow plate boasting an array of crumbs and gobs of peanut butter and strawberry jam rested unevenly on the round kitchen table. Two other matching sandwich-sized splotches on the blue-and-white check tablecloth suggested all three of her children had served themselves supper. Used glasses with orange juice residue rested on the table as well. A third of a loaf of bread remained in the open plastic bag. Jars of peanut butter and jam sat nearby, the hilts of table knives rising out of them.

"Douglas? Scotty? Janie?"

No answer.

One or more had likely gone down the block, given the distant sounds of a whiffle ball game underway in the empty lot at the end. Or off to the houses of those parents who still allowed their children to play with hers.

Leaving the mess for her despite all three knowing several clean-up spells.

She stretched, shaking her arms to ease sore muscles. The light outside turned golden as the sun inched down toward the horizon. Time enough for the children to linger before curfew.

A flash of white caught her eye—a sharp corner under the plate. An envelope. Just the right size for an overdue check from her ex-husband? The plate slid off, revealing a rectangle too long and thin, with her address typed rather than scrawled and bearing a harsh red stamp: Past Due.

Her nails pressed into her palms and she clenched her teeth. She drew in a hiss, and slapped the envelope. It vanished in a flash, going to join the other bills in the top drawer of her bureau, waiting for the weekend when she'd write checks and try not to curse her ex-husband literally or figuratively. Finger by finger, she uncurled her fists.

Only to startle at a hard rap on the door.

The curtains over the door window covered all but a sliver. A face appeared in the gap, one Marta had never expected to see there again in her lifetime: Bettina Bullen, the uncrowned queen of the Timms College faculty wives and a stalwart at the country club. Marta's next-door neighbor for nearly two decades, who once upon a time served as her mentor in adjusting to life as a faculty wife. Although Bettina was only a few years older than Marta, she'd always feared Bettina more than the dean's wife or the college president's—not because Bettina had more power, but she had less mercy.

As always, the other woman appeared exquisitely put together. Not a wavy, blonde hair out of place in her shoulder bob, nor any stray mark or flake of dust marring her makeup. The angle of the last sunlight turned her face into a burnished golden mask.

Even in the days when Marta didn't work outside the house, she'd never managed such a flawless appearance. Magic helped, but after a long, busy day, she had no chance of matching Bettina's physical perfection.

When the doorknob started to turn, Marta jerked in a moment's panic.

And vanity.

A few snaps and waves tidied the kitchen and laid on a glamor of cleanliness. The dishes and flatware turned clean and tucked themselves away in cupboards and drawers. The bag of bread and jars of peanut butter and preserves closed themselves and returned to their proper places. The counter and tablecloth restored to immediate post-laundering state.

Another spell refreshed her from head to toe. A few strands of hair still fell out of her chignon and her feet ached regardless, but wrinkles and spots vanished from her uniform along with the run in her left stocking. A faint clamminess on her cheeks indicated her makeup had returned to her normal work appearance.

Marta sank onto a chair. If she had ever thought this day might come, she'd have warded against it—or at least warded the door so Bettina couldn't walk in so easily.

The other woman stopped a step inside, the latch clicking as the door shut. Her pale blue shirtdress with elbow-length sleeves stood out against the white frame. Her legs gleamed under stockings, feet slipped into low-heeled shoes. All dressed up as though off to a dinner party. Her rose perfume filled the room within a matter of breaths.

But her face had a whitish cast under the light beige powder and base. Her hands knotted around the strings of a net bag so tight the knuckles turned bloodless in stark contrast to the deep pink of her nails.

The bag swayed, partially hidden by her calf-length skirt. Marta squinted, catching only fractured glimpses of the contents—something blue. Shoes perhaps.

Despite the strength of Bettina's favorite rose perfume, it mixed with grass and fallen leaves and even a hint of mold.

"Welcome, neighbor." Marta remained in place. "Have a seat." She waved a hand at the other chairs circling the table.

"How kind of you." The older woman didn't move from the door. "I fear this is not a social call."

Of course not. All social niceties ended the day Marta's husband moved to a boarding house on the other side of the college campus and word of the pending divorce leaked. Bettina's children were told not to play with Marta's. An extreme response, as other faculty wives might have dropped Marta but let their children remain friends.

Likewise Marta's kitchen privileges at the Bullen house, where she'd once freely entered after a knock as Bettina had just done, had been revoked.

"What do you need, a cup of sugar? An egg or two?" This time Marta waved at the refrigerator, lips pulling to one side.

"You misunderstand me."

"You haven't set foot in this house, or acknowledged my existence, for over five years. Why now?" Marta asked.

"I need *your* kind of help."

Breath catching in her throat, Marta stilled. Slid a hand discreetly along her side and pinched her thigh. After the brief flare of pain, nothing changed. "Oh?"

"You know what I mean." Bettina's white-knuckled hands shook, bag vibrating so hard the contents rustled.

Marta rested against the chair, crossing her arms over her chest. "You're going to have to spell it out."

"You believe in . . . magic."

Believed it, used it, and enjoyed using it.

"You don't." Then again, since their families had lived largely parallel lives for so long, perhaps things had changed. "You never did before."

When Marta first moved to Timms, Ohio, as a young faculty wife, she'd misread Bettina's cautious welcome.

She'd asked Bettina outright if she was a sorcerer. The other woman's mocking laughter still sometimes echoed in Marta's ears.

Most sorcerers grew up with magic, learning at the knees of one or both parents and knowing the sorcerers their families knew.

Yet every year a few magicless witnessed spells and managed not only to *not* talk themselves out of believing what they'd seen but accept the truth of magic. They turned sorcerer, the lucky meeting other sorcerers and being brought into the sorcerous communities. The unlucky struggled, often causing chaos and confusion.

Unfortunately, powerful magicians had driven magic underground during the Enlightenment—or so Marta had always been told. Nine times out of ten, disbelief in magic proved more powerful than belief. Every sorcerer had nightmare tales of casting familiar spells that had always worked before only to have them fail because a magicless person was around.

Even the most powerful spell could be broken by a magicless person who didn't realize it existed.

There was no easy way for sorcerers to identify each other without risk of ridicule or worse from the magicless when they guessed wrong. Sorcerers relied on hints, allusions, innuendo, and the occasional opportune catching of others in the act.

Under the circumstances, Marta had no qualms asking, "Have you turned sorcerer?"

"No." Bettina's nostrils flared and her eyes narrowed. She drew in a hissing breath, ire dissolving into disgust and discomfort. "Something happened that I have not been able to explain or fix."

Opening the bag, she pulled out a pair of blue kitten-heel shoes, releasing a hint of pine and leaf mold mixed with mud. The shoes were once lovely and suitable for wearing to festive occasions, complete with small ribbon bows over the toes, but no more. Clumps of muck and bracken covered one sole. Additional clods and drip marks clung to the sides of both. The impression was of someone having stepped into a mud puddle and not done anything to remove the resultant splatter.

The corners of Bettina's lips curled as she set the shoes atop the clean tablecloth.

They weren't Bettina's—too small—but she had three daughters. The eldest girl attended the college, and Bettina and her husband had for some reason agreed to let her live on campus. The youngest was no older than Marta's Janie.

That left Bettina's second child, Lois, as the likeliest owner of the shoes.

Lois. When younger, she'd seemed a shy child, and one who'd taken to heart the adage children should be seen and not heard. Brown of hair and eye, with pale quick-to-burn skin that meant she often stayed inside or lingered in the shadows. She'd become bookish, last Marta knew, though she tried to pay as little attention to her neighbors as possible.

Marta waited, legs crossed at the ankle, knees turned to one side, and hands folded neatly in her lap.

"Well?" Bettina crossed her arms, rapping red-tipped fingers against her elbows.

"I don't see the problem."

"Lois and Evelyn sleep in the back right bedroom. There is no way in or out except to pass by my bedroom and down the stairs, which creak. I would hear if either of them tried to sneak out." Bettina lifted her chin. "I've caught Charles every time he's tried."

That hardly served as evidence of Bettina's ability to wake at the creak of a step. Her cherished son had likely never stepped lightly in his life. Now, Marta's Scotty she wouldn't put past walking silently enough to sneak out.

"Evelyn swears her sister hasn't left the room in the night." Both sets of long fingernails rapped against Bettina's shoulders. Her whole body vibrated. "The shoes were clean and tidy when Lois went to bed last Saturday. The next morning . . ."

She waved a shaky hand, then gave up and finally perched on the edge of a chair. When she tapped the side of a shoe, clods of dirt fell off. A woodsy scent wafted through the room.

"The mud was fresh when I found them. Clinging to the shoes, covering them, though there was nothing on the carpet." Bettina nudged the dirt with her fingernails, sweeping it into a tidy pile albeit with dusty tracks left behind on the tablecloth. "I scolded Lois the first time it happened, though she insisted she hadn't been anywhere and couldn't explain how her shoes had been ruined—the lovely gold-and-white I bought her for prom last spring, too! This is the fourth pair. The other shoes at least were floppy sandals she wore for those horrid barn hops the theater club insisted on throwing this summer to raise money. Four pairs of shoes ruined, even after I locked the door from outside. She insists it wasn't her, yet it's only ever *her* shoes."

Marta picked up the left shoe, sliding her hand into it to avoid the mud. More clods flecked off to litter the tablecloth. Bettina swept them into the growing pile.

A few pine needles, one with a drop of resin, mixed with the earth on the sole. Marta coaxed a pine needle out with her own pale-pink nails. She set the shoe back on the table, might as well since the cloth would need laundering no matter how Bettina scraped up the dust.

Cupping the needle in a hand, Marta cast a small spell. She did her best to keep the gesture that triggered the spell—blowing on the needle—as innocuous as possible. If Bettina hadn't turned sorcerer, or accepted sorcery, then the only way Marta could work sorcery in her presence was to do so in a way the other woman wouldn't recognize.

Marta sought information. *Where did the needle come from? How did it come to attach to the shoe?*

For an instant, the dark of deep night wrapped around her. Slivers of moonlight flickered through trees. Shards of pain, despair, anger, zipped through Marta. Then her feet twitched and she tensed her legs, resisting the urge to rise and dance a circle around the table.

Bettina's gaze fixed on Marta, showing no signs of noticing Marta's sorcery.

"What do you want of me?" Marta set the pine needle down atop the shoe.

"I want this to stop. Whatever it is, whoever it is. If she's getting out despite all I've done to protect her until the right . . ."—Bettina sucked in breath with a sharp hiss, her hands rising and curling into claws—"then make it so she can't. If someone else is doing this, convince them to leave us alone."

"All of that, from someone you can't bear to acknowledge in public?" Marta dusted her fingers against the soft tablecloth.

"It's your own fault for getting a divorce. I don't want that rubbing off on my family." Bettina gave an overly sweet smile, mouth just wide enough to flash sharp, white teeth. "Isabel and Evelyn are both handfuls already, thinking they know better than me. I've enough to do keeping Charles from being too much like his father. Lois is my good child. She doesn't deserve this."

"Lois is a sweet girl." Marta nearly choked on this rendition of Bettina's family, as she opened her hands and stretched them out to either side. "But you've given me no reason to be of assistance."

"You enjoy your job, don't you?" Bettina cast a speaking look at Marta's uniform.

A cold sensation lodged at the base of Marta's spine. "Is that a crime?"

"You need it, too." The other woman sat back, hands and legs delicately crossed. "That makes it a vulnerability."

"How so?"

"Say I go to the dean of students, or perhaps the president. I'm troubled. I've heard such a horrid story about Dr. Thomson, what he likes to do in his free time and who with."

"Have you been peering into windows?" Marta mirrored Bettina's posture, leg muscles twitching.

"I have my sources. Are you going to tell me I'm wrong and he isn't perpetrating illegal and immoral acts?"

"He's a good man, and an excellent doctor," Marta said. "I've never seen him do anything that would be worth firing him for."

"That doesn't matter." Bettina gave a dismissive wave. "The point is, he's a bad influence. A word in the right ear, and the administration will investigate and find I'm correct. That's the end of him as the college's resident physician." She flicked motes of dust from her fingernails.

"That would be a pity." Marta swallowed, mouth gone dry. "Dr. Thomson's done very well here."

"It won't be just him they let go. There will be questions. About what you and the other nurses knew and why you didn't say anything. Hardly appropriate behavior for staff. Perhaps even a second look at last winter's tragedy, and whether there wasn't something else brewing behind it. I imagine most of you would go. No doubt the president would give orders to clean house and have a new doctor hire whomever he wanted, which would not include you." Bettina tilted her head, a half-smile on her face.

"Is that a threat?"

"Such a nasty little word." Bettina leaned in, gaze fixed on Marta. "It's a promise."

Marta licked her lips. Acquiesce to Bettina's demand, or suffer an investigation into Thomson's private life. The latter would result in much pain and many dismissals, and Marta needed her paycheck.

Equally, Marta needed to ensure Bettina never again endangered Marta's livelihood with tales, true or false.

To do that, she'd bend to the threat this once and find the answers Bettina sought. Tit for tat, uncover secrets to bind Bettina's mouth on other matters.

"I take it you're offering a bargain: I pledge to investigate the situation for you, and in return you commit to doing nothing to endanger my employment?" Marta asked.

"You find the answer, and I'll hold my tongue." Bettina scarcely blinked.

"I do everything within my power to find the answer, and in return you hold your tongue, head, and hands, and never jeopardize my livelihood again."

"Done." Bettina extended a smooth hand, her manicure perfect.

"Done." Marta matched it with her work-worn fingers and home-done nails.

Sorcerous spells could work on the magicless, one only had to be careful in casting them. Bettina had just agreed to keep her mouth shut . . . as long as Marta managed to unravel the puzzle of Lois's shoes.

Bettina gripped the edge of her chair, about to rise.

Marta forestalled her with a raised hand. "I will need more information. A chance to inspect Lois's room and speak to your family."

"You may have access to the house tomorrow night between the hours of seven and nine. No one will be home. We all have plans elsewhere." Bettina inclined her head, lips stretched in a thin, mirthless smile. "But you may not speak to anyone in my family. If you have questions for them, drop a line in the mailbox—in a sealed envelope, of course—and I will do the same with any replies."

With that, Bettina whisked herself up and out of the house, leaving the shoes behind.

# SHOES

*A* clod of dust dropped onto the tablecloth with Bettina's departure. Marta's hands and jaw ached. She unclenched her fingers one by one, then picked up the shoes. More mud flaked off the left toe, forming a dusty half-circle on the blue-and-white checked tablecloth. The leather beneath had a dull cast, but nothing a bit of elbow grease or a touch of sorcery couldn't tidy up quick. If the rest of the muck fell off as cleanly, the shoes would be quite wearable. The leather still had a new-shoe smell, albeit mixed with evergreen and fresh mud.

Bettina could clean them herself, if she cared. Blackmail only stretched so far.

Where the toes and heels pressed against the cloth, faint stains began to reappear. Orange juice, peanut butter, strawberry jam—the very mess Marta had banished before Bettina's arrival. Unfortunately, her cleanliness spell had been half illusion.

The shoes were soft along the top, stiff where the leather had gotten damp. They were just the right size for throwing, but no sense giving Bettina the satisfaction, or having to replace the glass in the door.

Instead, Marta set the shoes on a chair and yanked up the tablecloth. The well-worn fabric scrunched into a satisfactory ball, and then thudded nicely against the wringer-washer tucked away in the pantry. One more item for the next wash day.

Such a fuss over a pair of shoes. Threats. Blackmail. All so that Bettina didn't have to admit her daughter might sneak out at night without her knowing.

Marta wouldn't have expected it of Lois, but people changed. Even a worm might turn fierce or daring, whether or not Bettina liked it. No doubt why she was coming down harder on Lois, to the point of dragging Marta into the mess.

Head whirling, Marta slapped together a peanut butter and jelly sandwich using the fixings her children had left.

She ate over the sink, breadcrumbs dotting the piled dishes—the better to stare at out the window at the house next door.

Bettina's house sat on a large corner lot. Only the back portion was visible, but that sufficed. Beige stone lintels over windows and doors interrupted the red brick walls. Stones and bricks were rough, but set so that even a daredevil boy couldn't climb up or down without help, such as from a rope slung out a window.

How would Lois have gotten out? She couldn't have climbed down the wall, with no tree near. Especially not in those shoes if she wanted to keep them pretty—though apparently she hadn't, and hadn't minded having them discovered dirty.

So the girl must have crept along the stairs and gone in and out the front or back door. Bettina might insist she'd have woken, but so thought many parents. Though surely

Bettina would have noticed dirt tracked through the halls even if she slept through.

Then again, Lois might have removed her shoes and gone about in her stocking feet.

If so, why not have a care to clean the shoes as best she could?

Marta wrapped a yellowed apron over her front and washed the dishes by rote rather than spell. She was already tired and needed to conserve sorcerous energy. The ammoniac detergent and the clink of plates settling into the drainer to dry barely registered. Only the warm water penetrated, countering the chill running along her spine.

Surely Bettina hadn't stumbled across a true magical mystery.

The first rule of sorcery was that anything was possible—but possible didn't mean probable.

Spells required imagination, belief, magical power, and symbolic action to bring the ingredients together. Mess up one element, and failure was the result. Some failures proved fatal.

The best sorcerers either had really good imaginations or relied on spells learned from others, or both. Marta considered herself in the middle of the pack. She could innovate successfully, but didn't do it often. Everyday spells—cleaning, cooking, taking care of household chores—were her bread and butter.

Wiping her hands off, Marta removed the apron and hung it up, eyes scarcely leaving the shoes.

They were all she had. No chance to speak to Lois, or even ask Bettina for more details.

Seen at an angle, the dirt pattern differed. Lois had stepped heavily enough on her right foot for clods to fully encircle the sole. The left, however, only had mud marks around the toe, but thicker and higher. A full and a half step.

Where?

That, at least, should be simple enough to discover.

She doused the room with a more thorough cleaning spell, careful to exempt the shoes. The last dregs of sunlight gave the room a warm glow as shadows grew in corners the overhead light never fully reached. A distant, rousing cheer floated up from the whiffle ball game.

Licking the last film of peanut butter from her lips, Marta retrieved the newspaper from next to the fireplace. Laid pages to cover the table. Inked lines of print and images blurred as she waved her hands.

Swirls. Curls. Then the ink settled into lines and boxes with the occasional curve. Instead of text, an accurate map of the city covered the table. The town hall and intersection of Main and High Streets sat dead center. The college campus sprawled to the east, bounded by a mix of fields and farmhouses save for the remnants of a forest lingering to the south. A rail line bisected the northwest section, not quite neatly dividing the depot and central commercial district from a poorer neighborhood where most, but not all, of the Black citizens dwelt. The small but growing Jewish neighborhood was also near the railroad station, most of the residents having relatives in nearby Cincinnati, and they'd started building a synagogue. Residential houses, including Bettina's and Marta's, filled the southwest, with additional houses being built at the edge of the map. Apartment homes and boarding houses were scattered throughout.

Without glancing away from the map, Marta nabbed one of the shoes. A tap set dirt floating down to sprinkle the paper.

She bent. Closed her eyes as tight. Imagined the dust showing her where it came from. Believed the spell would work. Offered power.

Blew.

Opening her eyes, she straightened and stare at the map. There should be one pile, marking where Lois had stepped hard enough in wet earth to mark her shoe.

Instead, there were three.

Bettina's house. Well, the shoes had been there until Bettina discovered them.

A spot near the depot and close to the high school, but not near enough to be sure that was the place meant, even though it would make a glimmer of sense.

The largest pile marked the forest spur that curved around the women's dorms, or rather the White female students' dorms. Black students were not allowed to live in the residence halls, something Marta hadn't realized until she'd become acquainted with some of the town's Black citizens.

Nothing connected the three spots, not even the faintest trail of dust.

The light pouring through the windows darkened to orange-gray, as the sun sank below the horizon. Children's voices called in the streets, approaching nearer. Little time remained before hers would burst in.

Foot tapping restlessly against the floor, Marta bent again. Brushed dust and ink into a single pile, turning the paper blank save an immense blot at the center.

Bending low, she exhaled, with more energy this time and eyes wide open.

*Show Lois when she stepped in the mud.*

Nothing for the count of three . . . four . . . Then on five the pile blew up. Ink and dust splattered her head and neck, hands and arms.

"Ick." Marta stumbled to the sink, blinking and trying not to swallow any of the ink or dust coating her tongue. Before she did more than turn on the water, the door squeaked open and the thundering horde that was her two younger children tumbled in.

Scottie first, all arms and legs and dirty from shoes to eyebrows. Although fourteen, he was made of dust and spit, and carried a whiffle bat high. His younger sister huddled behind him, equally dusty but far less sure of herself thanks to her father's over-loud opinions on unacceptable pastimes for daughters.

Janie peered up, eyes and mouth wide at her mother's disarray.

"Looks like we all need to clean up." Despite the foul taste still coating her tongue, Marta opened her arms wide. Wrapped her children in a warm embrace. This, at least, couldn't be taken from her. She wouldn't let it.

For a half-hour or so, she set aside all thoughts of shoes and Bettina with great success.

Until, cleaned and changed and children put to bed, Marta descended the stairs to the living room and noted the kitchen light still on. Her blue cotton dressing robe floated around her ankles, weighted hem hitting her when she came to a stop.

Her older son stood in the center, his short brown hair wind-ruffled. Wrinkles marred Douglas's shirt, especially where the strap of his book bag weighed against his shoulder, but otherwise he was neatly dressed. He had her modest height, rather than his father's additional five inches, paired with her father's stocky build and a phlegmatic temperament from she-had-no-idea-where. Unfortunately, save in cases such as this, he also had more than his share of adolescent male cluelessness.

The skin around his eyes barely crinkled as he tilted his head. Brown eyes flashed behind thick glasses held on by wire frames, the lenses in need of cleaning as usual. "New shoes?

"Never you mind about those." She pushed the chair in, hiding the shoes under the table. "Had a good evening?"

"Yeah."

A one-word answer, typical these days. He hefted his bag and inched toward the door. The corner of a textbook poked out. No doubt he'd been studying, as he'd made no secret of wanting to get out of Timmsville, Ohio, as soon as he graduated high school at the end of the year. Preferably with a full scholarship to Arden College in Pennsylvania, where her parents lived, but ultimately he'd sworn to attend any college except Timms.

High school. Lois Bullen was in his year. Marta's hand tightened around the top of the chair.

"Do you see Lois much? Lois Bullen." She nodded in the direction of the Bullens' house.

"We have homeroom together." He jerked to a stop, elbows pressing against his sides. His torso faced the door, but he turned his head just enough to squint at her.

"And?"

"We don't talk. That is, she doesn't talk to me. Told me once that her mother didn't want her to and would know if she did, so she doesn't." A flush bloomed across his cheekbones.

"If you don't talk, do you do anything else?" Was he sweet on her?

The tips of his ears turned red, but his cheeks paled as he shook his head with a vengeance. "She's not . . . half the time she's hanging around the football players or the college guys."

Which didn't clarify how he felt about the girl, but indicated she had no interest in him. Yet it all went against what Marta would have expected of the quiet girl she remembered. "Lois? What is she, chasing a ring?"

"There's bets on she might wind up first to marry without even finishing out the year." He shrugged.

"What a switch." Marta shook her head. "She was always so quiet and studious. Now, her older sister? I wouldn't have put it past Isabel setting to marry and set up household as soon as she could. When she was a senior in high school, she had boys hanging all around their house." Several times Marta had had to inch the car out of her driveway, honking the whole way to keep from hitting them. "And went to every dance no matter where, high school, college, country club."

"Isabel's not a party girl anymore." Douglas lifted his chin. "She made Freshmen Dean's List last year."

"Did she?"

His ears turned redder. "I see her in the college library sometimes, when I study there."

"Well, tell her I say hi next time."

He ducked his head and stomped off up the stairs.

She watched, rubbing the smooth wood of the chair. His tidy clothes and book bag made more sense. Perhaps he'd been studying in the college library, maybe with Isabel, though even as a fond mother Marta couldn't envision that. Isabel would have had to change a lot more than turning scholar to take a fancy to Douglas. No matter how well Marta thought of her son, there were certain things expected of girls and boys in town.

Good looks matched to good looks.

Athletic success counted more than academic, as long as one made decent grades.

And girls went with older boys, or rather young men picked from girls a year or two younger.

Lois was evidently following in her sister's earlier path, favoring dances and fancy shoes and hanging around older boys.

Which still didn't explain why two-thirds of the dirt from her shoes had come from odd places. The pile on campus had been down near the women's dorms, not up by the men's.

Could she have witnessed magic and turned sorcerer? Yet if she had, surely whoever turned her would have taught her ways to avoid puzzling the magicless.

If only Bettina had agreed to let Marta talk to Lois! Yet little surprise that the mother kept her daughter away. From the very first, Bettina had contended Marta's merely filing for divorce made her a carrier of a moral disease and at risk of infecting others.

Marta picked up the shoes, dangling them and turning them around and around. They smelled of woods and mud, sweat and leather. Once pretty and highly suitable for dancing. More dirt flaked off, but otherwise the shoes didn't change.

More of a mystery than Marta expected—or wanted. But she had to uncover the answer, or at least find a way to stop whatever happened to Lois from happening again.

If not, Bettina would surely carry through on her threat to get Marta fired. One way or another.

# WARNING

Marta slipped through the back door into the infirmary. The stone walls retained some of the night's chill, as the building was slow to heat or cool. A whiff of ammonia cleared the early morning humidity from her lungs. The tiled floor was dry nearby, but half the floor gleamed wet under the harsh lights, and at the far end a Black cleaning woman wielded a mop and pail.

Marta stopped, her back against the thick wood door, and brushed any dust or grass cuttings from her uniform and stockings. Soft lines showed where the dress had hung awry in her closet, for she risen too late to touch it up with a hot iron.

Too late for anything, save a quick bite of cereal snatched between preparing her children's lunches. They'd left just enough bread and peanut butter and jam, but she'd have to stop by the grocery store after work.

Her hands trembled, nerves jangling. She plucked three times at a blade of grass that had gotten tangled in her hem. It broke, leaving an eighth of an inch behind. Despite the throbbing at her temples, she clapped her hands together in a quick cleansing spell.

Putting rather more power in than she'd meant.

Her uniform turned as fresh as when she'd first picked it up. All grass and dust vanished. The seams bore neatly pressed lines. The ladders starting to creep up her stockings reknit into solid, soft fabric covering her legs. Her nurse's cap settled more firmly atop her head. Even her white shoes glowed as though she'd risen in time to give them an extra polish.

"Good morning, Marta."

Marta jumped at the lyrical voice. She hadn't heard Esther Jacobsen emerge from the break room. The other nurse's shoes made little noise as she strode down the hall with mugs of coffee in both hands. Esther carried fewer inches than Marta and more years and pounds, but hustled twice as fast—a widow who lived with her brother and his family, she was always busy. Her cap bobbed, pinned atop a gray tichel that covered most of her hair and complemented her creamy complexion far more than the stark white of the uniform. Her dark brows rose inquiringly above soft brown eyes and ready smile, but she made no mention of Marta's spell.

"It's going to be a busy day. The semester has barely started, but already students fill the waiting room. The doctor is seeing a student with a broken ankle." Esther offered Marta one of the mugs.

The sharp taste and heady aroma drove away the last cobwebs of sleep. Following Esther a few steps down the hall, Marta tucked her lunch into the refrigerator in the break room, next to a tray of half-full vials. By the time she was done, she'd woken completely and registered Esther's unexpected presence.

"Good morning to you, too." Marta frowned and drained

her mug. The other nurse worked Sundays to Thursdays. "But whatever are you doing here? It's Friday. You should be off."

"Nancy asked me to cover for her. I can stay until early afternoon, but have to leave no later than three." Esther tilted her head as footsteps echoed down the hall and filled another mug with coffee. She set it on the battered metal table at the center of the room, then circled it. The chair legs squeaked against the floor as she tucked them under.

"Is she sick?"

"Again." Esther nodded, fingering the corner of her apron.

Nancy Davies, the youngest of the infirmary nurses, had called in sick at least three times since the start of classes, and looked pale and drawn the days she *had* worked. Marta had also twice caught her bent over a basin casting up her breakfast.

Easy to guess the cause, but not something for open speculation since pregnant nurses were subject to summary dismissal.

Married women had their husbands' wages to fall back on, or so the theory went.

Unmarried expectant women had best marry quickly, if they could.

"She promised she'll be back to work on Monday." Esther gave Marta a meaningful glance. Clearly the other nurse had also worked through the likely cause of Nancy's illness—and expected the younger woman to either announce an engagement and quick marriage on her return, or to come back without any further symptoms of pregnancy.

"To Nancy." Marta refilled her mug and lifted it, drinking deep.

Esther nodded and did likewise.

A moment later, Dr. Thomson strode in and grabbed the extra mug from the table. He'd drink or eat anything placed directly in front of him. Marta and the other nurses had learned early on to keep their food out of the way or lose it. Though where he put it all was a medical mystery, for he was tall, lean, and as cadaverous in appearance as old photos of Abraham Lincoln, whom he otherwise did not resemble at all. The doctor rejoiced in a shock of orange-brown hair atop his long, pale head, and matching whiskers that he never managed to completely shave away. His white lab coat swung open over a matching white shirt. The blue bowtie at his neck was a perfect match for the shade of his tailored pants. His hard-soled brown shoes ensured he couldn't sneak up on anyone in the infirmary.

"Morning, ladies. Ready for the day?" He left the emptied mug where he'd picked it up. He wove his fingers together, cracking them, and his brow furrowed.

"I need to speak to you at some point." Marta snatched the mug and set it in the sink to soak.

"Yes, yes. Later. Too many sick students for now. Four in the waiting room. No time to delay." He turned on his heels and strode out.

"Grab him at the end of the day, when he's too tired to run away." Esther patted Marta's arm as she followed in his wake.

Wise advice, but following it meant she'd have to wait through the whole day. Through sniffling student after student, half with bad colds or upset stomachs.

A White senior who'd stepped on a nail doing something stupid that he refused to admit.

Two likely cases of venereal disease although the young White men each, separately, insisted on only talking to the doctor and refused to tell her any symptoms she couldn't independently measure.

A female Black student with a twisted wrist accompanied by a much older White woman, one of the dean's secretaries, who didn't seem to hear the younger woman insisting she'd rather see Dr. Warren, the local Black doctor. Marta gently encouraged the secretary to return to her work, because only family members were allowed to accompany patients into the examination rooms. Once alone with Marta, the student again said she wanted to see the local Black doctor, with a dispirited air that suggested she was used to having to pick her battles. Marta checked to make sure the younger woman knew the way to Dr. Warren's office, then let her out the back door and disposed of the paperwork.

Just a normal weekday, made worse when Esther left at mid-afternoon with a cheery smile and wave. Despite the steady stream of patients, Marta kept one eye out for a chance to snatch a word with the doctor. Only a few words, enough to alert him—and maybe win her some mental ease?

By the end of the day, Marta's body ached from head to toe, despite a dose of paracetamol. Her stomach grumbled, unsatisfied with the tuna sandwich and apple she'd consumed hours earlier. She preferred to attribute her disinclination to approach the doctor to her physical condition rather than other causes.

The doctor's office resembled all the exam rooms, with white walls and a tall window although the panes were not glazed. A wide, wooden desk covered with papers sat at the center, with a cushioned chair for him and wooden for any visitors. Steel filing cabinets lined one wall. The other held a large painting of the building when first raised, a decade earlier.

His pen scratched at paper as he scrawled notes. It made noise, but not enough to cover the clatter of Marta's approach—or her knock on the doorframe.

The doctor's head jerked up as she entered, arms tightening at his side as he braced to rise.

"No more patients, at least not at the moment." She waved a hand to reassure him. "The rush seems to have slowed."

"Or the weekend begun. We'll see them on Monday instead." He sighed and laid the pen down, rubbing at his temples.

"Yes."

Marta closed the door almost all the way, leaving it a hair ajar. Stroking the wood, she imagined a sorcerous barrier infusing the doorway to ensure privacy and offer warning if a patient entered the waiting room.

"Have a seat." He waved at the wooden chairs. His chair creaked as he sat back, weaving his fingers together. Although not a sorcerer, he shivered as though sensitive to the magic floating in the air. It could be nothing—or perhaps he'd witnessed magic and managed to talk himself out of believing in it one too many times. "What's wrong? Your ex-husband giving you problems?"

"No, nothing in that line." She swallowed, mouth dry, as she settled onto the edge of the chair and gripped the sides. "I had a visitor the other night. An old acquaintance, you might call her. My next-door neighbor."

He frowned and shook his head.

"Bettina Bullen."

That got a reaction. His back straightened, jaw clicked shut, and eyes narrowed.

"She didn't come right out and say anything, but hinted at rumors,"—Marta stared at him, not moving her gaze so much as an inch—"and what might happen if they were reported to the president or the dean of students."

"Rumors about me." No doubt in his voice.

"Yes."

He yanked at his hair. "How long have you—"

Marta raised a hand, stopping him. "It's not my business whether you prefer women or men or sheep."

"No sheep." He met her gaze, chin high and throat muscles flexing.

"Just as well, since few of the farmers hereabouts raise them." She tried to grin, but it felt fake even to her.

He leaned back, eyes narrowing as he studied her. "You're taking this calmly."

"A few years ago, before my divorce, I might've taken this differently." Marta shrugged. "But you know what they say about divorcées, don't you?"

"Man hungry?"

She nodded. "Which I'm not, though no one seems willing to believe I'm not ever risking myself or my children under any man's thumb again." Her turn to narrow her eyes. "You've never hit anyone, have you?"

"Only in self defense." He shook his head, gaze softening for a moment.

"That makes you better than my ex."

"I keep my oaths to do no harm or injustice to my patients." He gripped the arms of his chair, knuckles white. "What I do in my personal life has nothing to do with that."

"But not everyone will believe it if it's reported to the president." Marta leaned forward. "Bettina wants me to do something for her. She promised to keep her mouth shut—if I succeed." She grimaced, snapping her jaw. "I thought you should be warned."

If one person had guessed, someone else might too. Still, better that he was on the alert.

Best of all would be for Marta to unspool the mystery of the shoes, seal the bargain with Bettina, and close her mouth on the matter.

# ENVY

Marta never envisioned being a housebreaker. She lacked the right kind of attire—her closets held no slinky outfits suitable for skulking about. A decorous mourning suit for funerals and a single little dress constituted her only black items. Instead, she took refuge in her gardening clothes: ratty blue shorts, a matching shirt, and a scarf tied over her hair. The warm late-summer breeze tickled her ankles, sockless feet slung into old canvas shoes. She'd spelled everything clean, the better not to track any dirt in, but it was hardly what most of her former friends donned on Friday nights.

So much for being the seductive divorcée. Then again, extra men were welcome at carefully planned faculty and country club dinner tables, but extra women were not.

Even lurking amidst the overgrown grass in the backyard, puttering over the vines clambering up a trellis, she couldn't avoid noticing neighbors' cars tooting about, men and women laughing and chattering. Dinner parties, bridge parties, meetings at the club, with younger children left behind in the care of their older siblings or sitters or off for overnights.

All things she'd left behind. Lost. Thrown away some said —her former mother-in-law among them—for a fuss and bother over a normal man's temperament.

She didn't miss them, except when she did.

The gray twilight helped hide the overgrown lawn. She'd have to haul out the mower herself, or nag Douglas to mow once more before winter. The growing cloud cover smelled of rain, so better to venture over to the Bullens' now than dally and risk tracking mud in or out.

She tried to focus on that and other mundane matters— her younger children in the house probably reading past their bedtimes and imagining she didn't know. Well, Janie reading, but Scottie more likely arranging and re-arranging his beloved baseball cards. Douglas off who-knew-where. The drug store, perhaps, and what she wouldn't give for a nice strawberry ice cream soda right now. Something to soothe her jumping nerves.

All because Bettina thought she could wave a hand and make Marta dance to her will. Worse, she was right. Marta had bound herself with the spell. No easy way back out now without a lot of misery.

Still, Marta had permission to go into the Bullens' house for the first time in years. She'd see how the other half lived again.

The outside of the Bullen house hadn't changed, apart from a coat of paint turning the trim from green to blue. The three-story Victorian brick edifice rose high against the darkening sky, oddly thin despite their having a corner lot. A small porch at the front, and none at the back. Just a narrow passage past the cellar entrance to the kitchen door. By no means an inviting residence, but rather an old dowager of a house pulling in her skirts to keep from being contaminated by encroaching neighbors. Rose bushes planted along the white picket fence edging the sidewalk only enhanced the effect, with luxuriant white and red blooms even this late in September.

A few lights on in the front room, giving off glints through the cracks between blue curtains.

No one home, Bettina had said.

"Where are the Bullens?" Turning over a shaky palm, Marta blew up a small globe with flickering images. Finger flicks cycled through them in order of age. The younger two off to sleepovers at friends' houses. The oldest curled up in her dorm room studying. Bettina and her husband at a bridge party, the kind Marta had once regularly attended. She didn't miss the cards, but the conviviality.

Marta paused in the middle, when checking on Lois's whereabouts. The girl sat in the movie theater, her pink shirtdress complementing the burgundy plush upholstery. Curvy and round-faced, the girl carried a dwindling layer of puppy fat, with soft brown hair and a creamy complexion that owed a little to artifice. Colors flickered in reflection against her face as she gazed up at the screen.

A young man slouched next to her as he slipped an arm around her waist, and she swallowed hard. He had a strong enough resemblance to the college president to be one of the sons—the same long face, wide nose, and square jaw. Marta couldn't recall his name, but surely the middle son had graduated from the high school a year or two earlier? Then again, no doubt he attended Timms, where freshmen and sophomore men tended to seek out dates from the high school, as the junior and senior men picked over the younger college women.

Her then-husband had nodded approvingly at the custom when they first moved to the town. The man should be the older, more responsible, in any marriage. That's what he'd done, picking her, and she'd gone along. One way or another, most of her bad luck traced back to agreeing to go out with him in the first place. Believing in fairy tales of happy ever after and handsome princes, never considering they might turn to frogs or worse after marriage.

But fretting over that got her nowhere further.

Staying in shadows, she slipped from yard to yard. The back door was unlocked. Her hand rested on cool metal as she paused long enough to cast a look-away spell. Not invisibility, but the next best thing. She'd touch little-to-nothing, stay only as long as she had to, and leave as soon as she could.

The hinges creaked as the door opened. Chill tremors rippled up and down her back. Drawing a deep breath, she ventured in. Winced when the door snapped shut hard on her heels. Her feet already hurt from her day's labors.

How long since she'd been in the house? Years, but some elements hadn't changed: the kitchen was immaculately clean, as always, and spacious. A big, gleaming refrigerator took pride of place in the kitchen, but not the one Marta remembered. This was their *second* new one since replacing the ice box. A full pantry with enough food stocked up to keep Marta and her children fed twice as long as what she had stored away.

The similarly tidy dining room gleamed, table bright as though freshly polished, likewise the immense hutch along one wall. Its beveled-glass doors allowed glimpses of the gold-rimmed dinnerware contained within, full service for twelve. A silver bowl atop the hutch offered a variety of apples. In contrast, the crystal vase in the center of the crisp-ironed, lace-edged white tablecloth featured a dozen red and white roses, their perfume filling the house.

The living room had changed the most. The Bullens had kept the thick blue-and-cream rug in the living room that Marta had always loved and envied. Its softness cushioned her shoes. The matching blue sofas and pale-wood end tables were new, likewise the walls papered with a light-blue and green pattern—and the television in a gilded wooden cabinet! No one could miss the fuss when it had been delivered or the party they'd thrown a few weeks later with all the faculty and their wives or girlfriends invited. Marta's ex-husband had stopped to pat his children on the head before sauntering off to join them.

Marta licked her lips. Her hands clenched and arms pressed so tight against her sides that her muscles ached. She unclamped her fingers one by one, then wove her hands together. Better to be in and out and done, without losing herself in bitterness. She pressed her thumbs against her lips and imagined a spell that would guide her, even if it drained her energy.

"Lead me to whatever information is here to be found. Show me whatever connects to the dirt on the shoes." Marta closed her eyes and held her breath, then opened wide. "Help me."

Nothing changed on the first floor. At first and second turn-around, her shoulders sank as she whirled seeking anything. It took a moment to register that the nothing included no footprints from front or back door, or on the stairs.

Whatever had ended in Lois's shoes being covered with dirt, she hadn't walked into the house wearing them. Could she have walked barefoot or in her stockings? But there were no *footprints*, not merely no shoe prints.

Yet at the top of the stair, a faint green luminescence beckoned.

Several steps groaned beneath her weight no matter how light Marta stepped as she tripped up. At the top, she rested one hand on the diamond-pointed newel for balance as she caught her breath, frowning all the while.

The luminescence split into three. One source, the strongest, lay down the hall toward the back of the house. Two others, both faint, came from the bedrooms to either side.

The second floor boasted four bedrooms and one bathroom, plus the stairway to the attic hidden behind a door. A quick glance there indicated nothing worth checking. Nor in the bathroom nor Bettina's son's bedroom—though he rivaled Marta's children for messiness.

The girls' bedroom matched the downstairs for tidiness. Both twin beds neatly made with pink-and-gold blankets tucked under fluffy gold-covered pillows. Whitewashed bureaus with the drawers closed and only a few trinkets atop each. A perfume stopper wasn't fully set, or perhaps a drop had been spilled, given the light rose fragrance permeating the chamber. One of the beds held a discarded outfit of a simple blue top with matching cardigan and a blue skirt, but otherwise all was neat.

A hint of luminescence surrounded that same bed, as though emanating from the sheets or mattress. Only a small, triangular shadow at the far corner of the mattress marred the light. It proved to be the corner of a piece of paper. Marta stooped and eased out a half-finished note addressed *Dearest, loveliest Sarah . . .*then tucked the paper back under the mattress.

A glow also lined the bottom of the closet door. Fingers cool despite the warm air, Marta cracked it open long enough to note the light came from the larger-size shoes—all of them, in unequal proportions.

If Lois hadn't turned sorcerer, she'd somehow gotten caught up in accidental magic. Marta wasn't sure which was worse.

Turned sorcerers were one set of headaches, requiring training from whichever sorcerer first realized they'd turned.

In contrast, accidental magic meant a sorcerer had put together all the ingredients for a spell—imagination, belief, power, action—without meaning to. Marta's mother had used the example of the Greek sorcerer Circe in reminding Marta, over and over and over again, to be careful with magic. Circe might have been merely venting, turning on the first man and calling him a pig without meaning to change him into one. But *not meaning to* was cold comfort for the man who became a pig.

The problem was, without talking to Lois, Marta had few ways of figuring out what was going on.

Though tempted to investigate further, a layer of sweat slicked her shirt to her back. Every moment she remained in the house risked discovery. It didn't matter that Bettina had given Marta permission. If someone other than she found Marta in the house, the other woman would hardly admit to it.

Marta stooped long enough to check the soles of Lois's shoes, and found all clear, although the sides of a few bore signs of thorough cleaning.

Hastening back down the hallway to the stairs, she paused and glanced at the other bedroom doors. Nothing ventured, nothing gained.

The master bedroom had the faintest light, but she moved into it first anyway. No light source on the big double bed with its fine lace coverlet, or the heavy matching mahogany furniture. Again, the light came from the closet. A full array of dresses filled the space, all requiring the kind of money or sewing time and skill that Marta no longer possessed.

But one of the many dress shoes emanated light. A little, and only from the left heel.

Quickstepping across the hall, Marta froze one step inside, hand wrapped around the doorframe.

This room had a double personality. Half was a sewing

room, with masses of cloth and ribbons ready to be fastened into delicious concoctions. A most definitively feminine space—and yet the single bed against the far wall was made with military simplicity and had a depression too large for Bettina or any of her daughters. As with Lois's room, the bed glowed—albeit far, far fainter—showing where a tall, heavy-set man had slept.

A matching line of luminescence shone at the bottom of the closet. While lighter than in Lois's room, it likewise came from an array of shoes. Men's shoes one and all. Men's shirts, jackets, and trousers' all neatly pressed, hung above. The closet held only one piece of female attire—an unfinished wedding dress pushed to the far end, but long enough that the raw silk hem glimmered in the faint green light of the shoes.

All of the shoes were polished to a fare-thee-well, with no sign of dirt. Yet whatever was going on had evidently ensnared Bettina's husband to some degree—if not her.

None of which she'd mentioned.

Shaking, Marta hustled down the stairs, flicking her fingers as she went to dissolve any and all evidence of her presence.

What had Lois got herself into?

# DREAMS

The smell of the woods. Evergreens as the base mixed with roses and anise. Earth warmed all day by the sun—but with the promise of rain, given the hint of the acrid smell preceding storms. Leaves turning, rustling overhead. Soft grass growing all around.

Marta lay on a bank of grass, on a small rise curving around the side of a clearing. A true grassy bed, of lush tender blades that bent and eased beneath her. A wind whistled—whispered—through the trees arching high. Their trunks and branches melded in the mix of moonlight and shadow. One stood out, a tall, old stump near the center. A few flowers rested against the thick roots still burrowing into rich earth: white roses and sprays of goldenrod.

The moon peeped over the edge of the trees, three-quarters strong and bright despite the shifting, growing cloud cover.

She did not move, felt no need. The ground eased her, offered rest and shelter.

She wasn't dead. She lived and breathed.

Thrum after thrum reverberated through her body and

the earth below. Her heartbeat, for it slowed as she lay slumped against the earth. Fabric rustled about her, light and filmy, but she lacked the strength to lift her head and peer about.

She lay back, slipping into the first easy sleep in longer than she could remember.

Cradled in a place of peace.

# CONNECTIONS

*M*arta paused, hands wrist-deep in hot water. Rubber gloves reduced the heat welling in her fingers, and her mobility. The sponge slipped from her hold to float down to the bottom of the kitchen sink, even as the last wisps of steam wreathed around her face. Loose strands of hair clung to her skin, though she'd wrapped a bandanna around her head before starting on the dishes. Damp spots made her yellow dimity apron cling to her blue shirt and knee-length shorts. Her stance shifted, feet slipping within the old flimsy shoes she'd donned without socks.

The back door stood open, screen door keeping out pests while offering a clear view of Scottie holding a bat and practicing his swing. The house lay silent behind her. Janie had gone over to a friend's right after lunch and Douglas likewise headed out.

Only Marta remained with the minor mess of lunch. Despite the harsh ammoniac scent filling the room, a hint of the forest whispered through. Her eyelids fluttered as a matching sense of peace wicked tension from her shoulders and neck.

She shook her head and plunged her hands back into the water. Grabbed the sponge and scrubbed the lunch dishes. Plate after plate—one, two, three, four—clinked as she rinsed them then set them in the drainer.

Yet all the while, peace lingered in her as though part of her remained at rest in the moonlit clearing she'd dreamt of two nights in a row.

"You wash up by hand?" A light rap on the kitchen door-frame was the only warning before the words broke Marta's reverie.

Marta jerked. Her fingers tightened on the butter knife, little help though it would be, until the tone registered. She gave the metal a sharp scrub, then set it in the drainer. "Come in, Ruby."

The young Black woman opened the door and strode through. Her dark hair was slicked along the sides of her skull and twisted into a tight bun at the back, and copper hoops a few shades lighter than her gleaming skin dangled from her ears. Her bright yellow shirt had elbow-length sleeves trimmed in orange that matched her shorts and the socks peeping above her brown shoes—not church attire but an outfit much more fitting for a Sunday than Marta's.

Ruby Warren's gaze traveled over Marta, making her aware of every drop of sweat and sticky hair. Such old hazel eyes in a round face, save for gentle curves under either cheekbone, otherwise young and unlined and suited to her status as a high school senior and one of Douglas's classmates.

His only sorcerous classmate, as far as Marta was aware, and she'd gone to trouble to find other sorcerers in town.

Magic was intensely personal, and unless sorcerers were particularly creative—which bore its own problems—they only learned or invented more spells by expanding their views of what was possible or working with other sorcerers.

The best sorcerers studied many different teachers, whether or not particularly creative. Marta's younger children were growing up quite inventive, but her oldest . . . imagination wasn't Douglas's strong suit.

Marta had scoured the town for sorcerers willing to teach Douglas. The few White sorcerers she'd knew of weren't interested for one reason or another. Three men had taken her husband's side in the divorce, fellow professors one and all, and declined unless Douglas's father made arrangements, which he somehow never got around to doing. The two female sorcerers she'd located, both librarians, pled too much work.

Only after all other avenues failed had she turned to the town's Black community. Coincidentally—or perhaps a beneficial instance of accidental magic?—at just that time Marta had noticed a Black nurse working a small spell to remove drops of blood from the hem of her otherwise pristine uniform.

Convincing the woman and her husband, the town's Black doctor, to take on Douglas had taken much negotiation. In the end, she'd arranged to trade. Douglas went to their house every Sunday afternoon for lessons, and in turn Ruby came to hers.

Marta had been nervous the first weeks, but Douglas never had any complaint about going to the Black neighborhood—not that he'd notice trouble unless it stood in front of him anyway. Likewise, Ruby had been a joy to teach.

And she hadn't been late once yet.

After checking the clock on the wall, Marta shook her head and gave a rueful wave at her dishevelment. "I'm running a little behind today. Bear with me, and we'll start your lesson soon."

"Sure thing, Mrs. Floding. It's your house." Ruby leaned against the kitchen cabinet. "You do the dishes by hand?"

"Sometimes." Marta swept a hand across the sink searching for the cups. "How do you do them at home?"

"By snap." Ruby matched action to word.

The cups vanished from the sink and reappeared—clean and dry—on the counter. The dirty pot and pan sitting nearby turned sparkling clean as well. Crumbs and stains dissolved from the kitchen table, leaving the tablecloth pristine blue-and-white.

"A handy spell." Turning to mirror the teenager's pose, Marta matched the snap. The dirty water in the sink disappeared. So too did every mote of sweat on her. Her apron flew across the room to hang on a hook by the door, leaving her shirt and shorts clean and tidy.

"So you know it, too." Ruby nodded, no surprise in her mellow voice.

"It's fine to use when one is alone, or when the only others around are known to be sorcerers," Marta put the cups away in the cabinet. "But a good idea to know how to do things by hand just in case there are those without magic watching."

"Of course. Mother has to hang out the laundry every Monday, or first thing Tuesday morning one of our neighbors will be over with a pot of chicken soup." The young woman said.

"Would you like something to drink?" Marta asked.

"Juice would be nice, if you have it." Ruby walked over to the table and ran a hand along the back of a chair. She didn't sit down until Marta set two tall glasses of orange juice out and took a seat herself.

As the other tilted her head back and drank, Marta shifted in her chair. The wood creaked under her, but her gaze caught on the reflection of the Bullen house in the door window. Only the farthest corner—but the timing was perfect to watch Lois sneak out the back and head off down the driveway.

Marta sipped her juice, enjoying the burst of cool flavor, and eyed the high-school senior in front of her. "By any chance do you have classes with Lois Bullen?"

"Lois?" Ruby set her glass down and leaned back against the chair, brow furrowed. "One or two."

Marta ignored the other's hard gaze, which all but asked why she wanted to know. "How does she seem to you?"

"She's smart enough, though she doesn't show it so much anymore. I've seen her in the public library a couple of times, if not so much of late. There's a college beau buzzing around, or was that last year?" Ruby waved a hand at the rest of the house. "Why don't you ask your son?"

"Douglas?"

"They pass each other notes." Ruby's expression remained serene, but light danced in her eyes.

"Douglas and Lois?" Marta shook her head, unable to envision them together. Or Douglas even pursuing a local girl considering his determination to kick the dust of Timms off his heels. He might be interested, though he'd denied fixing on Lois when she'd asked him.

"I'm not sure he's sweet on her," Ruby shrugged. "But he surely knows her as well as anyone."

"Or not." Marta rubbed her head, missing the peace of the clearing. "He made no mention of magic about her."

"Magic? She's no sorcerer." Ruby leaned forward, hands braced against the table. "Is she?"

"Not that I'm aware of. I thought Bettina might be, when I first moved here, but I was wrong, something she's never let me forget." Marta paused, gaze narrowing.

Bettina had forbidden Marta to talk to Lois, but said nothing of anyone else. Douglas wouldn't do, since he never spoke to her though he apparently wrote notes, something requiring further investigation. Ruby though . . . was Marta's student. Entrusted to Marta's teaching, not to be her assistant. Marta couldn't in good conscience ask her to spy on Lois.

On the other hand, she saw no issue in ensuring Ruby's family, who formed a sizable proportion of the other sorcerers in town, took an interest in the girl. "Yet there are traces of sorcery about Lois now."

Ruby blinked, then gave a slow nod. "My mother and Gramma Thelma and the others will want to know."

"Tell them what you need to." Marta rubbed her hands. She doubted they'd discover more or even as little as she had, but one never knew. "And I will talk to Douglas. In the meantime, why don't we tackle domestic magic applications this afternoon?"

Teaching Ruby kept Marta on her toes. Once she'd left, the need to speak to Douglas could have pressed on Marta, but didn't. A breeze blew through the few trees at the back of the yard, all pines, and carried the scent into the house. One whiff brought back the clearing, the woods, and the peace.

The house lay in good order, all neat and tidy after the spate of housekeeping spells. Dinner would be leftovers.

Marta had nothing to do but put up her feet for an hour or two and lie back on the sofa. Rest her head on one of the pretty cream chenille throw pillows she'd managed to keep mostly stain-free, as her body sank into the worn cushions.

Her eyes flickered shut.

In a breath, she returned to the clearing. Sunlight hardly changed it, save for painting grass and trees in their rightful array of greens rather than the drained shadows of night. Only birds calling in the distance, or occasionally swooping through, broke the stillness.

The peace.

The grass offered an excellent bed on which to rest.

Nearby, in daylight, the top of the stump was blackened, as though it had once caught fire or been struck by lightning. The rest of the tree had vanished, rotted or carried away, save for the rough three-foot trunk above ground.

Roses and anise from goldenrod mixed with the forest smells, making for a restful perfume. Two asters, two sprays of goldenrod, and three roses lay against the thickest root. Only the top-most rose appeared pure and fresh, the white petals delicately curved.

It hadn't been there the night before, or had it?

Marta sat up, pressing her hands against the grass. Rested her weight on them, then lifted—leaving no mark behind.

"Mother? What's for dinner?"

She returned to her home, her living room, her sofa, with a jerk. The sun had sunk notably in the sky. How long had she lost to the clearing?

"Lawn's done." Douglas bounded down the stairs into the room, only to stop and squint at her. "You okay, Ma?"

"Yes. Fine." She waved a hand at him as she patted her hair and brushed wrinkles from her shirt. "How was your lesson?"

"Good. It was with Mrs. Warren. The doc got called away on a consult." He dropped onto the other end of the sofa and propped bare feet on the ottoman. His damp hair clung to his head, a few rivulets trickling down his neck. His clean blue shirt and shorts stuck to his skin over the muscles he'd used mowing the lawn, which she'd somehow managed to doze through. "So she put me back through a primer on basics and called me out every time I got lazy. Not hard, you know, just pointing out how often I stick to the conventional and forget the first rule of magic."

"Anything is possible." Marta frowned. "True enough, though possible does not also mean probable or easy to accomplish."

"No, but Mrs. Warren wouldn't ever let me put it like that. She said it's accepting defeat before you even try. To make a new spell, you have to imagine it, want it, believe it, and put in the power. Saying it might not happen undermines believing just when you need it." Douglas rubbed his head. "Makes my brain hurt."

Such a difference from what Marta had done with Ruby, going through possible spells versus refining and strengthening the basics.

Then again, Cora Warren had her husband and a good two-dozen family members, most if not all sorcerers, around to help her out if she were ever in a jam. No doubt they had regular discussions about magic over tea or a quilting bee or Sunday social. She had the time to plan lessons, rather than figuring them out on the spot as Marta did whenever she forgot to spend time the night before.

Though Mrs. Warren had other burdens to bear that Marta did not, but Marta had to remind herself of that.

Marta's belly ached, from hunger but also the serpentine twists of envy. The same twists and turns as when she'd walked through Bettina's house seeing everything hers lacked.

Which brought the ticking risk of Bettina's blackmail back to mind.

"You said you never speak to Lois, or her to you." Marta rose and dusted herself off. The air about her legs shone with a momentary green tint. She'd tried to keep her tone even and casual, but Douglas popped to his feet, arms crossing over his chest.

"Yeah, what of it?"

"I hear you pass her notes."

"How? Oh, of course, Ruby," Douglas huffed and rolled his eyes. "I swear, she's got her nose everywhere and notices near everything, and now she's onto me about doing the same. What'd she have to do telling you? So what if I pass Lois notes? I'm not the one who writes them."

"Then who does?" Marta plumped the sofa pillows and set them at either end.

The pause stretched long enough for her to finish and turn around, to find Douglas still in place with arms crossed.

She set her hands on her hips and tilted her head. "It's a simple question."

He swallowed, then shrugged. "Isabel."

"Lois's *sister*?"

"She doesn't leave campus much, and Lois never gets over to the college, so sometimes they trade notes."

"Through you."

A hint of red shone across the tips of his ears. "I met up with Isabel once when I was studying over at the college library, and she asked me, as a favor . . ."

"That's very kind of you." Marta rolled her shoulders and loosened her stance. All was explained, without making Douglas a way to find out what Lois was thinking or doing.

"It's easy enough a thing." He ducked his head, scuffing sock-covered toes against the rug. The red stretched from his ears to his cheeks.

She let the matter go. He still wouldn't be a way to find out what Lois was thinking or how she'd gotten caught up in magic. Yet interesting to know he also wasn't quite as immune to local girls as she'd thought.

Even if that left her in the same mess as before.

# HEADACHES

*M*ondays always set the tone of the week.

Marta woke reluctant to leave the peace of the clearing. A hint of the woods lingered around her as she dressed in a clean uniform and saw her children fed and on their merry way. Janie, her baby grown so big, squeezed her mother tight and murmured "you smell good" before running off to school.

A fine beginning. The sense of peace and well-being carried Marta along on her walk to campus, despite the fog settling across the town. Mist clung to her skin, clammy and cool. A trickle condensed at the back of her collar and seeped down her spine. No matter how fast she moved—and she couldn't go too fast on slick pavement—she wound up damp and uncomfortable by the time she slipped through the back door to the infirmary.

Warm, dry air surrounded her, but she'd gone from the coal scuttle to the fire. A bare five feet inside the door stood John Martin, Dean of Students, looming over Nurse Davies. Literally towering, his long body clad in a dark gray suit and graying hair slicked back from his pale face. Black eyes, a thin nose, and high cheekbones made for an attractive prospect dampened only by thin lips that almost never smiled due to yellowed, mis-aligned teeth.

Nancy shrank in on herself. Her white uniform, pressed neatly save for a few wrinkles along the hem, hung loose about her thin body. Her knees squished tight together, feet slightly ajar, and she had her hands clasped against her belly. Her color came and went, from cream to red and back again, stark against the lush dark-brown curves of her bobbed hair. Although a good five years older than the students, she looked younger than them for the moment.

"Am I interrupting anything?" Marta let the door swing shut behind her, the wind slamming it the last inch. The thud echoed down the hall.

He said yes, she said no.

Checking her watch, Marta tsked as she inched closer to Nancy. "Time we were opening. Did you have any business for the doctor, Mr. Martin?"

The dean shook his head, giving her a thin-lipped smile. His teeth flashed when she didn't move, and his gaze shifted to Nancy's down-turned head. "We'll speak of this later, Miss Davies."

His hard-soled shoes echoed as he strode down the hall as though he owned the building.

Marta hustled Nancy into the break room and pressed a mug of coffee into the younger woman's chilly hands, noting her ringless fingers.

"You could have called in sick one more day." Marta's fingers shifted to assess Nancy's racing pulse. "The rest would do you good."

"I don't have any time left." Nancy shook her head. She slipped her wrist from Marta's grasp, chin lifting. "It wouldn't do any good anyway. I might as well work and be paid."

"Your choice. Was it him?" She snapped her mouth shut, not having planned on asking the question. Or any questions. The less she knew, the less to hide.

"He was nicer before," Nancy mumbled. She wrapped both shaky hands around the mug.

"Nicer?"

"When I first hired on. Checking to make sure I was okay working with the students, when I wasn't much older. That the male students weren't trying to cozen me." The younger nurse managed a smile as thin as the dean's. "Until I realized *he* was the one wanting to . . ."

"He's the kind of man with an eye for a pretty girl," Esther offered from the door.

"Not just an eye, but fingers and other parts as well." Marta grimaced. "We should report him."

"To whom?" Nancy's shoulders curved inward. "The president? He wouldn't care, and even if he did, Mr. Martin would only have to say I misunderstood him, or I was the one going after him and being unchaste—he likes that word —or something of that kind."

"He's so busy calling others unchaste." Esther shook her head. "But that's the way of the world. Still, the waiting room is full, again. At least we can make a difference for the students who come to us."

Nancy drained her mug and bustled off into action, brushing her hands against her skirts.

Esther hung back a moment, a grimace on her face. "I did not see him chasing after her. I wish I had, in time to drop a word of warning in her ear."

"So do I. We could have done better by her." All the night's peace drained from Marta, leaving her cold and damp.

"We did what we could. Now that we know better, we must do better. More warnings. Sharper eyes to catch signs of problems." Esther sucked in a sharp breath, shaking her head.

"Warnings and watching." Marta stuffed her lunch in the refrigerator. "You'd think the tragedy last spring would have put us on our guard." She didn't have to close her eyes to remember a once-laughing co-ed with bright green eyes, a sideways tilted nose, and a long brown braid, in a fancy dress nearly the same peaches-and-cream as her complexion. Or the same girl, shoulders hunched and gaze fearful as she perched on the edge of a chair rocking back and forth and whispering for help. Worst of all, touching flesh cold and pale as snow after a night in the wood.

"Do you think he was responsible for . . ." Esther gestured toward the outside.

"No. She said it was a student, easy enough to guess who though no one was ever named," Marta shivered at the memories. The dean's gaze had been dismissive when she'd handed over the doctor's report. "But think who got the report after the incident, whom she had to speak to? Who made the decision to expel? It was all hushed up, except *her* name getting out."

The stamp of feet down the hall called them to work rather than leave Nancy to handle the usual Monday morning hordes on her own.

The unsettling start to the day left Marta off her step.

Every little thing that could go wrong took the opportunity to do so. Hands slipped. Coffee spilled, as did any liquid she collected. Pills scattered when she tried to dole out one or two.

The clearing of her dreams seemed very far away save for moments between patients, when she leaned against a wall and caught her breath.

Her head ached well before the end of the day, despite having self-diagnosed and popped a few pain relievers. The only silver lining was that she got to leave a little early, in recompense for having worked late and alone the previous week. A departure made possible only because the press of students seeking care had dwindled through the day from the rush in the morning to a whimper in the afternoon.

Yet even that hint of grace curdled when she walked into her house and found Bettina Bullen ensconced at the kitchen table.

*Marta's* kitchen table. Marta's house. Granted she never locked the kitchen door, but even when she'd called Bettina a friend, they'd never swanned into the other's unoccupied house. Bettina couldn't claim she'd been let in by one of Marta's children, for they weren't in sight and they had manners enough to have stayed with her until their mother came home. They were home, too, given the chatter and ruckus in the living room and upstairs.

Of course Bettina was immaculately dressed. Her pale-pink sweater set gleamed with newness above a demure gray skirt and flawless hose and shoes. Hair in a demure updo, makeup pristine, and rose perfume pervasive.

Whereas Marta had worn off her lipstick hours ago and failed to reapply it. Her uniform remained intact and mostly unstained, save for a few spots of blood on her cuffs. Her hair had seen better days, and her hose had two runs. Lacking warning of Bettina's presence, she'd had no chance to conceal her dishevelment with a spell.

She stalked across the kitchen and wrenched open the refrigerator, filling a cup with orange juice and downing it. The sharp tang cleared any remaining cobwebs from her brain, while the sugar gave her an energy rush.

She set the cup down and turned around, leaning against the counter.

Bettina's hands rested demurely in her lap, legs crossed at the ankles and knees tilted to one side. Perfect ladylike posture. Her eyebrows narrowed, gaze fixed on Marta. "Well?"

"What are you here for?" Marta turned half away, careful not to turn her back on Bettina. With unsubtle bangs and crashes, she opened the cupboards and removed a pot and the first can of soup that came to hand.

A tic twitched to the left of Bettina's pink-painted lips. Otherwise, she didn't move a muscle. "What have you learned?"

"Somethings." Marta worked the can opener. The metal piercing the lid produced a soft grating noise, but she fancied it stood in for Bettina's response, which lightened her spirits a trifle.

"Such as?"

Marta dumped the can into the pot on the stove and added water. Grabbing a wooden spoon, she stirred the chicken and noodles over the warming flame. Her stomach rumbled, despite the juice.

"Well?" Bettina rose, heels clicking as she crossed the floor to stand only a few feet away. The air between them vibrated as tension rolled off the other woman.

Marta rolled her head on her neck, trying to ease the growing ache. Holding the dripping spoon, she shifted to face Bettina. "It's been four days, and you forbid me to even talk to Lois. What do you expect, a miracle? I have hints and threads, but I need time."

"Every day you take means one more my daughter spends caught up in this . . . nightmare." Bettina set her hands on her hips, fingers tapping against her belly. "You promised to free her."

"I promised to investigate what was going on, but it won't be done in a day or four." The pot hissed. Marta turned and stirred the warming soup before it could burn. Glancing back over her shoulder, she raised an eyebrow and asked, "Have any more shoes been dirtied?"

The other woman hissed, lips drawing back from sharp, white teeth. Then she swallowed, licked her lips, and admitted, "No."

"Take what you can get." Marta passed within an inch of Bettina to retrieve bowls and spoons and set the table. Returning to the stove, she stirred the soup while glaring at the other. "Either loosen my hands and let me get the information I need from whomever I need, and that means anyone in your family, or give me time."

Bettina's fingers rapped ever faster against her abdomen, then she lifted them. Flicked the tips, bright pink nail polish flashing under the harsh overhead light, and offered a bitter smile. "You have the week. Or I take things into my own hands."

Seven days. Not much. Marta set her hands on her hips, although the pose was likely weakened by the dripping spoon sticking out to one side. "And I can talk to Lois?"

The extension wouldn't do much good otherwise.

"No. I'll not have her contaminated when I'm trying to save her from being a failure. My girl will be more than a *college professor's* wife." Bettina stalked off without allowing any chance for a response—or even to savor Marta's wince— and slammed the door behind her.

Marta shivered at the disdain in Bettina's voice for her husband, or was that for the other woman's self?

A scorching hiss drew her back to the stove in time to rescue the soup. She served it up, with bread and butter, and called the children before dropping into the chair Bettina had left canted out from the table. The seat was still warm.

Her headache doubled as her children raced down the stairs for dinner.

The noise of her house and the pressure of her promise left her longing for the peace of the clearing. Or perhaps it was due to five minutes' conversation with Bettina. If Marta were Bettina's daughter, forced to live with her, she'd welcome refuge in the serenity of the woods, even if only in her dreams.

Marta remained forbidden to talk to Lois—which meant she couldn't learn if the girl even wanted to be rescued from whatever had enthralled her.

And was enchanting Marta, too.

Marta always managed to forget how much the porcelain mixing bowl weighed until she had to heft it from a lower cabinet to the counter. There it rested in splendor, a wide-lipped affair of cream and copper-colored stripes on the outside and smooth finish inside. The kitchen still smelled of chicken soup, but the pot and bowls were washed and put away, the table and counters wiped.

Douglas had gone off somewhere to study, and Scottie and Janie down the block for a few rounds of whiffle ball before bedtime.

Only Marta remained in the house, which made it an excellent time for magic. Much as she preferred to teach her children by having them watch or help cast with her, this spell she needed to do on her own.

It was for their sake, after all.

Her uniform rested in the laundry basket waiting the next round of cleaning spells or, if she kept using up sorcerous power on the mystery of Lois's shoes, Marta might actually have to drag out and use the wretched wringer-washer. The worn folds of her faded blue day dress whispered around her bare legs as she assembled base ingredients: flour, salt, and starter mixed with warm water and a little sugar and flour foamed in a small bowl.

Her arms ached as she stretched up to remove a cookbook from above the stove. When she laid it on the counter, it flopped open to the breads section with little prompting. The first recipe on the page was for potato rolls, something she hadn't tried before. Just what she needed.

The spell would take time and effort to bear proper results, but she needed something to help her meet Bettina's challenge.

The sorcery lesson Marta had given Ruby the day before had sprouted the idea. They'd mostly talked about different spells to take care of household tasks—sweeping, cleaning, laundry.

With a quarter hour left, Marta had shifted the topic. "Don't forget that housekeeping can also *be* magic."

Ruby had tilted her head, but said nothing.

"Sorcery requires a symbol—an action—to bring together power, belief, imagination, and will into magic. Most people focus on quick symbols. A drawing. A head tilt. A snap or a clap." She matched her action to her words. "Some spells are too complex to be encapsulated in such a simple action. They require time and thought. Cleaning or cooking by hand can help bring the ingredients together into a magical whole."

"That's not something I've seen much of." Ruby leaned back, watching Marta with narrowed eyes. "Most all the housework sorcery my family show me are ways to hide casting spells, make it look as though you're cleaning when you're doing much more because we've always got more work to do than we've time, but the cleaning isn't a spell."

"Cleaning's a hard one. You have to fit the nature of what you do to what magic you want to accomplish. Dust a room today, and tomorrow it'll need dusting again. If you use dusting to cast a spell, it had best be something you don't mind doing again, if necessary."

Ruby shuddered, and Marta laughed.

"That's why I prefer cooking spells, or baking." Marta went to the refrigerator and retrieved her sourdough starter. She set the jar on the table, turning it so that the frothy white contents were fully visible. A small layer of light amber liquid floated on top, alcohol she'd need to pour off sooner than later. "All I need to do is cook something I don't usually make, or something I've never made before, and I can whip up big results."

"Mom doesn't cook much, she's too busy."

"Your parents have a good practice," Marta said. "Every time I've driven by, there's been a line outside, and many students would rather see your father than come to the infirmary."

"The Black students." Ruby nodded. "They know they'll get good care from Dad and Mom."

"We'd take care of them, too," though Marta's voice trailed off halfway through. Most of the staff were devoted to making people healthier, but there was that night nurse who muttered about certain types of folks malingering, much like the town doctor who substituted for Dr. Thomson on his vacations.

"Maybe." Ruby shrugged, frowning as she studied the jar of starter. "Since Mom doesn't have much time, we get most of our meals from Aunt Hazel, who lives next door."

"Does she bake much bread?"

"Every day, seems like." Ruby unscrewed the top, nose wrinkling at the sour odor. "She runs a boarding house." The younger woman's gaze fixed on Marta again. "Some of the students who aren't allowed to live on campus stay with her."

"Good for her." Marta tapped the glass, keeping to her

point. "The thing about baking a spell in bread is, it takes a lot of time. Has to rise at least once if not twice, or you're likely not doing it properly, and that's before you set the dough in the pans to rise again. All that time lets a lot of power seep in, so the final product isn't just a loaf of bread but a powerful spell. You might ask your aunt if she ever casts spells when she's cooking, or we can work on cooking up magic at your next lesson."

Ruby'd gone home partly convinced, at least Marta hoped so. Though what kinds of spells she'd help the girl bake next time, she had yet to decide.

*This* spell was for *Marta.*

The ingredients represented what she did and didn't know about the situation, all the different elements. She tended the starter, grated potatoes, then mixed them with flour and salt, milk and lard, eggs and sugar. Her fingers ached as she worked the dough over and over. All the while, she ran over what she knew, what she didn't, and what she wanted to happen.

Which was a problem. She didn't know enough to know how things should end, how she wanted them to, other than freedom from Bettina's blackmail.

Once the dough was fully mixed, Marta covered the bowl with a white cloth and set it in the window where the last sunlight would warm it and make it rise. She set the oven to low heat, for the second rise, though she wouldn't cook the rolls until tomorrow.

She'd never made potato rolls before, didn't know how they'd come out. That made the recipe a good match with the spell. Cooking magic worked best when one knew exactly what one was making—and used a known, everyday spell— or tried something new. Or changed a recipe just enough to ensure the result was a new experience. Failure or success.

Make the rolls over two days—she'd expect the results under Bettina's deadline of a week.

Though Marta had no idea what she'd wrought.

# FEET

*A* potato roll sat heavy in Marta's stomach. It had tasted lovely. All of her children praised them, gobbling up two or three apiece. An extra zip in Marta's blood suggested the spell had started to work. She should be pleased with her success. Happy, even.

Yet as she lay on her bed, shivers rippled through her instead. A chilly night breeze snuck in where she'd left the window ajar. It blew over her bureau, making the perfume stopper shift and chime against the glass bottle. A lipstick or some other trinket fell over and rolled off to drop and skid across the floor—she couldn't see what in the dark, clouds having covered the sky.

The cool dissuaded her from rising to find out. Much better to remain cozy, cuddled under her soft, worn sheets and thick wool blanket. Her long cotton nightgown tangled around her legs as she pulled the blanket more securely around her shoulders and against her ears.

Her stomach kept her from slipping into rest—and into the peace of the clearing. A burp forced its way up and out, then the pressure eased. She longed for the clearing. It connected in some way to Lois and the dirt on her shoes, but how? There was no one there but Marta.

Except, when Marta slipped back to the clearing, the sky had changed. Clouds covered and hid the moon. Yet the opening was filled with light, which she saw through a mist. Green luminescence graced the trees surrounding the open area. More glowed from the trunk, obscuring the faint shadow of the flowers left against the base. White roses and goldenrod and asters and other autumn flowers, though the rose perfume still predominated.

Wisps of gray light danced in the air. Hither, thither, any-which-way. Some swirled in endless circles. Others wove up, down, and through as though bees drunk on nectar. Dozens —too many to count.

The grass verge offered a more comfortable resting place than any bed. Marta curled on it, head pillowed on her hands as she watched the flickering lights. Shoulders and arms ached, despite the warmth emanating up from the earth. She stretched and rolled to lie flat on her back.

To the accompaniment of silk rustling, and the soft scratch of cotton and lace against her body.

She lifted an arm, now covered in a thin sleeve that ended in a point on the back of her hand. Fingers brushed soft, rustling fabric from wrist to elbow to shoulder. There the neckline swooped across her upper chest to the other shoulder, where another sleeve attached.

A rope of pearls ringed her neck, warm to the touch.

Bit by bit, she sat up, hardly daring to breathe. Glorious skirts of gray silk pooled about her legs, formed of distinct panels of two different makes of silk, one heavy with embroidery and the other plain. Tiny stitches bound them together. Matching stitches held the bodice close to her body, although she'd gained some pounds since she'd worn the original.

Her wedding dress, pieced together from her grandmothers' gowns.

Somehow resized to fit her now . . . and dyed gray.

The same gray as the flecks of light dancing in the air.

A misty veil covered her head, falling to her waist. So thin and flyway that no matter how she reached for it, she couldn't grab hold—and yet fixed in place to the point it didn't slip no matter how she moved. She rose onto bare feet. Her soles pressed against the warm earth, drawing the heat upward to fill her.

Naked feet? This had to connect to Lois's shoes. How else, and yet Marta wore no shoes.

Nor did anyone else.

One by one, the flickers of light expanded into human forms, but veils obscured their features. Even the men had lengths of thin cloth over their heads and shoulders. Most wore fancy gowns, though one or two had on uniforms of some kind, or loose gowns, or even suits. Their veils—or Marta's—blurred the more she tried to look at anyone. The only parts she could view without obstruction were feet.

All exposed—and gray. No peach or beige or tan or brown, just lighter grays and darker.

Everyone danced. None to the same beat or in the same style. Two performed contra dance movements—swings and do-se-dos—but without any connection to each other. Others waltzed or boogied or just stood in place waving their arms and swaying.

No words. No voices. No songs.

No music but the pulse of her heart and the thrums through the earth below.

The warmth and beat pushed aside worries and fears and the nagging certainty that this made no sense. Instead, effervescence flooded her. Here she was safe. Secure.

Without conscious thought, her feet began to shift. First a

slow dance, but moving up to a foxtrot as sheer joy burst through her.

She danced.

When she woke, gritty-eyed and a hint of weariness remaining—as though she had, indeed, danced all night, none of her shoes showed so much as a hint of dirt. Nor did her feet.

Yet her bed gleamed for a moment with a faint green luminescence outlining where she'd lain.

Marta hadn't worked the spell for knowledge, as she had days earlier in Bettina's house, or at least she didn't remember doing so.

Nevertheless, if she closed her eyes and *looked*, her skin gleamed, too.

# NURSES

"Nurse Floding? You're wanted out front."

Marta stopped, laying a hand on the infirmary hall to brace herself. Wednesday hadn't been too bad thus far. Her feet didn't hurt much despite wearing her newest and least-broken-in work shoes, her uniform remained clean and tidy, and she'd had an easy day thus far. All of the nurses had, in an unusual midday slow-down. Nevertheless, her stomach rumbled and she'd been looking forward to a nice sit-down and lunch with the others. The hint of tunafish in the air suggested someone had already started lunch, likely the doctor. Though Marta couldn't care less for tunafish, the scent made her mouth water.

The young Black woman sent over to substitute for their usual receptionist nearly tripped racing after Marta, she glanced back at the door to the waiting area so often. Truly young, but lithe and able to move fast in a close-fitting dark-green dress. Dark curls cropped close surrounded a dark-brown, oval face with a steep nose and hesitant mouth.

"Is it a student?" Marta pushed away from the wall and covered her face to hide an unwanted yawn.

"No, it's Miz Cora." The girl dropped her eyes, shook her head, and started again. "Mrs Warren, that is. She says she wants a word with you."

"I'll be right there." Marta frowned. Mrs. Warren was no stranger to the infirmary, though she had more than enough work assisting in her husband's office and had never picked up a substitute shift at the infirmary. She could have come on medical business, but then why ask for Marta? Or wish to discuss the exchange of lessons for her Ruby and Marta's Douglas, but why come to work?

Then again, Marta could just trot over to the waiting room and find out. Her shoes squeaked as she turned around. The waiting room matched the rest of the infirmary for whitewashed walls and general lack of adornment. Wood chairs lined the side walls, with the receptionist's desk and chair controlling access to the infirmary proper. The far wall boasted glazed-glass double doors leading to the entrance hall and the rest of the building.

Cora Warren perched on one of the chairs, spine straight and well away from the seat back. Her face was oval rather than round and her soft black hair, with the merest hint of silver, pulled back in a chignon, and she barely topped five feet, but otherwise she shared a general appearance with her daughter in soft lines and curves and big, golden-brown eyes. Her navy-blue uniform complemented her light-brown coloring and she cradled a matching clutch purse in her left hand.

Yet all appreciation for her neat appearance fell away at the sight of her wrist-length gloves of a soft gray similar to the dancers in Marta's dreams.

Similar, not the same. All the same, Marta drew in a hissed breath.

A soft creak and the movement of air prompted Marta to

glance around. The receptionist nodded at Mrs. Warren then closed the door to leave Marta alone with her visitor.

"Mrs. Warren, it's a pleasure to see you." Marta jerked and stepped forward, hand out. "How may I help you?"

The other woman rose and shook her hand, then sat down.

The glove seemed regular cotton to the touch, but Marta rubbed her hands together as she took a seat one over so that they could face each other with ease. The smooth wood did not make for a comfortable seat.

"I'll not beat about the bush." Mrs. Warren met Marta's gaze. "I'm here about what you told my daughter last weekend, of sorcery and the Bullen girl."

"Lois."

"Yes. My grandmother sends her thanks for your word." The woman nodded, a gentle smile playing about her lips although her expression remained calm and serious. "We've investigated and there is quite a cloud of magic about her although the girl is not a sorcerer."

"Not a sorcerer." Marta shifted in her seat. Good information to have, and Marta had no complaints about having been of use to Mrs. Thelma Katy. The few times Marta had met the older woman, she could practically taste the magic boiling off her. "You're certain?"

Mrs. Warren sat straighter and lifted her head, glancing down at Marta despite being several inches shorter. "Yes."

"I meant no insult, I just . . ." Marta dipped her head. "It would have been so much simpler if she had turned, perhaps without whoever turned her knowing, because she's at the center of . . . something magical."

Moreover, how did Mrs. Warren know? Marta had never learned ways to tell sorcerers from the magicless except by asking or catching them doing magic, as she had the day she noticed Mrs. Warren removing spots of blood from her uniform.

A heavy stillness stretched between them, then the other nodded. "I asked the earth on which she stood whether she was a sorcerer, and so did my aunt, and the answer was no."

"You asked the earth?" Marta licked her lips, shivering at the unexpected taste of potato rolls.

"It relies on my family's having lived here for a long time and developed a connection with the land,"—Mrs. Warren tilted her head—"but it's quite accurate."

Marta had never heard of such a spell, nor did she dare ask for details on how to cast it. Her own spell was working, given the brief taste of potato rolls, yet she remained in a muddle.

Maybe she should have bargained with the Warrens for more than their teaching Douglas—for trading spells with her as well. But that would have to wait for another day.

"Then whatever is going on?" Marta asked.

"That is a very good question. I can't tell what the girl's been up to, only that she's wrapped in green-colored magic." Mrs. Warren's eyes narrowed as she leaned in to squint at Marta. "So are you."

"Green-colored magic? Not gray?"

"No."

Green had dozens of symbolical sorcerous meanings. It might relate to newness, growth, plants, the clearing, or too many other things. "Have you seen anyone else glowing the same?"

"I don't make a habit of going around checking people to see if they glow. Asking the earth about sorcerers is hardly an everyday matter." Mrs. Warren clicked her tongue. "You know something of what magic touches you and her."

"Nothing but dreams of dancers and clearings and dirty

shoes." Marta shook her head. "It's all still a mystery for now. If I knew more . . ."

"You might tell me but you might not?"

"I have a half-dozen details that do not make enough sense." Marta extended her hand. "Fair trade, knowledge for knowledge."

"That's not my call to make in this instance." Mrs. Warren shook her head and rose. "I'll get back to you. Or someone else will."

"Very well." Marta hefted to her feet, swaying slightly. A shiver rippled along her arms, and the hint of potato roll on her lips was wafted away by a quick whiff of roses and lilies.

The other woman had turned away, but hesitated and then swiveled back on one heel. "Dancers in a clearing, you said. Anyone you recognize?"

The look on her face, mostly confident but a hint of worry, suggested she asked as a mother, not a fellow sorcerer. "No. I couldn't even spot Lois among them."

A small sigh escaped Mrs. Warren.

"If I see any sign of Ruby, I'll let you know," Marta promised.

"I told her to stay away from the Bullen girl, but who's saying she'll listen this time," Mrs. Warren said. "Thank you."

Her departure left Marta with as many unanswered questions as before.

*A*gain Marta headed down the hall toward the break room. The scent of tunafish was even stronger than before, but mixed with peanut butter. Yech. Rustles and bangs of drawers opening and closing, and chairs moving, plus low voices, suggested at least two others taking their lunch break. Marta's steps slowed as she walked, one hand brushing the wall.

Cora Warren's information was welcome, but disappointing. Only with the possibility ruled out did Marta realize how much she'd hoped it would turn out that Lois had turned sorcerer and the whole mess with the shoes was her having done accidental magic because she was so new and didn't know any better. *That* at least would make this the kind of mess that many a sorcerer had to deal with. Sorcerers born to magical families far outnumbered the turned, but that still left thousands of them in existence, most of whom cast some impossible spell before they knew better.

If not Lois, then who had cast the spell that enthralled Marta to the extent that Cora Warren had been able to see it on her?

No matter how often she licked her lips, she failed to taste potato rolls. Might as well go have lunch.

Esther and Nancy were at the table, the former digging into a beef pastry of some kind and the latter a peanut butter sandwich. A plate atop the refrigerator held a half-eaten tunafish sandwich, evidence that the doctor had been summoned away. Marta threw a layer of plastic wrap over it and a napkin atop that to reduce the odor, before retrieving her own peanut-butter and jelly sandwich.

"You're looking better today," Esther said to Nancy, although she nodded at Marta and patted an empty chair.

"I've slept better lately, with such good dreams. I almost didn't want to wake up." Nancy left her sandwich on her plate and clasped her hands against her chest. Her complexion remained paler than usual, but her eyes were bright.

"A good night's sleep is one of life's greatest pleasures." Esther smiled and drank from a glass of orange juice.

"I usually sleep well, once I can find a way to my happy place, but the last dream was . . ." Nancy leaned back against her chair, head lolling to one side and sheer joy radiating from her face.

A smile stretched Marta's lips as she settled at the table, Nancy's delight nearly infectious.

"That good?" Esther clapped.

"Oh, yes." Nancy pressed a finger against her lips, glancing around. "You won't tell anyone, will you?

"Of course not." Esther shook her head, and Marta followed suit.

Nancy rose, chair legs scraping against the floor as she pushed back from the table and went over to the door. She peered down the hall in both directions and went so far as to close the door, though she didn't latch it, before sitting back down. Even with those precautions, she still dropped her voice to barely over a whisper. "I was floating around campus."

"Floating?" Marta blinked at the odd choice of word. Sorcerer though she might be, she'd never floated nor seen any magicless in any circumstance deserving the term—including Nancy.

"Hsh." Esther leveled a stern look at Marta, then turned back to Nancy. "Go on."

"Floating." Nancy tipped her chin out, then leaned toward Esther. "As though I were a ghost. No one could hear or see me, but I could hear and see them. It was sunny with a chill wind and the first fall leaves starting to turn. I saw all the college students bustling around in their little groups, you know how so many of them never go anywhere alone if they can go in threes or fours."

Esther nodded.

Marta bit into her sandwich and chewed to keep from saying anything.

"Except there was one student alone. One of the co-eds. New. Young. Pretty. Shy. She reminded me of . . ." Nancy pushed her plate toward the center of the table and wrapped her hands around her elbows.

*Of her*, Marta mouthed. Esther nodded, but pressed a finger against her lips.

"She was carrying several books and Dean Martin stopped her to ask a question. Or two. Or three. He leaned in to her, touching her arm." Nancy's hands ran up and down her own, fingers rustling against the soft fabric of her uniform. "She tried to pull back, but there was a wall behind. The side of the student center. They were over near the path leading to the women's dorms."

Marta had no trouble picturing it easily, swapping Nancy's image in for the unknown student. A hard surface blocking escape. No one around. An older man praising a younger woman, helping her, and working toward his reward.

Nancy stopped, teeth biting her lower lip. Her arms pressed tight against her torso, and her feet tapped restlessly against the tiled floor.

"What happened?" Esther stretched out a hand but rested it on the table near Nancy without touching the younger woman.

After staring at Esther's hand, Nancy grabbed hold. "He kept leaning in. Touching her. But there was a tree, on the other side of the path. That big old maple that turns red last of all. It dropped a branch out of nowhere, and somehow the wind twisted it around so that it fell between them and smacked him right . . . right . . ." She lifted her free hand high and tilted it, pointing a finger at her groin, then slapped her hand over her mouth to hush a spate of giggles.

"Oh, marvelous!" Esther laughed, squeezing Nancy's hand. "But you're so cold! Do you want something hot to warm you up? Coffee or tea?"

Nancy nearly choked on her giggles, but opted for coffee. Letting go, Esther rose and bustled about to heat up a pot. Water clanged in the pipes, and the fire hissed on the stovetop.

Marta finished her sandwich, wiping her fingers on a napkin.

The taste of the potato roll bloomed in her mouth, overriding the peanut butter and jelly.

Dreams. Very different from those she'd been having, and yet . . . Cora Warren had noticed Marta wrapped in green magic as well as Lois. And there were definitely more than two dancers in the last dream, though Marta hadn't been able to come up with any total.

Marta leaned back, studying Nancy and glorying in— envying—the younger woman's delight.

Then the other nurse's shoes caught Marta's gaze. Bits of dirt clung to the sides despite marks showing Nancy had tried to clean them off.

"You said you've had a lot of good dreams lately, not just this one." Marta smiled at Nancy. "That's good to hear. Shows you're getting better."

Nancy flushed at the reference to her recent "illness," glancing away then back. "A little better every day."

The clop of hard soles against the tiles echoed down the hall despite the closed door. The doctor no doubt returning for the remainder of his lunch. Only a little time left before they were interrupted. Marta leaned in toward Nancy. "If you don't mind, what else have you been dreaming? I love hearing good dreams."

"Nothing much. Just . . . dancing."

"In a clearing?" Marta asked.

The door burst open with the doctor on the other side, at the same moment as Esther dropped the coffee tin, which went rolling across the floor. No chance for any more questions, but Marta had found one more of the dancers. Though it left her nowhere nearer resolving the mystery. A high school senior likely headed to marriage sooner than later and a nurse nearly a decade older earning her living. Whatever did they have in common?

# VISITORS

That evening Marta settled onto one end of the sofa, the remainder covered by a wicker basket holding an assortment of threads and a pile of clothing. She kicked off her slippers and tucked her feet under her. This was the reason for house clothes—a worn but well-loved yellow shirt and soft blue lounging pants—to be able to sprawl in ways dresses didn't permit.

Even if it was for the purpose of doing the mending. Her least favorite task, but Scottie tore through his shirts and pants too quickly for her to put it off any longer. He lay truly sprawled across the orange carpet, legs and arms akimbo, as he glanced at the pile of mending and his beloved Cincinnati Reds shirt atop the rest. Grinned as he rolled dice, and gave a triumphant yelp as his sister moaned. The two warred over a board game, penned inside as rain drummed on the roof and trickled down the windows.

Only her elder son was missing, off somewhere as usual. The library, perhaps, though he'd counted out nickels from his store of cash and mumbled something about sodas at the drug store.

Heaving a sigh, she picked up the baseball jersey. Regular washing with a liberal helping of sorcery had mostly removed mud stains, but a rip marred the back. Scottie hadn't quite explained how, something about cleats and a bully.

She stirred the thread bobbins in the basket with a minor spell requiring little power or attention, and drew at random one that matched the white cloth. The loose end slipped through her fingers three times before she managed to align it with the top of the rip. Another spell linked thread and cloth, mending the rip as she carefully drew her finger along the tear.

Only to jerk and lose her place when a loud rap broke her concentration.

Janie popped up before Marta could say anything and ran to open the front door. The wind blew in a dozen raindrops around the two figures silhouetted against the wet street.

"Good evening, is your mother in?" An arch note tinged Esther's familiar voice. She glanced once over Janie's head at Marta before focusing on the girl.

"Mama?"

"Come in, come in." Marta set the mending aside, rising and brushing stray bits of thread off her pants.

"Thank you." Esther collapsed a black umbrella and set it in the umbrella stand by the door. A younger woman enveloped in a long tan raincoat followed, dripping on the linoleum as she doffed the wet fabric.

Marta swooped over to take the coat and hang it in the closet, well away from dryer apparel. The activity gave her opportunity to study the second woman. Esther's daughter Sarah, one of Douglas's classmates, had only stopped by the infirmary on a few occasions. Her dark hair and creamy complexion clearly came from her mother. Their many resemblances were clear since both wore long-sleeved white blouses and calf-length patterned skirts.

Tall and lithe, Sarah had an athletic figure and, on this occasion, a decided twitchiness. Fingers, shoulders, feet, some part of her was always moving. Dimples flashed in and out of existence in her cheeks, to either side of a button nose, rosebud lips, and a pointed chin. She reached back and wrung her kerchief and the braid underneath it.

"Would you like a seat?" Marta winced at the disarray in the room—the game spread across the floor, children staring, and pile of clothes on the sofa.

"If you don't mind, we'd like to speak with you privately," Esther glanced around, then gestured at the doorway to the dining room. "Perhaps in the kitchen?"

"I can offer something to drink, coffee or tea?" Marta led the way, her back itching as nervous energy swirled through her. What could she offer them that they were allowed to eat or drink?

"No, thank you." Esther shook her head as she settled at the kitchen table, giving an approving nod at the clean and tidy space. "But I would appreciate if you cast a spell to keep our words from your children."

"Spell?" Marta froze, one hand on the back of the chair opposite Esther.

A chuckle escaped Sarah as she moved a third chair far enough back to sit in her mother's wake.

"You are a sorcerer, are you not?" Esther leaned forward, eyebrows raising and eyes wide open. "I was so sure you were. So many times I've seen you warm your coffee with a flick of your fingers."

"But . . . are you?" Marta sank into the chair, letting it support legs weak as noodles. If Esther had seen Marta work sorcery, then Esther must not be magicless—either a born sorcerer or a turned one.

"No, it is too dangerous." The older woman shook her head.

"It's not *too* dangerous." Her daughter huffed, mouth tightening as her legs jiggled.

"My father would not allow magic in the house because of the risk of things going wrong." Esther sighed. "His first wife was a sorcerer, but she died young and he forswore sorcery after that. He loved my mother, but he also loved that she was not a sorcerer."

"But *my* father didn't mind." Sarah glared at her mother. "He liked magic, he said so often, he just didn't do it because learning how to do it well took time he'd rather spend playing the piano."

Esther stiffened, and Sarah shut her mouth with a snap. Her head tilted down and she shifted to hold her mother's hand. Marta bowed her head. Esther had let fall that her musician husband had enlisted in the Army during the Second World War and died at the Battle of the Bulge.

"Your father is no longer with us." The older woman shook her head and pulled her hands away, folding them in her lap. "We live with your uncle, in his house, so we honor him. When you have your own household, you may choose to do magic or not."

Sarah rolled her eyes. An old argument between them, no doubt.

The byplay between mother and daughter both eased and unnerved Marta. Eased because it seemed natural and unfeigned—and unnerved as they evidently appreciated the existence of magic. "You don't do magic? How? I was taught that there are only two kinds of people in the world, magically-speaking. Those who do magic, and are sorcerers, and those who do not. Magicless. If a magicless sees magic, they either become a sorcerer or find some way to forget it or excuse it."

"I only know that I believe in sorcery, but I also believe that doing spells is dangerous. I've never learned, and have no plans to change that," Esther said.

Marta frowned. If Esther was that adamant about not doing sorcery, power likely cooperated. Perhaps affirming over and over that one couldn't do sorcery because it was too dangerous became a spell that removed one's ability to work magic.

Though it was all a moot point, since they were here. "And so you're here because you want help from me?"

Esther tilted her head pointedly at the doorway to the front half of the house, and the children beyond.

With a snap of her fingers, Marta cast a spell to ensure the children could not hear them. Although she usually kept such things invisible, this time she added a twist that made the air in the entryway glitter silver.

Esther nodded in approval. Sarah shifted in her chair, leaning forward to study it until her mother coughed.

"Yes, I'm a sorcerer. What do you need of me?" Marta laid her own hands in her lap, rubbing chilly fingers against her pant legs.

"Four days ago, after Shabbat,"—Esther shuddered—"I went through Sarah's closet to make sure she had clean shoes for the week. I found pair of her shoes covered in dirt. Good shoes, mind."

Marta drew in a sharp breath as she tensed, and belatedly the taste of potato rolls filled her mouth.

"I asked her how this happened. She said—" The other woman waved a hand at her daughter.

Sarah crossed her arms over her chest, head turned away but words clear. "I don't know."

"But she admitted that she'd had dreams about dancing in a clearing for long time." Esther rubbed her forehead. "Several weeks at least."

"The first time was last spring." The younger woman said in a low voice.

"A clearing." Blood pounded through Marta's veins, pulsing at her temples. Three other dancers. She now had *three*, all of whom had had dirt appear on their shoes. Finally one she could question.

"Exactly! You asked Nancy about that the other day," Esther said, "and Sarah's not the only one. For the last three nights, I also have dreamt of dancing in a clearing."

"Both of you?" Marta licked her lips, but the potato roll taste had dissipated. Her mouth was dry. Leaving the table, she gathered three glasses and a pitcher of orange juice. Sarah refused the drink, but Esther filled a glass halfway and drained it in a matter of moments, even as Marta did.

"Both of us." Esther set the glass down, rubbing the condensation on the sides. "Our Rabbi has gone to Cincinnati and will not return until just before Shabbat. I am afraid to wait until then."

"Tell me more. Whatever details you remember." She set her cup down, fingers tracing the condensation forming on the outside of the glass. "What does the clearing look like? Are you alone?"

"It's a clearing in the woods." Esther threw her hands out. "There are a lot of trees, I don't know what kind. Flowers. Tall grass. The grass is soft underfoot, and just as well because I dance barefoot in my wedding gown. It still fits." Her gaze grew distant.

"There's an old, blasted tree, with flowers around it. Roses, white always, but the other flowers vary." Sarah scooted her chair closer to the table and poured a glass for herself. "Sometimes I'm alone, but usually there are others. The number changes, but we're all wearing veils, even the men, at least I think some are men, they're wearing suits. I've never recognized anyone, even my mother, or her wedding dress."

"What do you wear?" Marta asked.

"Not a wedding gown." Sarah glanced at her mother, shaking her head. "A dress, rather like one I wore to school on special days last year, except gray instead of blue."

Marta ran a hand over the condensation on the jug and used it to trace a gleaming square on the tablecloth. "If you don't mind, touch the table and think of what you've seen. That will let me see, too."

Sarah went first, leaning forward to brace her hands on either side. A range of trees formed a backdrop for a clearing that mostly resembled the one Marta remembered, although the dead tree and the flowers laid at its roots were far more detailed. A dozen or more veiled figures in gray danced around as the image whirled and dissipated.

The daughter had to prod her mother to touch the table. A much fuzzier image formed with far fewer details. Shadowy trees loomed around an open space empty of all save a dark stump. Then the image shifted to focus on a heavily embroidered gown in silvery gray.

"When did you first dream this?" Marta waited until both had a chance to drink more juice. Sarah's twitchiness had returned, while Esther's shoulders slumped.

"Last spring, around the end of the school year, but only once or twice then. Same for the summer." Sarah's feet started tapping against the floor, one faster than the other. "Then it started up heavier a couple weeks ago."

"Was there anything different about the night your shoes got dirtied?"

Sarah shrugged.

Esther set a hand on her daughter's knee, stilling the tapping. "Please share anything that might help her figure out what's going on."

"Nothing much, just . . . the first time, I'd gone to bed early that night. There was a dance, a hop at school that I couldn't go to." Sarah glanced at her mother. "So, funny thing, I dreamed about it instead, somehow at the same time as I dreamt about the clearing. As though I were at the dance but not there, as an invisible spirit able to see and hear everything without anyone seeing or hearing me."

"That hadn't happened before?" Marta renewed the viewing spell.

"No." Staying well back, Sarah brushed a finger against the table cloth.

The same image of the dancers in the clearing manifested. This time it was not quite so sharp and clear. There might be a second image underneath, but no matter how Marta adjusted the spell, she couldn't refocus on it. She sat back, lips tight. "So you went to the dance, without going to it."

"Floated around, mostly outside. I see enough of the gym during school, and it's no nicer just because someone strung ribbons along the walls." The younger woman sat back, crossing her arms over her chest. "Though there was . . . some of the guys got pushy, seeing how far they could go. One in particular. You could tell his date didn't really like it, was just going along. She was really pretty, with long brown hair and sad eyes and skin so soft and creamy . . ." Her gaze turned distant, lips curving up then down. "And he kept swishing her hair and running a finger down her cheek even when she winced away. It made me so mad. I wanted to whap him one good."

"And?" Marta asked.

"I did." One hand fisted, then a satisfied smile passed over Sarah's face. Her tension eased, and arms slipped to hang at her sides. "Then I was back in the clearing, dancing."

Esther frowned. "Did you actually hit him?"

"No . . . I don't know? I didn't touch him, my fist sort of

kept going. Into him. It was odd and gooey." Sarah shivered head to toe. "He made the weirdest face, but that was all I saw."

Marta and Esther's gazes met. The details varied, but the base story resembled Nancy's dream of a tree hitting the dean. Both Sarah and Nancy had wound up with dirty shoes afterward.

Had the same happened with Lois and her shoes?

# PEEPING

*A*gain Marta dreamed of the grassy sward. A clear sky overhead shone dark blue against the deeper shadows of the surrounding trees. She lay sprawled, a breeze teasing the silk skirts covering her legs. The same flowers perfumed the air, and the thrum of dancing feet reverberated through her.

She rose to find herself dressed as before in her long-lost wedding gown, gone gray and a long veil. Her feet and ankles below the hem were a matching gray.

Others, also in gray dresses and a few suits, whirled about, all of them veiled and their hands and feet gray. Were there more this time? She couldn't keep count. Even the smaller number of men refused to settle at three or four or even five, although she tried to track the different suits twirling around.

None resembled Esther or Sarah, or Lois or Nancy for that matter. She tried to call their names, but nothing came out of her throat. All was silent except for the insistent beat of feet pounding against grass that never showed any sign of being stepped on.

Dancers passed near but never close enough to touch.

Yet something had changed with this dream. One person didn't dance. A woman—at least she wore a gray dress and veil similar to others as she knelt by the stump. On second glance, her gown was unfinished, with bits of thread dangling from some of the seams and pins sparkling along the turned hemline. Gray hands pressed against the earth near the roses and lilies, and sparkling diamond tears fell on them.

The sweet taste of potato rolls manifested in Marta's mouth, but when she swallowed it vanished.

The kneeling woman turned hazy, transparent, as the dancers whirled and twirled and caught Marta up among them.

She swirled in circles, arms out and head back the better to rejoice in the magic flowing around the clearing. Around and around, this way and that, filled with twists and turns.

Everything in the clearing glowed green. Peace flooded through her, and surety that here she was safe. This one clearing offered sanctuary and shone with power.

Tendrils of the clearing's serenity clung to her as she woke to her alarm clock, rested and yet a bit weary. Rote memory guided her dressing, picking up the usual pieces of her uniform: cap, dress, hose, shoes, and underthings.

Calling her younger children to wake and dress, as Douglas had likely already headed out to deliver newspapers, she headed down to start breakfast—only to stop on the last step at a knock on the door.

As with the night before, two women stood on the other side, but not a mother and daughter.

Marta stiffened, elbows tight against her sides at the sight of an unfamiliar Black woman. An older woman, tallish, in a soft green dress with medium brown skin and graying black hair pulled into a soft knot under a green hat with a floppy brim. She had a round face with few lines or wrinkles, unre-markable save for the warm golden-brown of her eyes.

The same as Ruby's, and Ruby's mother.

And Ruby, in a pale-pink sweater set and black skirt, stood by the older woman's side.

"Good morning." Marta remained in front of the door rather than stepping back to allow them in.

"Aunt Hazel, this is Marta Floding." Ruby had a stiff smile. "Mrs. Floding, my great-aunt Hazel Gregson."

"I realize you have to work soon, but Ruby will see your children readied for school if you permit." Mrs. Gregson's smile was far more genuine. "I need you to come with me to see something."

"See something?" Marta crossed her arms over her chest.

Mrs. Gregson cupped her hands. Miniature trees glimmered green and brown around the sides and in the center rose a stump. "A clearing in the woods."

# PART II
# HAZEL

Saturday 7 September –
Saturday 22 September 1951

# RIPPLES OR TREMORS

The lacy hem of Hazel's white nightgown fluttered around her calves under her yellow terrycloth robe as she sped down the darkened stairway. Her right hand slid along the railing, wood worn silky from years of use, just as her bare feet landed on smooth step after step. The thick braid of her hair swayed against her back, and the blue silk head scarf she'd been on the verge of wrapping around her head trailed from her left hand and whistled as she whipped around the landing halfway down.

She never missed a step or raised more than a dull thud. Not a single creak. Nearly fifty years of living in the house had left her with sure knowledge of exactly where to set her feet, so she descended far quieter than when any of her young boarders tried to sneak up after having come in late. Leaving her head scarf draped over the newel post, she turned to the back of the house. A lamp shone from the kitchen, beams falling warm and yellow on the oval braided rug covering the long hall floor.

The blue-and-white wallpaper appeared as shades of gray as she trailed her fingers along the wall—save for the emptiness where the door to her mother's room lay ajar. The sheets and blankets were in disarray, and were the fuzzy lumps under the bed her mother's slippers? Pausing only for a breath and a glance, Hazel hurried on.

Shadows filled the corners of the kitchen, for the lamp atop the pie safe near the door, a pretty thing of amber glass and yellow-fringed shade, couldn't fill the full expanse. It was kept burning through the night to offer a welcome to late arrivals or boarders sneaking in after curfew. Some always did, no matter how often she warned them that Timms might be safer than surrounding towns but that didn't mean it was safe.

All remained clean and tidy. The counters stood bare with dishes put away in the oak cupboards lining the walls and leftovers tucked in pantry or the big refrigerator whirring in one corner. A hint of Lysol lingered, bitter on the tongue. She licked her lips and grimaced as she hurried across the yellow-and-white linoleum to where the back door lay ajar. The screen door kept out whining mosquitoes but let in the chill of near midnight.

Hazel yanked the door wide open and filled the doorway, face pressed against the screen. Her body blocked most of the light. Blinking helped her eyes adjust to the dark. The lamp in her bedroom high above cast a faint glow from right above, muffled by the curtains she'd been adjusting moments earlier. The moon hid behind thick clouds, but a few stars glittered in the sky and bits of light fell from the windows of her house and the one next door.

Just enough illumination to show her mother, Thelma Katy, kneeling on the back lawn in her nightgown. Hazel, her youngest, had never learned her mother's exact age, but Thelma was a great-grandmother several times over. Her slight frame and delicate features were a pretty covering for a woman unbowed by time or life's cruelty. A woman who'd held her family's land in her own right for decades, and played a central role in ensuring the town welcomed Black people by day and by night.

But now her mother's hands, usually fawn with gold undertones several shades lighter than Hazel's russet-toned brown, trembled as they rested on grass. Her slender torso curved, revealing the line of backbones through her dimity nightgown. Her pink sleep bonnet had fallen forward and short white hairs curled along the nape of her neck.

The same sight, from above, had sent Hazel pitching down the stairs in hopes she'd hallucinated, but no.

"It's late, Mother." The chill of near midnight made Hazel's joints ache, and her body had four decades or so less wear. "I would have sworn you were in bed."

"I was, but then I felt it. Distant, but . . . I had to be sure." Thelma sat back on her knees. Grunting, she shifted to sit on her bottom with her legs curved to one side.

Hazel winced, her feet pressing against cool grass as she hurried to her mother's side. A stiff hip protested as Hazel settled down. Pulling off her bed robe, she wrapped it around the older woman's shoulders and tried to hide the shivers trickling down her back.

Then stilled. Something deep within the earth reverberated in curvy, winding lines that multiplied the farther they went. Sorcery. Power. The faintest hint of lightning branching a thousand times as it darted through the dirt? She couldn't tell what, only the experience of a . . . thrum . . . passing through the ground in twists and turns—yet without disturbing anything above ground. No other sign of change. The grass remained overlong and due for another mow. The big old oak tree with the plank swing swaying in the breeze was the same as she'd enjoyed in her youth, and her sons in their time, and their children someday. The tree rested close the property line with the next house, all but one window dark, no changes there. The home behind them looked the same, down to the yellow beams of the lamp through the screen.

"You feel it too, don't you?" Thelma's chilly fingers wrapped around Hazel's wrist.

"Yes." Hazel covered her mother's hand with her own. "Some new magic at work. But surely it can wait until tomorrow?"

"That's what I thought, last spring."

"Spring?" Hazel bent her leg and set a bare foot against the earth. Whatever had passed through had ceased, leaving only faint twinges of energy behind. "That long?"

"April it was, sometime, when I noticed the first ripple." The older woman shivered. "Just the one, nothing near the torrent today."

"You consider this a torrent?" Easing to her knees, Hazel urged Thelma to rise and return to the house. Step by step up to the kitchen, with one of Hazel's arms wrapped around a bird-thin waist making her very aware of her mother's fragility.

"It is in contrast." The older woman shrugged off Hazel's support as the outside door clicked behind them. She tottered across the linoleum to the hall, then turned into her new bedroom. The former sitting room she'd fought moving into until all her living children insisted she stop scaring them with the way she gasped when climbing the stairs. A comfy space even in near-dark, with sheets and blankets thrown half-off the mattress. A large braided rug in shades of blue and green covered most of the floor.

Hazel counted to three. Right on time, her mother clicked her tongue. "I can still smell the paint."

"You, but no one else." Rather, Hazel found the room redolent of lavender from the potpourri bowl on her mother's bureau.

Her mother paused and sniffed, leaning close to the wall where she was most likely to smell paint. Hazel turned on the light then hurried around to plump the feather pillows and straighten the mussed bed. She unfolded the red-and-blue quilt hanging from the brass footboard and laid it atop the blue woolen blanket. Her mother tsked again, for the quilt was an heirloom once used to identify the house as a stop on the Underground Railroad, but she didn't say anything as she slipped under the covers and lay back with a sigh.

"My fault."

"Yours?"

"There've been other instances since the first, all small. Fewer in the summer, or fainter. No one walking the wanders or bounds mentioned anything different. No new sorcerers arrived in town that I can tell, no one turning sorcerer either, and the power—what little I could touch of it —didn't remind me of anyone." Her hands played with the sheet drawn up over her chest. "It seemed a small thing, harmless, so I let it go."

Hazel settled sideways on the foot of the bed. She cast a quick spell to check on the other occupants of the house. Two boarders resting and talking in their room. A third deep, as always, in her studies. The last two still out-and-about. No one near to hear her mother's words. Such a rare occurrence for the older woman to speak without herself first checking, as she usually took the lead in avoiding exposing magicless people to even talk of sorcery lest it contribute to their turning sorcerer and acquiring magic whether they wished or no.

"No one was hurt today." Hazel laid a hand over her mother's, then wrapped them between hers to warm the chilly fingers.

"That we know of." Her mother pulled away long enough to shake a finger. Then tucked her hands under her covers, shoulders hunched. "Somewhere, someone cast a spell and this is the result. But who, and where, and for what purpose?"

"How much do the details matter?" Hazel shook her head, bracing against the expected reaction. "We don't know every spell every sorcerer casts, or even most. That way lies madness. The point is it's new, so we need to find who's come to town—or if some magicless has turned sorcerer."

"Also—" Again, the finger raised and shook. "How they cast a spell with such an . . . after effect as to be felt far away. For it wasn't a spell itself running through the ground, but something more akin to ripples as when someone drops something in a pool of water."

Ripples. Hazel pursed her lips, for the description didn't fit what she'd felt. Too circular, though she couldn't think of a better description. She yawned and shook her head. "Whatever it is or was, it's done for the night for all we know. Sleep, and things'll seem clearer in the morning. Time enough to make plans in daylight."

Words her mother had said to her a thousand times over the years, but the turn-around didn't make the older woman smile. Her thin brows drew together and she lifted her chin. "Have Cora come over, first thing tomorrow."

Hazel's elbows pressed hard against her torso, shoulders tight. Of course, the first person her mother would ask for would be Cora, oldest of her grandchildren. This time, though, she'd have to wait, as Cora's husband had dropped her and Hazel's husband off at the train station together early that morning. "Don't you remember? Cora's out of town for the week, at a gathering of midwives."

"How wonderful for her!" The older woman clapped her hands. "A nurse and a doctor in the family, we are so fortunate. But . . . how is she to find out what happened when any remaining signs will be gone. She won't know what to look for." Her legs moved restlessly under the covers, sending tremors through the mattress.

Laying a hand flat, Hazel noted the agitation. More akin to ripples than the power she'd felt flowing through the earth. Softer, too, without the edge of the magic earlier. Nervous energy coiled in her belly as she threw her shoulders back. "I'll investigate for you."

"No, no, I'll find a way." Her mother removed a hand from under the covers to flutter dismissive fingers. "Perhaps Luther—"

"He'll be busy enough without Cora around." Hazel swallowed, unclenching her teeth. Why did her mother's second thought go to Cora's doctor husband rather than the daughter at hand? "I'm walking the wanders this week, so I'll be out and about anyway. After tonight I know what it feels like. I'll do it."

"You're taking the wanders again?" The older woman clicked her tongue. "Cora should be doing them, building up her familiarity so she can take over as landward. I can't hold it forever."

"Why must Cora be the landward?" Hazel leaned forward. "There's plenty others of us at hand. Me, for one."

"The landward serves as the center of those who care for the land and its health, and holds the web of spells laid down and remade year after year, to keep us safe and make this a haven. To be the landward one must belong here, and pledge to remain. Work with others, for the land is too vast for any one person to tend alone. Have the strength and fortitude to hold strong against storms and troubles. Keep a sharp eye for changes in the land, that they be welcome and not ill. Watch those who walk on it that they show due respect. Render judgment when needed, on themselves as well as others." Always the same reply, hardly varying in the words—or the conclusion as Hazel's mother adjusted her bonnet and gave a sharp nod. "All of which Cora can do, if she would only stop playing coy and insisting she's not ready."

"Maybe she isn't," Hazel said. Her niece was busy accomplishing other things.

"She must be, if I am ever to lay down this load." Frail bones and sinews showed through skin grown thin as the older woman planted fists against the blanket over her belly.

Hazel froze, body stiff and heavy. Her mother had dwelt on distant "somedays" in the years since Cora had moved back to town with her husband and new baby, now near grown. Somedays—but never until now drawn so clear a line to the desired end: setting down a responsibility assumed when Hazel was little. The better to rest and breathe easier?

"Let me take the burden." Hazel grasped her mother's hands, warmer than before but barely. "I went away for two years, but I came back and never wish to stray again. I have years of experience keeping this house, and guiding and guarding the students who board here. I love the land and would do anything to—"

"Oh, baby, no, I couldn't burden you so." Her mother's fingers slipped through and cupped Hazel's face. "You've enough to do as is, keeping this house and boarders, and hosting family Sunday after Sunday, no matter where your husband's ridden off to."

"He's a Pullman porter on the railroad. It's his job to ride off," Hazel said, "but he always comes back. And he carries messages and news to our people near and far."

"Yes, yes, he does good work." Her mother nodded. "But he's so rarely here."

"He's always here." Hazel touched her chest, but her shoulders slumped. Somehow they always wound up with the same ending: Hazel offering and her mother declining, over and over. Hazel drew a sharp breath, ready to challenge the decision—but the older woman's chilly fingers shook as they pressed against Hazel's cheeks. Her mother's eyelids lowered and head rolled on her neck.

"At least let me look into this for you." The argument could wait for another time.

Her mother nodded, lying back and pulling the covers up. "Until Cora's back."

# MAYBE THIS TIME

Cora, always Cora.

The door closed with a soft click and Hazel leaned back against the cool wood. Glimmers of yellow light escaped along the bottom, and more shone at the far end from the kitchen light. Otherwise she stood in the midst of shadows. Left in her nightgown, as her robe remained with her mother, she ran her hands over her arms to warm away goosebumps..

The grandmother clock in the nearby living room ticked away the seconds and minutes. Farther away, a whistle blew, followed by the chug of the train pulling out of the station and heading south to Cincinnati. The last passenger train until early morning, but there was no one on it for her.

She let her shoulders droop and her body sag against the creaking wood. Her eyesight had adjusted, allowing her to distinguish the lines of the hallway in the dark, from her head scarf hanging off the newel post to the umbrella rack by the front door. Closing her eyes turned the world back into grayness.

A soft snore suggested her mother had slipped readily

into sleep. Why would she not, having passed over the duty of investigating the odd power shift? To Hazel, not Cora, but the burden was lifted from the older woman's shoulders regardless. Hazel hadn't even had to argue long, since Cora was away.

In the silence and darkness, she reached for her husband.

*Jake. Where are you?*

The vast distance between their bodies made her muscles ache, but in the stillness hearts might speak to hearts.

*Twenty minutes out of Chicago, bound for Denver.* His deep voice resounded in her head, not her ears. *You?*

*Home, where else? How've you been?*

*Lost track of how many times I got called a boy. Twenty or more.*

*Not a good day, then.* She clasped her hands, imagining they were wrapped in his warm fingers. That his broad and decidedly un-boyish body rested against the wall opposite, shoulders slightly stooped. His face turned to hers, wire-framed glasses glinting atop a long, steep nose and black skin gleaming with umber highlights. Gray mixed with short black curls atop his head, his matching beard trim along his chiseled chin. Vibrations ran through the floor beneath her, an echo of his place in a carriage riding the rails. Likewise, a hint of coal smoke tainted the air, in sympathy with what he breathed.

*I've had worse, but no, it wasn't good. You?*

*One of the clerks at the grocery store followed me around during my shopping even though she knows I pay cash for what I buy. But what else isn't new?*

*Not a day gone and I wish I were back.* Tendrils of hair shifted against her cheek, as though blown by his sigh. *It'll be a long two-three weeks before I'm home.*

*I'll be busy, though that's not to say I won't miss you. I always do.* Worth saying, though he knew it for truth without. It was hard to tell lies speaking heart to heart. Something always leaked through. His joy in traveling, her love of home, and the countless ways they kept balance between the two.

*Always. What kind of busyness are you up to now?* he asked.

*Investigating something for Mother.*

*You, not Cora?* His delight came through, but nearly overwhelmed by surprise.

*Such encouragement. It cannot be Cora, as she's away.*

*Will you get to keep on once she's back?*

A sharp silence stretched between them. He'd asked nothing more than what she wondered, but it stung all the same. A decade separated Hazel and Cora, the years in Hazel's favor, and yet her mother always turned to the younger first when seeking assistance on magical matters. No matter how much Hazel studied and learned and served.

*She doesn't see you that way, darling,* Jake said.

Before Hazel could respond, door hinges squeaked in the kitchen followed by a giggle and the soft patter of people trying to sneak in. Another giggle, or a hiccup, or even a sob. Little enough sounds, but they broke the stillness.

Talking with Jake would have to wait. First, to deal with the late arrivals.

She pushed away from the wall, the hem of her nightgown swaying around her ankles. Hardly the picture she'd want to present. Snatching up the scarf from the banister, she quickly wrapped it around her head in a turban. The silk sighed as it slithered through her fingers, but she had the ends tucked under a moment before two young women tiptoed through the kitchen doorway.

One giggled.

"Ssh!" The other pointed at the floor. "Step here, not here."

Hazel waited until both had cleared the doorway. Shielding her eyes with one hand, she reached over and turned on the hall light. A strategically placed mirror magnified the illumination. Both girls froze, faces tilted away and eyes shut—their stocking feet rested on the wood floor as they held their dancing shoes high above.

The elder stood a half-step ahead of the other. Grace was starting her third year boarding with Hazel and studying mathematics at the college. Small and solid, she'd ruthlessly tamed her hair into a modest chignon that drew attention to her long nose and high cheekbones. With her almost-beige skin, she could probably have passed and lived with the White female students on campus. The hem of her deep purple dress hung at a slant due to a loose shoulder strap.

In contrast, Frances, the newest and youngest of the boarders, was tall and lithe. The skirt of her orange dress swayed, brushing her calves. The color brought out umber undertones in her deep black skin, and hinted at russet highlights in the braids wrapped around her head. On second glance, however, a glaze of dust clung to the skirt hem with a few matching splotches across her front.

"Grace, Frances, whatever happened?"

"It's only just past eleven." Grace shivered, a burp escaping her. A sharp, fruity odor quickly dissipated. "Classes start this week. Frances likely won't get a chance to do much for weeks, until she gets her feet under her. And there were others at the hop—in Farmer Collins's field!"

Hazel nodded, appreciating their choice of venue. The Collinses were one of three Black families farming in the area, the others being her family and some of Jake's distant cousins. She'd met her husband at a farm dance when he'd come up from Cincinnati to visit, many years earlier. Her lips curved as Grace oohed over everyone they'd met at the dance.

"One of the newcomers was Samuel Baker, who's from Frances's hometown so she had to stop and be sociable.

Especially to such a fine-looking man. But we're back, safe, in good time."

Frances slipped to Grace's side, head down and eyes peeping up through thick lashes at Hazel. "Are you going to tell my mother?"

"That depends." Hazel crossed her arms over her chest. Safe they were, and hale—but for the dust splotches and torn strap. "Samuel Baker, hmm?"

They nodded, Grace giving a second, smaller, burp. The name meant nothing to Hazel, but Frances said, "he's an accountant."

"Ah." Hazel nodded, faint memory of a handsome young Black man sweeping the front stoop at the edge of the business district. "Did he escort you home?"

"He did, and it was so good of him." Grace clasped her hands, leaning her chin on them. "For there were three, four White men, college students, in the square who'd been drinking, but Samuel hurried us along when they got grabby."

Hazel leaned over to take a closer look at the tear on Frances' gown, while giving Grace a side-eye. Frances was still learning which areas to avoid, but Grace . . . "You came back through the center of town?"

"I know we shouldn't't've. Samuel hasn't been here long enough to know all the ins and outs, which I didn't figure out until too late." The student ducked her head. "But we're fine. One of the students tripped and fell into that big evergreen near the bandstand, knocking the others in, and they all got caught in the branches while we made our escape. We could still hear them grumbling a block or more away."

Frances giggled, clapping her hands over her mouth.

At least they were safe home. Perhaps, in the light of the morning, they'd see their adventure in a more serious light as a warning to be more careful in the future. But Hazel agreed not to tell their mothers—this time—and let them trip and stumble up the stairs.

Hazel waited until they were all the way up, their steps trekking between their rooms and the bath, before she made the rounds of the first floor. She touched each corner of the house and the well-wishing protections built into it. Even sorcerers couldn't rely solely on magic to protect them, but her family kept their homes as safe as possible.

Leaving the light on in the kitchen but not the hall, she made her way up the darkened stairs to her room. The bed was too big and empty without Jake. The sheets and blankets had lost any heat from earlier, but she snuggled under the layers.

Here, in the dark, it was even easier to slip into the stillness of the heart and reach out across distances. Jake was busy for a few minutes. She waited, verging on sleep, until he matched her. Again the faint hint of smoke from the engines wreathed about them, and the rattle of wheels rolling over rails.

She lay on her side of the bed, one hand straying into the center. Warmth enveloped her fingers, as though he did the same in his narrow bunk.

*All well?*

*As before, though one more man a decade my junior just called me boy.* Air blew across her forehead, as though he'd huffed right next to her, and a hint of a thumb brushed the back of her hand. *You?*

*Classes start this week, so the boarders are up to their usual parties and pushing the curfew,* Hazel said.

*Nothing out of the ordinary, then.*

*Only the mystery Mother's letting me investigate.* She shared what little she knew, the feel of sorcerous power flashing through the earth beneath her. This, at least, was something far easier to do in the stillness. *It's a chance to show her I can be the landward when she steps away.*

*Perhaps.* Hope and doubt flowed back from him.

*Cora's a decade younger than me!* The old complaint escaped her.

His chuckle in response blew across her shoulder. *But Cora's the oldest of Thelma's grandchildren while you're her last born. Her baby. All those years ago, when we moved back to Timmsville, the first thing out of her mouth was "Thank you for bringing my baby back to me."*

*She called me that today. Again. Marriage, raising two sons to successful adulthood, and managing house and church duties and boarding dozens of young women successfully and safely through their college years doesn't make me an adult?* All of which Hazel's mother had seen firsthand, since Hazel had lived in the same house apart from those two first years of married life in Chicago, having hated the density of the city and the feel of all the tall buildings pressing down on the earth.

*For me, yes, but I am not the one you have to convince.* Another squeeze of her hand, and a caress along her arm.

The stillness, and comfort of his presence despite the distance, eased Hazel toward sleep. A last hope sizzled through the connection before she succumbed. *Maybe this time.*

# BEFORE WANDERING

azel finished her coffee, then donned a modest straw hat before leaving the house. The ends of the light-blue ribbon decorating it almost matched the color of her calf-length dress. The low heels of her sensible wedges thumped against the wood stairs, and then softened to dull thuds when she reached pavement. The sun shone low in the sky, air still cool but her dark-blue half-cloak kept her warm —and she'd layered some of her favorite silky foundation garments beneath where no one would see. A covered basket hung from one elbow, the better to create the image of a housewife off to market.

Or a housekeeper or maid off to work—the better to do sorcery under the noses of town citizens who didn't look close enough.

She didn't know where she would go in specific, but sooner or later she'd have to pass through certain neighborhoods if she wanted to do a proper wander—and find the source of the strange sorcery—and had dressed accordingly.

At the street, she paused. Drew in the mix of dust and smoke and exhaust, and let out a long, low breath. Nothing pulled at her any which way in a magical sense. Her arms tightened against her sides, and the basket swayed. Lacking any other sign, she turned to the left. Might as well head to the farthest-away neighborhoods first and check off the worst so as to save the best for last.

The door to the house one over—a modest bungalow with a full-length porch—burst open and her great-niece rushed out. A frilled white collar topped a soft beige dress nipped in at the waist with a leather-and-bronze belt that brought out copper highlights in her gleaming skin. Instead of the sleek updo she'd worn to church the previous day, Ruby had crimped her thick locks into shoulder-length waves held back from her face by bronze hairpins. White socks peeped over the tops of her brown pumps.

Her lips thinned into a straight line as she crossed the wide porch, tripped down the stairs, and marched toward Hazel. Her hands gripped tight to the leather strap binding her schoolbooks. Head high, she nodded. "Morning, Aunt Hazel."

"Good morning to you too, Ruby."

Taking this as a subtle sign that she headed the right way, Hazel fell in with Ruby. They waved and smiled at neighbors tending gardens or heading to work—Hazel smiled, Ruby barely loosened her expression—as they made their way toward the high school at the edge of the town center.

"How's your father doing with your mother away?" Hazel asked.

"Fine."

"Is he opening the clinic as usual?"

"Nope."

"Taking the day to sleep in?"

"Never."

"Then whatever is he up to?"

This morning, Ruby showed no appreciation for the sun,

warming air, or new sidewalks, too busy casting sullen looks in her aunt's direction. It took Hazel several blocks and one-word answers to extract that Ruby's father had gone off in the night to deliver a baby whose mother hadn't managed to wait until Ruby's mother, the local nurse and midwife, was back from her trip. Hazel persevered, hoping the ordinariness of the conversation would ease the girl—or prompt her to let loose with her aunt rather than once she in class.

The high school loomed in the distance, a Victorian monstrosity in white with blue and red trim standing three stories high, if one didn't count the gabled attic that had recently been put to use while the town councilors argued over where to raise a new school. The distant chatter of students gathering on the grounds wafted along the street, as did savory scents of bacon and coffee from the two diners on the main street.

Except, Ruby stopped short a block away. When Hazel paused too, the girl managed a stiff smile and waved a hand. "I won't be here long. Just waiting."

"Waiting?"

Ruby nodded at two young Black women turning onto the street several blocks down. "It's easier, walking into the school when I'm not alone. You can tell Mom I didn't skip."

"Why would I do that?"

"You mean you're not walking me over because *they* asked?" Ruby tilted her head to the side, drawing back.

"No, I'm going this way." Hazel pursed her lips, catching on the word Ruby had stressed. "They?"

"Mom and Gramma Thelma." The girl crossed her arms over her chest. "I know Mom told Gramma Thelma about my bad grade in chemistry, which was my fault. That teacher's pretty fair across the board. It's the English teacher who grades me down for doing better than she thinks I should."

"We'll have to keep an eye on her, as this isn't the first complaint I've heard about her. Be sure to let your parents know."

"Of course." Ruby nodded, lips tight.

Then implication of Ruby's earlier comments hit Hazel. "You thought I was checking up on whether you went to school?"

"If Gramma Thelma asked, yes." A sharp nod. "You always do what she says. You snuck me treats when Mom sent me to bed without my supper, those couple years back, until Gramma Thelma caught you and you stopped."

"In truth, it was your father who caught me in the act and asked me to stop before your mother did." Hazel licked the last hint of coffee from her lips. However had Ruby got that view of her, as her mother's handmaiden . . . "Your mother's upset about your grades?"

"I got a C in chemistry. It was only a quiz! Still, all I heard from her before she left was how important it was to keep my grades up, especially in science. She'd rather think I'm skipping and not living up to my potential than that I'm not good at biology or chemistry, or don't want to go into medicine. Dad wasn't any too happy either, but he didn't come down as hard." Ruby let out a whistling breath, some of her tension easing. "I was so sure she'd got Gramma Thelma to have you make sure I didn't skip."

"No, nothing of that kind." Hazel shook her head, gesturing at the mix of houses and businesses lining the street. "I'm out for a wander."

Ruby scrunched her nose as she looked Hazel over head to toe, as though she hadn't before. "That's why you're dressed so . . ."

"It's one way not to be noticed." Dressing as though headed to work as a domestic followed the rule of sorcery working best on the magicless when it hid just under the surface. Often the easiest way was to appear as the expected thing, and let people's assumptions lead them the wrong way. "Doesn't your mother do the same?"

"Mom does her wanders on nursing rounds, so she's in her uniform. Sometimes she'll sneak trousers under her skirts when she bikes, though."

"Part of the point of wanders is to go slow and keep an eye out for places that have changed. You can't do that if you go fast. Much better to keep one's feet on the ground and in touch with the earth." Hazel's turn to stiffen, elbows so tight they dug into her side. Wandering meant taking one's time to survey surroundings and see what had changed and if anything was going wrong. It was a sacred practice dating back well over a century to when their freeborn ancestors had settled in the area, some marrying or adopting into the Shawnee tribes, who claimed the territory until the growing United States had forcibly removed most of them. Others remained or returned, and several of their descendants tended lands nearby. "She bikes?"

"Sure she does. She used grumble whenever she had to do a wander, because it slowed her down, having to follow whims while walking." Ruby swung her book bag, leather strap whistling through the air. "Then she started biking so she could swing off on a whim and still get where she was going in good time, and the grumbling stopped. Mostly."

Such airiness. It might be her youth and impatience, or perhaps unfamiliarity? "Doesn't Cora ever take you with her on wanders?"

"Not much. Gramma Thelma used to once in a while, but she always spent half the time telling me what everything used to look like when she was young. All the houses and buildings that weren't here, or were smaller. Who lived where and what they did." A bell rang out from the school.

With a wave, Ruby dashed across the street to join her friends and headed in.

A car honked as it passed, Ruby's father nodding and smiling from behind the wheel, no doubt headed for home. Hazel meandered past the school and the last students streaming in through the doors, on toward to the town center.

Cora biked her wanders. The news came second-hand, not straight from her. There was no sign that she didn't do her duty, but there was a difference between doing the wanders placing foot after foot as something to be done, and doing them out of care for the land.

Would Cora even have noticed changes such as produced the tremors?

Then again, Hazel had missed them in her wanders, as her mother evidently had on hers before letting others take the bulk of the work when the summer's heat slowed her down.

Whatever had flourished without their awareness, they knew now. She had to find it so they could decide whether it belonged in their town or not.

# WANDERING IN TOWN

Hazel started her search in the heart of town, or near it. A square park occupied the actual center, featuring a trellis bandstand next to a mighty evergreen that wore garlands every December, along with several flower beds and a massive oval water fountain with a big fish squirting water into the air. A few droplets fell on her face and cape as she passed by.

Businesses lined two sides of the square. All boasted clean-swept sidewalks before them and were situated in neat buildings pressed close against each other. None had more than two stories although most had false fronts rising ten or fifteen fight higher.

Diners and clothing stores. A jeweler next to a dime shop, with the new bakery beyond run by a Jewish family down from Cleveland. The line out the door suggested that the delicious smells wafting out had overcome peoples' hesitation about patronizing it.

On another side stood three banks and two florists with a bookstore between. One of the florists, an older White woman, arranged a bouquet of carnations for display and watched Hazel pass.

The college owned the block edging the last side, and had raised an inn and an art museum fronting the park.

In the distance, a train whistled and a hint of coal smoke belched from the engine betokened freight traveling through. The ground rumbled, though most might not notice it this far from the tracks and station—all of three blocks.

Sound and smell moved Hazel to slip back and lean against the darkened windows of the closed bookstore. Without sacrificing awareness of her present—no sense risking danger—she reached for the stillness of the heart and Jake. A snore vibrated through her, rumbling in her bones stronger than the train passing. To be expected, given how far west he likely was, and that he snatched rest when he could between duties.

Pushing away from the wall, she planted her feet flat against the sidewalk and used the stillness to begin the wander.

Exactly when her family had begun the practice no one knew, though papers left by the ancestors who'd moved here suggested they'd adapted older patterns to suit their new home. They'd focused first on walking the boundaries of the lands they claimed—seeking to ward off slave takers and others who wished them ill, and at the same time to set a beacon for those in need of refuge. Even before they built a house, now occupied by her cousins who farmed some of the same fields, they'd made their home a stop on the Underground Railroad.

Yet at some point, the sorcerous practices had split in two. Hazel's aunts and uncles and cousins still marked the boundaries of their land for protection against theft and ill-wishers. For that matter, she and her mother did the same with their house.

By the time of her grandparents, the practice of the landward was set with the landward and their helpers wandering to care for hill and dale, fields and woods, to note what flourished, what faded, and what changed. Wandering involved having a general idea of where one was headed yet allowing oneself to step off the trail at any time for an inkling that here or there was something worth noting.

And so they continued, even when little of the town belonged to them according to government records. A few houses within the town proper, and a few farms outside.

Leaving the business district behind, Hazel ventured into the residential neighborhood lining the fourth side of the park. The houses themselves she paid little notice to. They changed slowly, a new coat of paint here or a porch added there. Nothing very different from where she lived except that these were one-and-all well-kept to a competitive degree. This house had one gable picked out with trim in two colors, and the next might have a gabled porch decorated with three layers of trim.

The gardens she studied with more care. Great swathes of green lawn kept ruthlessly neat mixed with fenced yards boasting bushes still blooming and giving off sweet perfumes. Lavender asters with dots of gold at their center. Bright yellow, orange, and pink chrysanthemums. Similar colors on the pansies with their delicate petals. Most were nurtured with love and fertilizer, but the occasional sorcerer residing there added a spell or three to encourage their plants.

Lovely to the eye and sometimes to the nose—but what Hazel watched for most was signs of blight or anything else presaging trouble such as a flash of sorcerous power running through the ground. The land mourned grass cut short with regular mowing, and though she could do little to stop the practice, she at least stood witness and grieved with it.

She let her feet wind back and forth through the blocks, passing from the richest sections to middle class neighborhoods. The sizes of the houses diminished, though all boasted at least three or four bedrooms. The women who lived here did for themselves, but occasionally hired help for parties. Some curtains twitched as Hazel went by, but no one challenged her.

Many yards were simpler, but others as elaborate as those of the rich. One corner lot edged by a white picket fence on both sides boasted fountains of red and white rose bushes carefully trained along the edges. The house itself was a simple, narrow affair set back from the streets, the better to allow room for the flowers. Enough bloomed, even this late in the year, to perfume the air.

The woman of the house tended her yard herself. She'd pulled her gold hair back from her face with a blue kerchief that matched her gardening outfit—a light blouse and dark pants—both in color and dirt stains. Heavy green gloves covered her arms nearly to the elbow as she wielded pruning shears and removed dead or dying blooms.

"Good morning Mrs. Gregson." She straightened as Hazel passed, looking right at her.

"To you, too, Mrs. Bullen." Hazel nodded and stopped. Between the fence and the bushes, a good three or four feet separated them. No more or less than those civic occasions when they'd met in support of one cause or another. The other usually provided flowers and ordered people about while Hazel and her family brought food.

"You're out early." Mrs. Bullen rubbed her forehead with the back of a hand and left a smear of dirt behind.

"Just paying a call or two." Hazel patted the basket hanging off her arm. Rarely did she need to actually cast a spell, so long as she created the conditions for people to make their own assumptions.

"Anyone I know?"

"Someone on the far side," Hazel said and nodded in the direction of the edge of town.

The other woman also nodded, shoulders easing slightly.

"I couldn't help but stop to see your roses still blooming," Hazel said. "Every year you grow the prettiest blossoms and your bushes bloom longer than anyone else's."

"My family and my roses are my pride and joy. The roses are doing well this year—so well I've a rose thief of late." The other woman set hands on hips and surveyed the roses with satisfaction, but with a tilt to her head that promised woe to the thief if she caught him. "Would you care to take some to your mother? I trust she's well." The two had served together several years earlier on a committee picking the designs of the park flower beds.

"That would be lovely. I'm sure she'd appreciate it." Hazel handed over her basket, receiving it back a few minutes later with several white and red blooms. The perfume accompanied her on the remainder of her wanders—the one bright touch to the morning.

For she found nothing. No signs of decay as most of the vegetation grew green and healthy. Yet neither could she locate any hint of the strange magic that had flashed through her yard so recently.

All was well. Usual. Customary.

And yet by the end of the day wandering, she was left with every nerve on edge and the surety that she'd missed *something*.

It hardly helped that when she presented the roses and her findings, or rather the lack, to her mother, the older woman patted her hand.

"You tried, that's what matters." Hazel's mother buried her face in the roses, hands cradling a simple cream vase. "When is Cora back?"

# STARTING WITH A TREE

The question of Cora's return weighed on Hazel. Day after day she wandered through different parts of town, each time seeking and failing to find any sign of the flashing power.

The business district—nothing.

The college—likewise.

The other residential districts, leaving her own for last the better to look at it with determination to see beyond everyday familiarity—failure again.

Friday morning, Hazel sat at the big, scarred kitchen table. She'd dressed for wandering, this time in a light-yellow blouse and soft orange skirt with sensible shoes below. Her hands twisted in her lap, where no one could see. Her breakfast lay before her, partially eaten. A few bites of apple, cream, and cinnamon remained in the lump of oatmeal so thick the spoon stuck straight up. What she'd consumed rested heavy in her belly. The rest of the table was clear and clean, three boarders having headed off to campus while the two remaining did the dishes and chattered amidst the clatter.

Her mother had eaten and gone into the parlor to reread the latest letters from family and friends, and to write her responses. She'd shared highlights about grandchildren doing well in school, a tailor cousin thinking about moving back to Timms, but Hazel knew she hadn't given sufficiently enthusiastic responses. No doubt her mother would be happier farther away from Hazel's despondency.

Only the outlying farms remained to check. A bitter prospect, as Cora was due back anytime. Her husband and daughter had come over for dinner the night before. He'd flourished a telegram from Cora providing details, which Hazel's mother had snatched up to study.

Failure.

True, Cora likely wouldn't find any more success than Hazel. She'd have to wait to experience the flickers herself before even knowing what to search for. Still, without any sign of success, Hazel had no reason to protest if her mother handed the duty over to Cora. The older woman might not even wait a day after her arrival.

A crashing noise startled Hazel from her reverie. She jerked, sitting straight and feet flat on the floor—only to realize the oldest of her boarders had just deposited an array of spoons into the dish drainer. The young woman, in a long white apron over a simple gray and white dress that flattered her dark complexion, turned to face Frances, the youngest of the boarders. The two were distant cousins and looked it, even with the one dressed simply and the other in a lace-trimmed blouse and smartly cut skirt under an enveloping apron.

"Don't you 'but Grace' me." The older wagged a finger at the younger. "Grace is a fine person and a good student, but she can do things that won't *do* for you or me, not without getting the wrong kind of notice."

"Everything's gone well so far." Frances lifted her chin as

she wiped down the counter. The wet cloth squeaked, high enough to make Hazel's teeth hurt.

"If you consider a close call or two going well." Her cousin picked up a bowl and plunged it into the sink. A few bubbles rose and floated in the air, gleaming rainbow colors until they burst in a harsh blast of soap. "What about last Saturday?"

"We were saved by a tree." The younger student sniffed and kept her head turned away.

Their conversation continued. Voices sounded in Hazel's ears, but words didn't register in her head for she was too full of Frances's defiant phrase echoing in her head.

*Saved by a tree.*

Hazel rose and scraped her remaining breakfast into the trash. She managed to exchange pleasantries with the young women as she did so, though she never after remembered what she or they said—only that she had time to search for any sign of sorcery in Frances and found none.

Expected to find none, for only one of the many boarders she'd hosted over the years had been a sorcerer, and he a third cousin up from Kentucky who stayed several years earlier when she'd only accepted male students. She hadn't changed to taking female until her younger son left for college, and none of the young women were or had been sorcerers.

It was possible Frances had turned sorcerer, but unlikely. She lacked the usual signs—startling easily, suddenly noticing things that the magicless ignored or talked themselves out of accepting, plus an increased tendency to burst into static electricity whether or not the weather warranted it.

*Saved by a tree.*

Still, that one phrase stuck with Hazel. A dramatic interpretation of an attacker—how many had there been?—stumbling into a tree rather than the tree reaching out to help. Yet, whatever had happened to help Frances and Grace and their young swain escape took place at much the same time as Hazel and her mother had sat on the grass sensing flickers rippling through the earth.

Or passing root to root?

Likely it was only Hazel grasping at faint hope. All the same, when she left home she turned her feet toward the center of town and the tree that had saved Frances and Grace.

She knew which tree, for they'd mentioned the big evergreen in the town square.

Big it was, towering high above as she approached bare minutes later, having grabbed hat and cloak and rushed out the door. Wide, too, with dozens, even hundreds, of branches swaying in a light breeze. The morning was cooler than earlier in the week, just enough to raise a few goosebumps along Hazel's arms.

Or was that hope and nerves?

At the far end of the square, someone started a lawn mower. The smell of cut grass carried, along with a hint of exhaust. The tree's branches rustled all the more.

Hazel stood on the paved path leading to the bandstand. No one near, but the few other trees growing on the square —mostly elms, oaks, and maples—offered little in the way of concealment. Anyone passing around the edge of the park, patronizing a business or going into the college inn, could glance her way.

Summoning up power, she pulled at the shadow cast by a nearby elm and stretched it to include her. Let her movement be unseen, her actions unheard and unwitnessed, and might she leave no trace behind.

The shadow cloak cooled her skin and dimmed colors to barely seen variations on gray.

She hurried across the grass to the big evergreen. Brushed a branch, the needles soft to the touch. Nothing unusual, no leap of magic. Still, chills flickered along her spine. Drawing a deep breath, she bent and laid her palm against cool grass and damp earth. For the first moment, nothing. A lump formed in her throat, making it hard to breathe.

A tiny bolt of energy blasted through her, palm to elbow to shoulder. Up and out the top of her head. She clapped her other hand to her head, nearly crushing the crown of her hat as she made sure it hadn't been blown off.

Deep in the ground below, flickers of energy dashed this way and that. Nowhere near the extent of the previous weekend. This was a trickle to that storm—yet noticeable. As though mini lightning bolts zigged in unpredictable frequency this way and that from the tree's root ball.

Her legs weakened beneath her and she tumbled to the ground. The tree's shadow still protected her, but she glanced around all the same.

No one near, no one to see.

Just the tree, with flickering energy hidden in the earth below. Energy that slowed even as she noted, from a trickle to a drip.

Her skirts soaked up dew, growing damp and uncomfortable beneath her. Her palm reddened where it pressed against the earth, but otherwise showed no sign of the bolt.

Success! She'd found it!

But . . . found what? Not an answer, merely a first step toward an answer.

Dozens of questions flooded her, pounding one after another. She tried to rise, but her legs refused to cooperate.

Turning onto her hands and knees, she kept the elm's shadow tucked close about her as she crawled back to its side.

Risking her other palm, she laid it against the earth at the base of the trunk. Again, nothing at first. Then a zing of power, this much smaller and slighter than before. More of a twinge. Fewer darts of energy about this root ball, going out or in.

Out or in.

Swallowing, she set her other palm next to the first. She traced one flicker after another, and for nearly every one going in, another darted out.

How many trees were connected? Rolling onto her bottom and leaning back against the elm, she tried to count the trees on the square alone and gave up after reaching thirty. There were far too many to check individually, even if she could guarantee no one would notice.

Hazel clapped her hands, summoning a sheet of paper from her house. She laid it on her lap, the better to keep dry, and clapped again. A bottle of ink formed within her grasp, the glass warm and smooth to the touch as the ink sloshed within.

The stopper came out easily, with a soft sucking sound. Tilting the vial, she let fall just enough ink to make a blob in the center of the paper. Restopping the bottle, she sent it back home with another clap.

The ink blot slowly seeped into paper. Hazel closed her eyes and waved her hands over the surface, careful to leave space between skin and ink. In her mind's eye she imagined that a map of the connections between the trees existed on her paper. First the one connecting the evergreen and the elm, then any other trees with the same in or out flickers.

The ink smell grew stronger. Although she kept the paper

flat, a sloshing sound accompanied the scent. A breath, two, three, then scent and sound diminished. Hazel counted to ten. Leaning forward and away from the trunk, she opened her eyes.

An intricate map covered the paper. Soft gray lines so faint as to be almost illegible laid out streets and buildings for the whole town on an incredibly small and detailed level. Even sheds in back yards manifested as minute gray dots. Each and every tree in the city also appeared, as green dots although she'd only used black ink.

Yet nowhere appeared any connections between the trees.

She sank back against the elm. The paper fluttered on her lap, then went still. Bending over, she searched for any change, for how long she didn't know, before she noticed a tiny silver circle around one of the green dots, a circle with seven minuscule spikes pointing in different directions.

Hazel pinched the edge of the paper between two fingers, in one of the few places with no ink. Her legs wavered beneath her but supported her as she rose and tottered over to the evergreen.

One brush of a hand against a branch, and another circle, this one in gold, appeared around a different green dot, this boasting a dozen or so minute spikes. A dotted line connected one of the evergreen's spikes to the elm. Additional dotted lines stretched from the spikes around each to other trees, which now had their own circles with spikes— but those spikes led nowhere.

Sweat beaded her forehead and slicked her spine. Her legs ached as she stumbled from tree to tree until she'd visited a dozen on the square. After touching leaf or bark, each tree manifested a circle with spikes, and connections to other trees. Most were silver, only the evergreen's dot showing any hint of gold. She tried every way she could think of to make the connections ripple out, but for each tree she touched, she identified only those trees to which it was connected.

God gave with one hand and made things more complicated with the other.

She could map the network of trees by touching each tree individually—but that would take ages.

Unless there was another way?

# ROOTS AND STARS

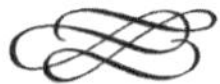

*L*ight blazed from the Warren house that evening, bright electric yellow mingling with the rosy glow of the setting sun to fully illuminate the couple cuddling on the porch. Luther Warren rested sideways, his long back against the railing spokes. He'd doffed his jacket and was casual, for him, in shirtsleeves and slacks and bare feet. A neatly trimmed beard, half-grizzled with gray, hid most of the pinkish-brown lines scarring one cheek. Otherwise his skin was deep brown with the same copper highlights as his daughter.

The angle of his body offered a place for Cora to lean. She'd changed to a short-sleeved green top and knee-length shorts in dark green, certainly not the clothes she'd traveled in. A green-and-yellow silk turban covered her hair, and the way the fabric angled over her face made her appear round and full-cheeked. Small and curvy, she nestled into her husband in a way that spoke of tiredness and comfort.

Didn't keep her golden-brown eyes from flashing at Hazel's approach. But if they'd wanted privacy on this fine warm evening, they'd have stayed inside or sat on the back steps. They might have to go inside soon enough, for the clouds gathering between the horizon and overhead suggested rain on the way.

"Welcome back, Cora." Hazel stopped halfway up the walk, the better to not hover over them. She hadn't changed after dinner, and in contrast to her niece, her linen dress appeared both too formal in cut and too informal with all the creases and wear from the day.

"It's good to be home. The trip back was rough. I swear the ticket clerk in Cincinnati studied my bags as though he thought I'd stolen them." The younger woman nodded, then tucked her head more securely into the crook of Luther's neck. "I don't know how Uncle Jake manages riding the rails week after week."

"It's easier on the longer stretches." Or so Jake had often assured Hazel, for she had never gone farther than Chicago. Still, some of his pleasure in gloriously different country-sides always slipped through when they talked in the stillness.

"Do tell." Cora waved at the lower steps leading up their bungalow. "Come to sit a spell?"

Hazel hadn't, but she did. It was only good manners to settle on warm wood. She angled her legs to catch the last of the sun's rays and warmth, to ease muscles still aching from the morning's exertion, all the while listening to new developments in midwifery. "Marvelous. Just marvelous."

"And how much of that did you understand?" Cora shook her head.

"Enough." Hazel clapped her hands together. "Since no one is likely to ask me to deliver a baby any day soon. But where is Ruby?"

"Down at the drug store," Luther said with his usual soft drawl, and jerked his head in the general direction. "Were you wanting her for something?"

"I need a bit of help on a project." Hazel dabbed at sweat beading her forehead. "A few hours, maybe a little more, this weekend if she can spare it."

Cora frowned. "Can't one of your boarders lend a hand?"

"It's a project for Mother." Hazel stared at her niece, brows raised.

"Oh." The younger woman's lips tightened. "Grandmother did say she'd have work for me, some new magic knot to be unsnarled."

Hazel's breath caught in her throat. She clasped her hands, the better to keep her fingers from twitching. Mother had started handing off the mystery to Cora already? She coughed. "No need for you to jump-to, first thing home. I have a good thread, I just need a little help following it. If not Ruby, then I can call over to the farm to see if one of the cousins can assist."

Before she could rise more than halfway, Luther gestured for her to settle back down. "Ruby can help."

"She needs to study. Two Cs in a row." Cora shook her head.

"It's still early days in the school year. She'll have to finish her homework first, of course, but after." Luther wrapped his hands around Cora's, then smiled at Hazel. "I'm sure Ruby would be glad to assist."

*And that was that,* Hazel shared with Jake, hours later when she lay in her half-empty bed. The air in the darkened room was stuffy, every hint of breeze having died down with the sunset. She'd kicked the covers to the foot and lay sprawled, though keeping to her own side. Her soft nightgown clung to her skin save for extra folds that pooled at her sides.

*Isn't it what you wanted?* A similar warmth came through with his voice. He was out back of one of the cars, leaning against the metal. The clacking of the wheels rumbled through her, loosening tight muscles.

*It is.*

*But?*

*Nothing. Just seemed I hit a sore spot or something. Over Ruby's schooling, of all things.* She hadn't meant to spark an argument. *I'd have thought Luther would be all for her keeping her nose to her books as much as Cora. He's a doctor after all!*

*Good for him. I'd never have made it, even if I tried. Too much sitting in one place.* A gentle laugh. *But he's got sense to see some women do better if they're not being pushed.*

*And just what are you saying about Cora?*

*Nothing against Cora, but sounds as though she's bent on pushing Ruby rather than coaxing. Too much of the stick, not enough of the honey. Ruby's a strong woman, just like her mamma and great-grandmother and great-aunt.* A brief gust of air fluttered over her shoulders as, far away, he tilted his head further back to take in an expanse filled with thousands of twinkling stars. *There, you ever see the like?*

*Only through your eyes.* She closed her own, the better to appreciate the vista. Those who wondered why she'd never pushed Jake to take only short, local routes—apart from the years their sons needed him most—didn't understand that with him free to leave and return, they both enjoyed traveling far and staying home.

Though she missed him more now, and not only because he'd be a help in tracking down the mystery.

*In all your travels, did you ever see magical roots connecting trees?* She shared an image of the map and the small array of glittering lines connecting trees.

*Roots . . .* He paused, and images filtered through their connection. A stand of white trees with golden leaves against a bright blue sky. Firs not unlike the big evergreen in the town square, but smaller and clustered together on a rocky hillside. Thick trunks sprouting from swampy waters with smaller lumps of roots protruding around them. *There's lots of trees growing close together, sometimes with their roots clear twining, but I never saw sign of magic running in them. Still I can believe it. You take care, now.*

*I'm so close. I just need something to show Mother I can be landward in her place.*

*You've done as much for her before.* A shooting star blazed across the sky over Jake, dazzling in its brightness. *What if this isn't enough?*

Hazel's hands fisted in her nightgown. *It has to be.*

# MAPPING ROOTS AND MAGIC

"Father said you asked for me?" Ruby appeared at the kitchen door early in the morning.

"I did indeed." Hazel jerked, then finished hanging up her apron. She rubbed her hands again on her slacks, last few drops of dish water darkening the blue. Her shirt likewise showed a little damp along the neckline, where it had risen above the apron. "I've a task, if you've time."

The girl shrugged, hands stuck in the pockets of her shorts and mouth a thin line. Her hair hung loose around her head in curls, the ends bobbing above the collar of her red-and-white shirt. Her nostrils flared and she glanced sideways at a cloth-covered plate on the counter.

Hazel whipped the napkin off the still-warm breakfast leftovers. "Care for a biscuit first?"

"You bribing me?" Her lips quirked to the side, a hint of a smile dancing in her eyes.

"Would it work if I did?"

"Maybe."

Within moments, Hazel had her great-niece seated at the kitchen table with a biscuit cracked open and slathered with butter and honey. The last of the spring's clover honey perfumed the air. Hazel's mouth watered, although she'd fed well enough that she settled on the other side of the table with not even a glass of water.

"Don't tell my mother, but you do make better biscuits." Ruby cleaned up after herself, then returned to her chair. "So, what is it you want of me?"

"You're willing?"

"It's got to be better than staying at home risking another lecture about my chem quiz grades." The girl's shoulders slumped, and a thump from below suggested she'd kicked the table leg. "Two weeks in, and already she's gone on and on about how am I ever going to get into a good nursing school if I don't do better, no matter how many times I tell her I don't want to be a nurse. I'd do anything to get away from that." Her head tilted to one side and she pursed her lips, shrugging. "Well, almost anything."

"I need your help mapping magic."

"Cool." Ruby nodded, fingers rapping against the table.

Hazel summoned the map she'd started and laid it out on the table. None of the colors had dimmed since the day before. "These are trees, and these are magical connections between them." She touched the green dots. "I had to touch each individually to establish even these few lines and spikes. I need help filling out the map. You'll need to go to the park, to the big evergreen, to get an idea of what the magic feels like."

"Wait a minute, you want me to go around touching trees?" Ruby studied the dots, then rocked back in her chair. "That's a lot of trees."

"It is. I don't need them all." Though Hazel preferred to be as detailed as possible, the town did, indeed, have a lot of trees. Hundreds at a minimum, and that without including the wooded areas on campus which appeared as a large green smudge rather than individual dots on the map.

"Good, because I'd go back to studying chem if you did." The girl crossed her arms. Leaning forward, she gazed straight into Hazel's eyes. "What do you want me to bring back? Give me the bottom line."

"I want to know the source, or where this all started. Or the center, at least, and the extent. How far it has spread." Hazel pushed the map toward Ruby.

The younger woman picked it up and studied it, then gave a decisive nod. "Okay, I have some ideas. Is it all right if I take this?"

"That's the original." Hazel bit her lip, breath hissing in. "Let me make a copy and tie them together, so I'll have whatever you gather even if it rains."

"Eh, not today." Ruby glanced at the window, sunshine clear on the other side. "Make a couple copies? I'm thinking I'll bike out to the farm and get cousins in on this, if that's all right with you?"

"Certainly." Hazel's oldest brother had inherited the family farm from an uncle, and worked it alongside two grown sons and their families; if Ruby hadn't agreed to help, Hazel had planned to ask them anyway. Hazel summoned additional pieces of paper and matched them to the map one at a time, ending with three copies and one original. She kept a copy, though she itched to snatch the original back as Ruby carried off the rest.

"Might have something for you tomorrow, might not, but I'll let you know." The papers fluttered between Ruby's fingers as she waved farewell, a wide smile on her face and gleam in her eye. "This should be fun."

Should be, if her enthusiasm stayed strong.

Hazel could hope.

And keep watch, albeit at a distance. Scuttling upstairs,

she set her copy of the map on her bureau. It would be safe there from prying, magicless eyes.

But not from her own. Time after time, she paused between tasks to dart into her room and check the map. She tidied the living room and dusted furniture, then consulted the map—no change. Gathered up laundry and ran the clothing through the wringer with a touch of magic to ease the labor—no change. Hung the wash out on the line to dry —no change. Prepared lunch and served her mother—no change.

Then, on second glance in early afternoon, a silver spiked circle appeared on a tree dot near the top of the map. It was within the town limits, not so far north as the family farm. No lines connected the circle to any other tree dot, but it was there.

Over the hours more such circles manifested around trees edging the north, west, and south—but still no dotted lines between trees.

And no word from Ruby.

The usual bedlam of Saturday night distracted Hazel for a while, as the boarders bustled around getting ready to go to a dance.

Likewise, Sunday morning kept her hopping between church and hosting half her brother's family along with the boarders for lunch. Ruby and her parents joined them, too, but Hazel had no chance to get the girl alone amidst the hustle and press of people. Most crowded around Cora, hearing all about her adventures at the midwifery conference.

The best Hazel got was that evening, rising from an after-dinner nap and coming downstairs still yawning to find Ruby and Cora leaving the house without Hazel having woken to their arrival in the first place.

"One more day." Ruby held up a finger as she followed her mother down the hall. "Tomorrow night, I promise."

"One more day then what?" Hazel's mother asked from her perch on her favorite chair, deep in her room. Warm slippers covered her feet, and she'd pulled a quilted jacket over her green day dress, but she looked pale and tired after a day of boasting about Cora's accomplishments, and those of her other descendants. She'd already wrapped a silk scarf around her head and, although her fingers dug into the soft, padded arms of the chair, she didn't rise.

"I'm making progress on the tree magic. Ruby's been giving me some help." Hazel patted the scarf covering her own hair, straightened the casual shirt and slacks she'd donned after the family meal, and then entered the room.

The windows were shut and curtains pulled, making the lavender potpourri scent all the stronger. A lamp high atop the bureau cast warm light, but left half of her mother's face in shadow. A hard chair of wood slats had been moved from the wall to angle facing her mother, and wrinkles on the foot of the bed suggested Ruby or Cora, but more likely the younger, had perched there for a while.

"Good to hear." The older woman nodded, reaching down the far side of the chair to pick up her knitting. The steel needles clacked and flashed in the light as she added rows of silvery yarn to what would soon be a shawl. The color resembled that on the map, but softer and more subdued. "Cora will be back to report in a day or two, so you can share what you've done then."

Hazel sank onto the bed, layers of blanket compressing and springs squeaking. So much in that simple sentence, but the first registered more strongly. "Report? On what?"

"Some strangeness about a magicless girl, one of Ruby's classmates. Or perhaps not, it wasn't clear." Hazel's mother stopped knitting long enough to wave a dismissive hand.

"Ruby brought the news. Cora plans to check on the girl, see if she's turned sorcerer or stumbled into something, or if it's a rumor."

Of course her mother would ask Cora. "Let me know if there's anything I can do."

"You do so much already, darling." Thelma shook her head. "No, Cora knows what to do. She's done it often enough before when strangers come to town, to see whether they're sorcerers and worth allowing to stay or encourage to move on."

"So have I."

Hazel's mother didn't seem to have heard, head up and view distant as she shifted the needles and started another row. "Good practice. I'm not getting any younger or spryer."

"You're not sickening?" Hazel leaned forward, searching for signs of fever or chill, sweat or pain.

"No more than I have been, but it's time. I've waited for Cora to be ready—to ask—but she'll have to be." A hiss and her mother lifted up the rows, scowling over a dropped stitch. A few tries, and she slipped it back on the needle. "Someone must become the landward, before I am forced to let go."

Hazel closed her eyes. Her body rocked as though seated in a wagon on a pile of clean rags. Booties on her feet, and the rest of her encased in layers of gowns handed down from her older siblings. Winter and summer, fall and spring, she'd ridden along—or toddled after, for as long as she could walk —while her mother wandered the town. Thelma had taken on the role when younger than Hazel, younger than Cora.

Her mother had flourished in it. She'd been one of the powers behind the town's election of not one but two Black council members. She'd mobilized citizens in supporting soldiers at war with boxes of warm socks and mittens and home-made goods. Raised healthy, happy children. And all the while served as landward coordinating care for the land during times of flood and famine. She deserved to rest if she wished.

"If Cora's not ready, let me take it." Hazel dropped to her knees on the soft braided rug. "Please?"

"Oh, child." Her mother returned the knitting into the bag next to the chair and cupped Hazel's warm cheeks in cool hands. "It's not so dire a matter. I can hold a while longer. No need to sacrifice yourself."

"It would be an honor!" Hazel laid her own hot, sweaty palms over her mother's. "Let me do this for you."

"You were such a sweet baby, so quiet and serene after my first girl and all the bumptious boys between, plus that sad last miscarriage—God rest the little angel." Thelma twisted her wrists and captured Hazel's hands in a gentle, frail, but unbreakable hold. "But I'd be a poor mother to make you bear such an unsuitable burden. No."

Such a simple, implacable word. Hazel remained on her knees swaying, until a faint breeze along her cheeks registered. Caused by her mother struggling to her feet. Hazel leapt up and slipped hands under Thelma's, easing her to the bed.

"I can tuck myself in." Her mother pulled the cover over her legs. "You go enjoy the evening."

A huff escaped Hazel as she turned the light off and pulled the door closed behind her. Leaning back against the wood, she closed her eyes and sought Jake. *She said no. Again.*

No words came in answer. A sense of busyness and need for concentration; hands rushing through cleaning a berth for the next occupant. All the same, a wealth of love wrapped around her heart as she stumbled up the stairs to her room to hide.

# WANDERING IN WOODS

*H*azel studied the map. The battered kitchen table offered a fine background, wiped clean after dinner. She had the room to herself, and no work remaining. Dinner dishes cleaned and put away, Monday laundry brought in and folded, and the boarders chatting in the living room under her mother's indulgent eye or off studying in the library. Her back ached, but a mug of tea and a paracetamol tablet would ease it soon enough. A cool breeze snuck through the window over the sink, chilling the back of her neck, but the rest of her was warm enough in shirt and slacks as she perched on a chair and traced the dozens of jagged dotted lines arcing from the north, west, and south into the town and intersecting in a steeply-angled triangle on the college campus.

"Aunt Hazel?"

"Come in, come in." Hazel rushed to open the door. Ruby blew by, whirling over to the table to lay out three replicas of the map beside the original to make a large square.

"We had ourselves a fine time getting these." Delight shone from her round face, curls bouncing with energy. A few faint dirt smears marred the sleeves of her yellow shirt, though she'd rolled it up near the elbows. Elsewise her clothes looked clear and clean, and her solid black shoes tracked no dirt. "We've found three spots that might be the center—at least they've all got many many connections to other trees—and we visited them this afternoon, each of us going to one, and they're all . . ." She dropped into a chair opposite Hazel, a shiver rippling through her body and voice lowering. "Uncanny."

"These three." Hazel touched the points on the original map.

"I checked this one." Ruby pointed at a ring of dots in the middle. "It's that circle of trees near the center of campus, around where they put the college seal in the ground? There're a ton of superstitions about not touching it. I swear, the White students watched me like hawks as though daring me to so much as breathe on it. There's no tales about the trees, that I know of. I almost heard them whispering, just out of hearing, but they didn't mind me being around."

"The seal." Hazel made a circle around the spot with her fingers and then slowly pulled her hands apart. The image grew—larger and clearer—as long as she kept her hands in place. Three of the dozen in the circle had golden circlets around their dots. The rest were silver, but each tree linked to all the others and dozens more besides. "Interesting. What about the others?"

The northernmost proved to be an immense oak tree near a cluster of men's dorms. A teenaged male cousin had visited it and called it creepy to the nth degree. Worse than the White students sneering at him for thinking he belonged there. He noticed they kept well clear of the tree. "According to him, the tree's branches twitched when he came near, or any of the students walking around, although they didn't seem to notice. He didn't see anyone he recognized as a sorcerer among them, though."

Last but not least, another male cousin had ventured into the woods in search of the third spot. He'd found a clearing and thought it a nice enough place, "if you like woods," until he touched an old, dead tree and then he couldn't get out of there fast enough. "And he swears you couldn't pay him to go back. He'd rather face down the students at the dorms."

Even before Hazel enlarged the southern spot, it appeared to have the most connections. Once made bigger, all the lines led, albeit in jagged darts through other trees, to a single dot surrounded by many others. This dot, though, was greenish-brown rather than solely green. An intense circle surrounded it with too many spikes to count. Most led to the nearby woods, but others led . . . nowhere. Worse, they blurred as though changing in number, defeating the few tries she made at estimating them.

"This is excellent work. Thank you." Hazel stroked the paper. "Did you have any trouble?"

Ruby beamed. "It was just the kind of project I like. Moving pieces, and figuring out ways to get people to want to do what I wanted rather than going off on weird ideas."

"I'll make sure your parents know what a help you've been."

"Thank *you*." The girl slumped back in her chair. "I swear, the only thing Mom cares about these days is my chemistry grades. You know I aced my math test last Friday? And got second place in a history debate, where I should've got first but Mr. Plunkett's never going to hand that to anyone who's not White and male. Father griped about that, when I told him, but Mamma just keeps going and going about that C on a quiz."

"Because you'll need it to be a nurse," Hazel said,

squinting and drawing on vague memories of talking with Cora, though she also noted down the teacher's name.

"Yeah."

Such a lack of enthusiasm. Hazel took the first opportunity to keep her promise, but ran into Ruby's father sooner than her mother.

Early Tuesday morning, with the sun casting sharp shadows, Hazel left the house. She licked the last drops of coffee from her lips as she settled her hat over her chignon. Her sensible shoes clopped against the pavement, skirts swirling around her calves and leather purse a firm weight at her side, as she prepared to walk the long way across town to the wooded southern part of the college campus.

Only to jerk as a car rolling down the street stopped right in front. Exhaust steamed out of the rear. Luther, in suit and tie under a white coat, rolled down the front window to wave. "Morning, Hazel, you're up early."

"I'd say the same of you." She'd strapped on a watch, and the time was a good half-hour before she'd usually noted him leaving. "Going far?"

To the campus, it turned out, for he'd been asked to consult with Dr. Thomson, the college physician. "A nice enough fellow for what that's worth, with some odd ideas that he tends to try out on me before going to the other doctors in town. He says I'm less likely to laugh at him." Luther shook his head, and on learning she was campus-bound, too, gave her a ride.

A chance to express her gratitude for Ruby's help.

And an opportunity to ask, discreetly, about Cora's preoccupation with Ruby's chemistry grades. At which he shook his head and deflected, "that's between Cora and Ruby. I'm sure they'll settle it out soon enough."

The matter didn't sit as well with Hazel. She let it drop, though it remained on her mind until she found the clearing.

It wasn't hard to locate. Ruby had provided directions, based on the cousin's report.

Start at the college library. Turn right, away from the main academic buildings, and follow the paved path curving toward the student center. Before reaching it, keep right onto the stepping stones that marked a short-cut through the woods to the women's dorms. About a quarter of a mile in, there was a dirt trail leading a short distance to the clearing. If she reached the dorms, she'd gone too far.

This early in the morning, Hazel encountered no one else on the trail. Breakfast smells of eggs and bacon cooking vied with the greenery for dominance, and a few young voices rang out in the distance. She kept alert, poised to step off the path and conceal herself by stretching shadows, but it wasn't necessary.

A few birds sang, yet their high notes faded as she moved from stepping stones to packed dirt. The month had seen little rain, but the dry earth at the edge of the trail retained a few crumbling shoe prints from when someone had passed this way in mud season. Bushes grew close along either side.

Only after she passed several feet did it occur that she hadn't had to push through any branches. There was clear room for at least one person, perhaps two, to walk without touching the greenery. Someone used the path regularly, unless the grounds crew tended it or the plants themselves left it bare for passage.

Then she reached the clearing and even that thought left her.

A host of trees—elms, maples, oaks, and a few evergreens—formed an uneven oval around beds of lush grass grown long but bending low. Birds called in the distance and breezes danced about the open air in circles and twists. Her skirts were tugged in different directions at the same time. A lovely place for a picnic, if one brought a blanket to spread over the soft grasses.

An old stump stood in the center, its roots still thick as they dove under the earth. Cut flowers lay among them, roses and goldenrod and asters, a few just beginning to fade atop others long decayed. Rose and anise perfumed the air. Unlike her nephew, she felt no revulsion, no need to leave, but a cautious welcome.

Then again, she hadn't touched the stump. Yet.

"I come here for the land, with care." She stretched her hands out, palms up. "I bring nothing but myself. I seek nothing but information, knowledge. I will take only that away."

All became still. The distant voices and bird calls ended abruptly. Her skirts fell limp against her legs.

"What are you willing to share with me?"

The breezes began again. Sound returned, but only the rustle of grass and branches swaying.

She moved further in—and patterns appeared in the grass. Here and there lay depressions as though one or more persons had lain down to rest. Elsewhere blades lay crumpled in overlapping circles that matched some of the breezes whistling by her. Yet even as she watched, the grass restored to knee-high, only to shift into yet another arrangement of depressions and tracks. And another, and another.

Approaching the gnarled old trunk, she bent over the flowers without touching them. The mix of live and decaying blooms gave off a sweet perfume that eased her aching midsection.

Blinking back unexpected tears, Hazel straightened only to lose her balance. Throwing her hands out to catch herself, she braced against the stump. The morning had warmed, sun shining strong overhead, but the bark under her fingers nearly burned her with chill. Much as she wanted to draw away, she resisted.

For with that touch, the clearing had changed further.

The breezes turned to ghostly forms of gray whirling as they danced with and through each other.

The trunk itself burned as gold as the circlet on her map. Gold and silver outlined its roots, tangling with those of the encircling trees. Its former glory stretched high above, branches glowing in the same colors.

Still more lines, glowing green twined with gold or silver and sparkling in the sun, rayed out from mid-way up the trunk. Waist height. Some tied the tree to the dancers. Others stretched into the distance, their ends unknown.

Hazel brushed one with a fingertip, ready to recoil. Images and senses flew through her, too many to grasp the whole. Only shards.

A White woman. Young, girl? Magicless. Flowing pink dress. Arm held behind back. Sloppy kisses dripping against her neck. Tears on her face.

Touching a second brought another whirl, leaving as much or as little information. A Black woman or girl. Magicless. Blue dress. A wall behind her. A hard hand on her shoulder, another at her waist.

And a third: a White man this time. Magicless. Cowering. Bitter words pouring into his ears. Fingers grasping his jaw, forcing his mouth wide.

Each thread resulted in frozen images of all manner of peoples, a full range of humanity varying in sex, race, age, and more—and each suffering from assault by words or deeds or both.

The dancing breezes or ghosts were silent, raising hardly a rustle of grass. Underneath the quiet, her ears rang as though recovering from a harsh, throat-destroying scream.

Steeling herself, Hazel gave up after testing so many of

the glowing ties with similar results. One hand remained braced against the trunk, fingers growing gray with chill. Every tie led to a magicless person.

"Are there no sorcerers?"

A pause. One flashed. One, out of dozens or hundreds.

Hazel ran a finger along it.

A White woman lay atop orange carpet surrounded by shards of glass, streaks of dirt, and liquid splotches redolent of alcohol. More alcohol stained her blue-and-white dress. Hanks of brown hair hung loose over a face marred by a swelling bruise along one cheek. A young White child in dirty shorts and shirt with a muddy face and hands huddled against the far wall, half-under a table. Clods of dirt marred their knees. A tall White man in disheveled shirt sleeves and formal pants dragged the child out by the ankle, arm raised to slap. The woman lurched up, face twisted in a grimace as she made a desperate attempt to dart between them.

Hazel jerked back, retreating. She pressed her near-frozen fingers against her chest, covering them with her other to warm them. Words of thanks and peace dropped from her lips, a broken babble she never afterward remembered. Only that, as the magic in the clearing diminished, the tree trunk glowed gold. She could still see bits of it whenever she glanced back, as she hurried along the dirt path to the stones.

Only much later did she realize nothing in the vision identified who the sorcerer was.

# MAGICLESS WITH MAGIC

The whole point of being without magic was protection from it. This principle of magical philosophy weighed on Hazel throughout that day and well into the evening. Needle in hand, she presided over those boarders studying in the living room. The gentle sway of the rocker helped keep away an impending headache, and she enjoyed the swish of her skirts around her legs with each forward roll. A basket of mending sat on a table next to her, and a lamp provided ample illumination as she plied her needle repairing tears and unraveled hems. The living room was an oasis of light and comfort in contrast to the dark chill of the night outside. Well-loved photographs and portraits lined the walls in their modest wooden frames. The students had popped corn and they clustered on the sofa alternating between chatter and spates of silence broken only by crunching kernels.

Thus leaving Hazel to her needle—and her thoughts. She'd reported to her mother and answered questions, but left with them still vexing her.

How could so many magicless have gotten caught up in

magic without word having spread? They should be immune, or there should have been some outcry about the impossible. Unless, perhaps, they didn't realize what they were involved in? The sorcerous could bewitch the magicless, but only so long as any spell didn't violate the magicless person's beliefs. Yet even that boggled the mind given the sheer number of magicless involved.

Worse, how had Hazel, her mother, Cora, and the rest of the family *missed* it? They wandered the campus, if not so regularly as the town.

Still, Hazel had noticed little to no sign of magic until she entered the clearing despite being aware, now, of power at work. Surely the trees in the clearing had connected to most, even all, of the other trees in the woods, but nothing of that had manifested above ground. Indeed, she'd walked home past the town square without seeing anything of the magic lurking within the roots of the evergreens and elms, despite *knowing* it was there. The same with the big oak in the back-yard—she'd had to walk over, lay her hands against the bark, and seek to find even the merest signs.

Except, the only thing they knew the trees had done was —*good*. The big evergreen had helped three people escape from men who meant them ill. Hazel had fallen so easily into thinking this was bad, but though the tree trunk had shown her pain and hurt, it hadn't hurt her. Maybe this was something to be encouraged and helped to grow.

Which might excuse and explain her mother's not noticing for so long. All the same, Hazel would not presume that was the case.

Worrying over the unknowns set her moving faster, the wooden rockers creaking as they rubbed against the floor.

Whatever was going on, by design or by accident it took the perfect form to hide in plain sight and grow.

Into what? And who could have nurtured it? The town

boasted less than a hundred and fifty sorcerers, nearly a third members of her family and all the rest known and vouched for one way or another save for a handful whom the family considered potential threats they hadn't—yet—convinced to move on peaceably.

Finishing a skirt with ripped waistband, she set it atop the small pile of completed work. Stuck the needle into the pin cushion, thread trailing behind, and rested entwined fingers atop her belly. She drew in deep breaths, deliberately slowing the pace of her rocking. Tension slipped from her shoulders and back as she leaned against the chair.

Until she heard the soft clicks of the door to her mother's room opening and shutting. Footsteps underscored the chatter among the students—except they headed for her, not the door. She looked up as Cora settled into an armchair near the rocker.

The younger woman was dressed for dinner in a pretty peach skirt and cream sweater set, and smelled of a dash of rose perfume. Pearls dangled at her ears, clearly visible as she'd pulled her hair into an updo. Her lips showed evidence of having chewed off most of her lipstick, but otherwise her makeup remained. She should be enjoying after-dinner conversation with friends or cozying with her husband at home, not visiting here to report.

"How's Mother?" Hazel considered reaching for more mending, but kept her hands where they were instead. They might shake too much to ply the needle.

"Resting well." Cora kept her voice low. "She told me about what you've uncovered—"

"With Ruby's help."

"With my daughter's help, yes." Cora smiled briefly. Her fingers flexed, then she set her hands on her knees. "We know at least one person likely caught up in it, but we need to verify. Will you come with me tomorrow morning?"

"Of course. When?"

"A little after eight." Her lips quirked to one side. "We can walk Ruby to school."

Ruby showed much less appreciation of this than her mother, when morning came. Hazel and Cora strolled in the wake of Ruby's stiff back. Despite the thin layer of clouds hiding the sun, all three dressed for the late-summer heat in light shirts and skirts, though Hazel preferred the looser fit of hers to how close the girl's skimmed her figure.

They walked in silence. The only noises they made were the clomp of shoes and rustle of hose, both mostly swallowed by the cars rolling down the road or the chatter of other students headed to school.

"You haven't told me what you want me to do," Hazel said, a block away from the school.

"Ask the earth if Lois Bullen is a sorcerer and see what you see." Cora didn't turn her head, stride unchanging.

"Bullen . . ." Hazel blinked.

"He teaches something at the college—" Cora said.

"Math," came from four feet ahead.

"And she has her finger in a lot of pies."

"She helped organized the joint prayer service after the tragedy last winter." Hazel nodded. "She and Mother used to work together on beautification projects, planting flowers in the square and such."

"Her daughter's evidently caught up in something. I don't have all the details, but . . . well, tell me what you see."

What Hazel saw first was a mass of students scattered around the front of the school. Boys in lettered jackets leaning against the stone railings leading up to the door, all White. Girls clustering around them, likewise. Other groups here, there, and everywhere. Most of the Black students in a few groups on the far side. A bunch of Jewish on another, and several Shawnee further along. Adults were scarce.

"Lois's over by the stairs. With the green bow in her hair," Ruby said before dashing off to join several of her cousins on the far side.

"Green ribbon." Cora elbowed Hazel, although her own eyes followed her daughter.

Hazel touched the corner of the shadow cast by a nearby church and drew it over them, since they intended to linger.

Green ribbon, green ribbon. But which? At length, she located a curvy and round-faced young woman with light beige skin and gilt-touched brown hair caught up in a ponytail, dressed in a green sweater set and bright yellow skirt.

Hazel set her feet square on the pavement, concentrating on the ground beneath. Cement counted for contact with the earth—better if it was cracked to allow the land beneath to breathe, as the earth disliked the substance. The spell required calm, peace, and persuasiveness, for the earth was not always willing to share information about other people.

All Hazel needed was to see if the young woman was a sorcerer.

The sudden drain of energy warned her the spell might take a turn even before light flared across the schoolyard and a full third of the students glowed with green light as though paint buckets had upended over them. Something separate enfolding them.

Tangling them in its roots.

Most were girls, plus a handful of boys. Cora and Hazel were free of the green, but a faint haze hung about Ruby, although in undulating lines of light floating around her rather than limning her body.

"Do you see?" Hazel grabbed Cora's hand, willing the spell to extend to her.

"So many." Cora's eyes widened, mouth hanging agape. "And Ruby!"

"It's trying to touch her." Hazel squinted and adjusted her

vision to check her great-niece closer. The ribbons hung a good inch or more away from her. "But she seems to be protected."

"Her father and I ward her every way we can." Cora pressed fingers against her lips, then blew her daughter a kiss. It flew through the air to land on Ruby's cheek. The girl jerked and glanced at her mother, then frowned and waved a hand as though swatting an insect. The ribbons tattered, moving further away from her. "We are not putting her at risk merely for knowledge."

"Not with so many others touched. And none of them sorcerers, though we know there has to be at least one involved in this, behind it." Hazel rubbed her temples, letting the spell go and the lights fade. "It only gets stranger by the day."

# COMBINING FORCES

One mystery solved, except Hazel hated coincidences. For the third day in a row, she'd risen early to venture out. The purse slung over one shoulder bumped against her hip as her pace sped up with every step as much out of irritation as to keep warm in the chilly morning air. Her shoes clumped against the stone pathway through the woods, echoed a heartbeat after by a second pair. As before, a few birds called overhead. Bacon cooked in the distance, and her stomach reminded her she hadn't consumed much more than a cup of coffee yet.

The cause: the woman following her so close her breath stirred the back of Hazel's blouse. Marta Floding. A White woman of roughly Cora's age wearing a nurse's uniform. A sorcerer whom Hazel had only met a few times in passing, despite the other having lived in town for nearly two decades, and whom Cora had vetted and decided should be allowed to remain in town way back when she first arrived. The very person whose question about Lois Bullen had drawn Cora and Hazel's mother's attention to the students in the first place. Last but not least, a woman caught up in the tree-root magic according to Cora, who'd visited her after discovering so many magicless students were.

All according to Cora, who had then declined to accompany Hazel and Marta Floding to the clearing this morning because the clinic was overbooked with appointments and her husband needed her. Asking Hazel's mother was completely out, Ruby likewise, and therefore Hazel the logical person.

Which meant Hazel led Mrs. Floding through the woods as much by default as because she'd stepped up to lead the investigation.

"I still don't understand why we couldn't have discussed this over breakfast." Mrs. Floding's teeth chattered, although she wore a navy-blue half-cloak over her uniform.

"You'll see once we get there. Only a little farther." Hazel pointed at the dirt trail a few feet ahead.

If only she knew more about Mrs. Floding, and how active a part she likely played in this complexity. Yet most of what Hazel did know could be condensed into a single fact: Marta Floding was an accepted town sorcerer. That meant she hadn't caused problems thus far and hadn't done anything worthy of censure or banishment, or hadn't been caught. This even though she, most unusually, had managed to figure out Cora and Luther were sorcerers and convinced them to bargain with her for an exchange of magic lessons for their children.

The sum should place her on the side of the angels, but Hazel preferred to reserve judgment. Though, in truth, the other woman had taken being whisked off to campus before breakfast with admirable calm—and even a measure of curiosity.

Hence her keeping step with Hazel, to the point her breath warmed the back of Hazel's neck and she risked stepping on the backs of Hazel's shoes.

"Here," Hazel moved aside, gesturing at the path. "You go first, if you like."

Mrs. Floding hesitated. Her hands twitched, wrapped within the hem of her cloak. "It's real?"

"There's a connection between you and it, that's all I can say for certain."

The clearing hadn't changed in the intervening time. Birds called from the treetops. A few breezes danced in circles atop the swathes of luxuriant grass. The stump remained as before, with another white rose lying atop the others.

Stepping back and following meant Hazel didn't see the expression on Mrs. Floding's face when they arrived. The other woman's posture made up for that. Her arms swept up and out to the sides, the folds of her cloak falling down her back. Her head tilted back and breath caught audibly in her throat.

"Oh!" The nurse tottered forward, balance shaky as she turned in circles. "It does exist!"

She whirled around in clear delight. Once, twice, three times. Then dropped down to caress the bed of grass. She even laid back, arms at her side, as though ready to go to sleep.

No matter how soft the thick growths of grass appeared, Hazel couldn't imagine doing so herself. Or if she did, only after laying down a blanket first. Surely the grass must prickle along the other woman's legs and hands.

As if sensing Hazel's response, Mrs. Floding sat up, confusion clear on her face. "Why did you bring me here?"

"I didn't expect that kind of reaction."

"What did you expect?" Mrs. Floding asked. "This is a place of such peace and ease . . ."

"Is it? What kind of peace?" Hazel pointed at the roses,

goldenrod, and asters, with the fresh laid atop those showing signs of decay. "Have you touched the stump?"

"No." The other woman stood, dusting herself off. Green stained the back of her uniform for only a few seconds before falling away as easily as dust. The depression where she'd lain remained, but the blades slowly—visibly—returned to their former luxuriant state. Chin up and eyes narrowed, Mrs. Floding stared at Hazel. "What will happen then?"

"I don't know."

"What do you suspect?"

Hazel sighed and shrugged. "Something less pleasant, but if I tell you, that might affect things."

Mrs. Floding grunted. Drawing in a deep breath, she pressed a hand against the trunk. The next instant, she dropped to her knees. Her arms wrapped around her chest, head bowed. Sobs racked her body as tears streamed down her face.

Whatever she experienced far exceeded the few scenes Hazel had seen. Guilt forming a lump in her belly, Hazel hurried over. Crouching nearby, she laid an arm around Mrs. Floding's shoulders. The other woman's tremors shook Hazel, head to toe. She stumbled and sat on goldenrod, releasing a strong whiff of anise.

The thread connecting the sorcerer to the stump flickered into view, green and silver. Swallowing hard, Hazel brushed a fingertip along it.

Despair washed over her, pulling her under. Everything she knew was washed away, replaced with a gaping emptiness. Nothing remained but loss and anger roiling in her belly. No safe place. Nowhere to go.

Until movement replaced nothing with a warm shoulder under her arm, then arms wrapping around her. A soft shoulder on which to lay her head. A body rocking her, and soft words of comfort, sweet nothings, whispered in her ears.

From a distance, a flash of concern rippled through her alongside the image of a man's face and feel of an embrace. Short salt-and-pepper hair and matching trim beard, with dark brown eyes warm behind glasses.

Both closer and farther, cool hands cupped her cheeks and a forehead pressed against hers. Love flooded through her. A soft voice whispered "my baby."

Hazel Gregson. She was Hazel Gregson, daughter of Thelma and Rudolph Katy, wife of Jake Gregson, mother of two wonderful men, housemother of a dozen or more men and women, would-be landward.

She shuddered, eyes sore from weeping. Her torso rested against Mrs. Floding, whose damp shoulder wicked up Hazel's tears even as a few more slid down the other woman's face.

"You didn't know it would be that bad." Mrs. Floding fumbled under her cloak and pulled out a white lawn handkerchief with her initials embroidered in green. She gazed at it and laughed, then dabbed at her eyes. Her makeup had run, leaving dark spots on her face and the cloth. "Tell me you didn't."

"No, or I'd have warned you." Something squeaked under Hazel as she settled backward. She felt around, pulling out her purse. Laughed a little, just as the other woman had, as she retrieved her blue handkerchief and wiped her face. "It did something else last time. Showed me images from people's lives."

Hazel's purse also yielded a compact with mirror and supplies to restore her makeup, as did the smaller purse the other woman had kept somewhere under her cloak, perhaps stored by magic since she didn't appear to have any pockets. Both restored their faces and tucked purses back away.

Mrs. Floding stuck out her hand, head high and shoulders

back. "It seems odd to be formal with someone whose shoulder I've cried on, so. Please call me Marta."

Hazel gazed at the hand for a moment, then put her own in it, both warm and a little slick with sweat. "I'm Hazel."

Marta nodded, then bit her lip. "You said the tree gave you images last time. Were any of me?"

"You divorced your husband for cruelty, didn't you?" Hazel preferred not to recall that particular instance.

"I filed the first time he hit one of our children." The other woman met Hazel's gaze, throat muscles tight.

Fear and desperation surged through Hazel at a remove—not hers, but the visceral memory of watching the woman lurch to intervene and protect her child. "Good for you."

"There are many who don't agree, so . . . Thank you." Marta shuddered, rising and nearly crushing a rose in the process. She gasped and lurched back. "I think . . . I know what this place is, now."

Hazel got up, careful to do no further damage to the flowers. The goldenrod she'd landed on was lost, pieces of the flower clinging to her skirts. She stepped back, brushing at the greenery with a touch of magic, and waited.

Marta had her hands palm to palm, head bent, clearly praying.

Only after she finished, and wiped away another tear, did Hazel ask, "what is it?"

"Where *she* died last winter, on the ninth of February."

"She?" Then the date registered. The Friday before Valentine's Day, when the temperature hadn't gone above freezing —and the hunt for a missing girl.

"Jean Neville."

"What happened?" Hazel frowned. The parts of the tragedy she'd heard could well lead to the wave of despair that had emanated from the stump—but made no sense with respect to the network connecting trees and magicless dancers. "I heard rumors she said she'd been raped, but the man claimed she'd seduced him."

"I don't know what took place in truth, but she came to the infirmary the day after and . . . the bruises on her body, the tearing along her . . ." Marta stooped and nudged the undamaged flowers around the stump into a wavy line. The movement released an extra burst of rose scent. "I believe she was forced."

Yet there was a hesitancy in her voice.

"But?" Hazel asked.

Straightening, Marta held up a finger. "I never heard the full report, but word came down that the dean,"—her lips drew back from her teeth as she snarled the word—"decided she'd been unchaste and expelled her."

"Not the man." Hazel knew that much.

"No, he graduated last summer, full honors." The other woman grimaced. "She was supposed to be sent home that weekend, immediately after being expelled, but the night before, the coldest night, she left her room and went out and lay down in the woods near her dorm." She turned in a circle, waving at the trees. "Her roommate reported her missing that evening, but it took hours to find her."

Hazel waited, but the tension in Marta's body suggested the tale wasn't finished. "And?"

"I was there, when they brought her in. Dr. Thomson did the first examination, before the coroner came—" She rubbed her chin, gaze considering as she watched Hazel. "This is . . ."

"I will keep what you share as secret as I can." Hazel turned her hands out. "But my mother and I need to know, to care for the land."

After a lengthy pause, Marta nodded. "There were signs . . . Dr. Thomson thought she might have been pregnant. Two, maybe three months along."

Far enough to likely have some suspicion at the least. Hazel laid a hand over her belly. The round weight was all her own now, but her body well remembered the weight of the two sons she'd carried to term, and the two babes who'd lasted only a few months in her womb before miscarrying. She, however, had been ready for children, with a home and partner.

"If she was . . ." Marta bent and adjusted the freshest rose again. "She must have been more afraid of going home than death."

The girl had died in February. Tragic indeed, but Hazel's mother hadn't felt the first inklings of sorcery at work in earth until a few months later, in spring. How could the two be connected?

"Oh." Marta clapped a hand over her mouth, eyes big. "Maybe that's why . . ."

"What?"

"I haven't had this happen to me, but I know a few others caught up in this." She waved at the stump.

"Sorcerers or magicless?"

"Magicless, although two who believe in sorcery but don't do it."

Hazel nodded.

"Two of them have recounted incidents where they were dancing in the clearing, in spirit, not truly here, you understand?"

A glance around caught two or three breezes whirling in different parts of the clearing, one over the grassy swathe Marta had lain on earlier—which had almost recovered—and another on the far side of the stump. She pointed at one, then the other.

"But some times they've also somehow floated or otherwise noted events around town. Men putting the moves on women and making them uncomfortable. Each wanted to intervene, although they weren't actually there, and . . . something happened. A tree or bush struck the man instead, in the groin." A dark smile crossed Marta's face. "But the women had dirt on their shoes after, though they'd been inside, even in bed, at the time."

The tale in part resembled the incident where a tree had helped Frances and Grace get away, though Hazel had no idea who might have intervened. Yet it also required reconsidering the network of connections between trees and people. "Then this may somehow be an immense spell, a growing spell, that uses nature to respond to the kind of incident that might have led to the girl . . . to Jean Neville's death."

"Good." Marta smiled again, only to have it turn into a grimace.

"Perhaps, but where does it draw the power to connect so many . . . dreamers . . . with the trees, much less the power for the trees to intervene?" Blood throbbed at Hazel's temple as she tried to grasp the many complications tying the whole together.

"The dancers." Marta shrugged and patted her chest. "Us."

"And now *you* know something of what's happening, but none of the others are aware. They give up power, energy, and may not even realize what they're doing. Which makes this a theft." Hazel turned a slow circle, counting the dancing breezes which had increased to four.

"What are you going to do?" Marta asked.

"Nothing, yet. I will bring this to the landward, but . . ." Hazel winced. It was a good cause, a protective cause, but built on stolen energy. "It's a mess."

# A CHILD'S INTERESTS

"*L*et me think on this." Hazel's mother's words echoed in her head over and over. Pensive, patient, and private with no room for sharing the load.

Alone in the tidy kitchen, Hazel loaded supper leftovers into a casserole dish. Thick slices of meatloaf covered in gravy rested next to generous spoonfuls of mac-n-cheese and beans, all mouthwateringly good. After covering the top with aluminum foil, she stripped off her apron and hung it to dry. A quick check of her dress—clean and dry—and her hair in the bathroom mirror—still largely in the curls shaped in the morning—and she lifted the dish and let the kitchen door swing shut behind her.

She stopped on the top step for a moment to drink in the glory of the sunset, with puffy clouds in pinks and oranges scattered across the sky. Less than a minute's walk brought her to Cora and Luther's house. Their car sat in the driveway, and lights shone from kitchen.

The door opened on the count of five after she knocked. Cora wore a pretty rose-colored dinner dress, but she'd wrapped her hair in a silk turban in a clashing shade of pink suggesting a degree of exhaustion. An empty bowl and four eggs sat out on the counter near the refrigerator, otherwise there was no sign of dinner in the works.

"Oh glory be." Cora took the casserole dish and set it on the counter. "This is a lifesaver. I've been fighting with the hospital all day, some stupid clerk who refuses to let me have the bandages I ordered just because they were delivered there by mistake. Luther—" She turned and called down the hall. "Dinner's served."

"Already?" He'd taken off his jacket and tie and loosened his collar, jaunty green suspenders bright against his white shirt and gray slacks. "Thank you, Hazel."

"You just sit yourselves down and let me serve you." She herded them to the dining room.

The chime of plates and flatware from the big sideboard suggested Cora wasn't ready to let Hazel do all the work. Still, Hazel made short work of grabbing a serving spoon and getting the food on the table. She tucked the eggs back away, then returned to the dining room with glasses of apple juice for three.

Husband and wife had already started to eat. There was plenty of room for Hazel to bustle around, with the dining table sized for four. The warm yellow walls bore simple drawings of fruit, for the walnut dining set was the star of the room. She settled into the chair opposite the empty spot where Ruby usually sat and waited. Didn't take long for Cora to pause and rest her fork against the plate.

"Where's Ruby?"

"At the movies." The boarders had swept Ruby away with them, happy as a clam.

"But surely she had homework." Cora's fork and knife scraped the plate as she cut a bite of meatloaf.

"She did, and she finished it." Hazel sipped her juice.

"Grace, who's studying to be a teacher, checked it over, so all's well."

"And?" Cora asked.

"She did fine."

"Chemistry too?"

"Of course." Hazel shook her head at the clear relief on both faces. "Such a fuss about a single subject and a few quiz grades."

"She'll need to do well in it if she wants to be a nurse." Cora lifted her glass and drank deep.

"Or a doctor," Luther grinned at Cora.

"And if she doesn't want to be either?" Hazel asked.

"That will come." Cora waved a dismissive hand. "We're grateful for the food, but did you come over just to deliver it? What's the situation with the magicless surrounded by magic?"

"You mean Mother hasn't told you?" Hazel threw up her hands, shaking her head. "No, no, I know you haven't seen her today."

"I can ask her, if you prefer." Cora's fork grated on the plate as she stabbed beans.

"No need. We know more about the spell now, though there's much still unknown." Hazel tucked her hands in her lap. "Marta Floding and the magicless are somehow connected to a stump in a clearing on campus, the one where the co-ed froze to death last winter."

Cora and Luther both froze, utensils in the air and mouths wide open. A moment later, they burst into questions but their voices overlapped to the point Hazel couldn't understand a word.

Hazel raised a hand, and they quieted. "We don't know if the spell started then, or later. The first time Mother felt magic in the roots was at least six weeks after. The spirits of those tied to the tree dance around the clearing. They apparently find it a place of joy and peace—and as they dance, they pour energy into the stump and the trees."

"How?" Luther set his fork and knife down, plate nearly empty, and steepled his hands. "Is it spiritual energy the trees are drawing rather than physical? That would make more sense, though they're still funneling the energy separate from their bodies."

"Your guess is as good as mine," Hazel said, "but apart from how there's also the matter that the people doing this don't know they're contributing energy.

"Gramma won't like that." Cora scooped up a last spoonful of mac-n-cheese.

"She doesn't." Hazel took another sip of juice, cool down her throat.

"If they're giving energy, what do the trees *do* with it?" Cora asked.

"That's more guesswork, though we have a theory." Hazel pushed the casserole dish with its remaining food closer to Cora and Luther. "Seconds?"

"How about an answer, instead?" Cora leveled a straight look at Hazel.

Luther helped himself to more food, wielding the serving spoon with as little noise as possible.

"The connection between trees and spirits apparently also allows the spirits to sometimes see what's going on around the trees, in the clearing but also elsewhere in town." Hazel rubbed her temples to ease the sudden throbbing. "Marta reported hearing of instances where the spirits saw men encroaching on young women who were visibly uncomfortable with the attention. In each case, the spirit somehow prompted a tree or bush to hit the man."

Something about her expression prompted both to look at her curiously.

"And?" Cora asked.

"In the . . ." Hazel pointed at her lap.

A laugh escaped Cora, but Luther dropped his fork and sat bolt upright.

"That's all she knows." Hazel wrapped her hands around her cool glass. "It's similar to an incident last weekend. A tree grabbed men who were harassing Frances and Grace on their way home from a party. Still, we don't know for certain that there is a connection or how it all happens."

"The trees hit men in the groin?" Luther asked, eyes narrowed and gaze abstract. "How many times has this happened? How many students?"

"Marta only mentioned two instances."

"But there may be more?" he asked.

"May," Hazel agreed.

"Why so curious?" Cora touched her husband's shoulder.

"I may have the answer to what the trees are doing." Luther grimaced even as he chuckled. "Earlier this week, Dr. Thomson at the college asked me for a consult. He's had an unusual number of cases of an unusual disease presenting muscular and vascular weakness, but the primary symptom is . . . sexual incapacity."

Cora drew in a breath on a hiss. Hazel glanced at her, trying to puzzle it out, then her niece leaned over and whispered. "They can't get an erection."

"Thomson's been trying various approaches. One of the students seems to be getting better but others aren't. Thomson's magicless, so sorcery wouldn't occur to him," Luther continued, ignoring the exchange apart from a raised eyebrow. "I haven't had any reports to share with him, but this . . ." He frowned.

"What next?" Cora asked, turning to Hazel.

"Mother's considering the matter." A sharp laugh escaped Hazel. "She'll probably tell you first."

"Lovely. More work, as if I hadn't enough already." The

younger woman rubbed her forehead just below where the silk crossed.

"Then how will you handle being landward?" Hazel pushed back, chair legs squeaking against the floor. Tension flowed off her niece in waves.

"I don't know." Cora glared at her. "If you're so concerned, why don't you take the position?"

"I've offered time and again, but Mother wants you." Hazel's jaw hurt from clenching.

"Well, I don't want it. I've too much work and would rather not tie myself to this corner of the state for the rest of my life and never have a chance to visit family elsewhere, so offer again and do a better job this time."

"Better job?" Hazel rose to her feet, fists pressing against her thighs. "I've told her I want to be landward, told her I'm willing to take it, and every time she pats me on the head or cups my face and says she can't burden her baby."

"Make her see you as more than her baby." Cora leaned back in her chair, but a muscle in her cheek jerked.

"I'm trying." Hazel swallowed hard and licked her lips. "I've taken more wanders, tracked down new sorcerers moving to town, investigated this mess of trees and spirits, but she still calls me baby."

"That's not the sticking point." Cora waved a hand as though swatting a mosquito.

"What is?"

Cora stood, muscle still twitching in her cheek. "You have to show Gramma that you can make hard decisions on the spot and make them stick, and not let them eat you up after with guilt. When she says the landward passes judgment, she means on others and on themselves with kindness for human weakness. Talk to her. Ask her what you can do to show you're the right person." Her niece sighed and slid down into her chair.

Hazel closed her eyes and counted to ten. She lost contact with the world, air whirling around her in the dark as Cora's words echoed and re-echoed in her head. The problem was making Mother see that Hazel was an adult capable of making hard decisions? Easier to say than do. Still, what had Hazel said in the past when making the offer? That she wanted it? Surely she'd gone over why she was a good choice —but she'd try again. The goal was worth it.

But if she had to follow Cora's advice . . . Hazel eased back down and perched on the edge of the seat. "I'll try again to make her see me as I am, but you have to do the same for Ruby."

"What?" Cora frowned, almost-empty glass poised before her mouth.

"You want Ruby to be a nurse—" Hazel said.

"Or a doctor." Luther added.

"Or doctor,"—Hazel nodded at him—"just as Mother considers me as her baby, but that's what you see, not who Ruby is. Have you ever considered that she doesn't want to go into medicine? That she has different interests?"

The couple exchanged glances in silence. Cora set her glass back on the table with a muted chime. "Has she said anything?"

Hazel stood, mouth quirking as she offered a variant on the advice she'd just received. "Ask her, and listen to what she says."

# A PARENT'S PROTECTION

o time like the present. Hazel marched back across the yards to her home. Her heels clicked against the floor as she passed through kitchen and hall to the living room. Two lamps shed warm, yellow light as her mother rocked in the corner. Her needles flashed as she knit a sweater sleeve. The ends dangled over her lap, delicate stitches a turquoise blue against the pink of her mother's best dressing gown. She'd already wrapped her hair for the night in a matching silk scarf.

Such a cozy scene.

Needles clicking, Hazel's mother smiled at her, then tilted her head peering around. "I thought you'd bring Cora back with you."

"You did?" Hazel settled on the edge of the sofa, sinking into the soft cushions.

"So that we can talk about the situation." The older woman counted stitches, then switched needles and started another row.

A framed portrait of Hazel's parents on their wedding day hung halfway between sofa and rocking chair. Both looked so young and stiff in their best clothes. Sometimes it was hard to see the youthful image in her mother, who stooped a little more each year, but other times Hazel had no trouble. Young and old, she led with her chin up and face full of determination to make the world do better by her. "You didn't ask me to invite Cora back."

"It went without saying." Her mother leveled a glance at Hazel.

"No, it didn't." Perhaps too many things had been left unsaid and assumed. Cora had a point that Hazel hadn't pushed her mother to explain why she wouldn't let her daughter be landward. "Mother, do you know Cora doesn't want to be landward?"

"She's just tired, with all she's been doing." Thelma sighed, wrapping on to another row. "Once she takes over, it'll work out. It did for me."

"What if it doesn't?"

"It will." There was the mother in the wedding picture, ready to force the world to cooperate. "My father wasn't supposed to die so young." Thelma set her knitting aside, head shaking. "But he was always doing, and then all of a sudden he wasn't, and I had to step into his shoes. It wasn't easy, but I'll be there for Cora, if she doesn't wait too much longer, ready to hold her hand and help her ease in. She'll be one in a long chain of us, carrying on."

"She doesn't want it." Hazel leaned forward, elbows on her knees. "But I do."

"That's sweet of you, baby, but—"

"Do you hear what I'm saying? I *want* to be landward after you." Hazel pressed a hand to her chest, fingers cold. "I always have. One of my oldest memories is of you taking me with you on wanders, after your father died. You used to talk to me as you went, describing what you saw and what it meant."

"You want to be landward because you've always gone on wanders?" The older woman rocked a little faster.

"I've spent my life watching you, wanting to be like you." Hazel rose and dragged an upholstered footstool over in front of her mother and squatted on it. Grabbed her mother's hands, fingers as cold as her own. "I want the responsibility and the right to listen to the land and tend its needs, to keep this town a place where our family and friends and neighbors belong."

"You don't know what you're asking." Her mother cupped her cheeks, eyes glistening.

"Then tell me, show me, put me to the test."

"Have you ever had to stop a sorcerer from casting a spell?" The older woman asked. "Pass judgment on someone who injured the land through magic? Forgive yourself for being human and unable to prevent all ills?"

"No." Hazel lifted her head, Mother's fingers slipping away. "But I'm willing."

"If you become landward, you'll likely have to do all that and more." Hazel's mother tucked her hands in her lap. "I've tried to protect you."

"I'm a grown woman, a decade older than Cora." Hazel caught and kept her mother's gaze. "You don't need to ward me."

"You will always be my baby." Again, chilly fingers caressed Hazel's cheek—this time only one hand. The older woman's fingers trembled, short nails lightly scraping.

"Can I be your baby *and* take after you as landward?"

The caress ceased. Fingers pinched Hazel's chin instead as they stared into each other's eyes. "Can you?"

"Let me try," Hazel said without pause.

Her mother let go and leaned back in the chair. She stared at Hazel for a long moment. "Not so fast, but . . ."

Hands wrapped around the chair's arms, Thelma heaved

herself to her feet slowly. The chair rocked a few times as she moved away. Soft, pink mule slippers covered her feet, their soles whispering against the floor with each step.

"Follow me." Hazel's mother turned and crooked a finger, then continued on her way without glancing backward. She shuffled down the hall and through the kitchen.

Hazel kept enough space between them that she wouldn't slam into her mother if the older woman stopped suddenly. Her breath caught in her throat. Could it really be so easy? She'd owe Cora an apology in that case.

A damp smell and a hint of cigarette smoke from the distance blew in as the older woman opened the door. She paused long enough to kick off her slippers, then descended the stairs and strode out into the recently cut grass.

Hazel followed, stopping to remove her footwear. The earth was cool and damp. Blades of cut grass clung to her skin and stuck between her toes.

Her mother raised a hand for her to stop once both had moved far enough from the house to stand in shadow. Stillness surrounded them, just as it had for a moment earlier in the day when they'd connected. Despite the darkness, the older woman's stance clearly shifted. She stood straighter, and so did Hazel.

The earth warmed beneath Hazel's feet. A rising wind twisted around her, very different from the dancing breezes in the clearing. This brought the scent of impending fall, and a single maple leaf edged in bright red that glowed just enough she couldn't fail to catch it.

"You want to step into my shoes and ask to be tested? Very well." Her mother moved right in front of Hazel and set her hands on Hazel's shoulders. "This matter of trees and spirits, it's yours. I will watch, listen, and advise if asked, but you must take it to the end, however bitter, and impose a satisfactory solution. It does not have to be happy, but it must be fair and just, and you have to make sure it holds. If you do all this, I will step aside and help you take my place at the center."

"I will." Elation at finally having the chance rippled through her, followed immediately by a sense of pressure as though her mother's hands pressed down with two or three times her weight.

Magic wreathed around them. Her response added to her mother's words and actions formed a spell. Hazel had one chance. The storm would break soon—the spell ensured that it must—and Hazel had to be ready pass judgment.

*I have my chance,* she exulted to Jake in the dark of the night. His pleasure twined with hers, for a wonderful night's sleep and dreams that let her wake refreshed . . . to frustration.

Nothing happened that day.

Or the next.

Until the phone rang late Saturday evening with Marta's voice on the other end. "In the clearing—please help, they're going to kill my son!"

# PART III
# DOUGLAS

Thursday 13 September –
Saturday 22 September 1951

# IN THE LIBRARY

They weren't laughing at him, but Douglas stiffened all the same, back pressing against the slatted wooden chair. His battered loafers rested flat on the thin industrial carpet. He rubbed sweaty hands against the smooth, worn fabric of his dark-blue trousers. Swallowed hard, the collar of his light-blue button-down shirt tighter around his neck than before. Heat flushed up his neck and cheeks, and ears as well, no doubt making them ruddy beacons since his mother had trimmed his hair back to a crew cut only a few days earlier. His wire-frame glasses slipped halfway down his nose.

Not him. He wasn't the reason for the soft giggles that had the librarian on duty raising an inquisitive eyebrow. All the same, he sucked in a hard breath and let it out slowly.

He had a sheltered place with a wall behind him and a table spread with books laid open in addition to his note-book. A high, arched window with a view of the lake offered further security to one side. Metal stacks bearing thousands of books stretched out to the other. Although the library's exterior resembled a Gothic castle, the interior was simple metal shelving, wood furniture, and gray carpeting.

The other three chairs around his table were empty of anything but the smell of furniture polish. So too were two matching tables separating his from where the female students crowded around a third. An equal distance beyond lay the librarian's station, but the cluster of giggling women blocked most of it.

Most dismissed him after a single glance. Nothing more than to be expected when a high schooler—even a senior— ventured into the college library to study despite the inconvenience. Even those high schoolers who didn't use the town library often clustered on its concrete steps, which lay so conveniently halfway between the drug store and the movie theater, while the college library sat on the far side of town. Nevertheless, Douglas preferred the relative anonymity it offered. The vast majority of college students didn't know him from Adam and didn't care.

Admittedly, the staff knew him, or rather knew of him, but to the extent any of them thought of him it was as one of *them*. The children of the college professors. A faculty brat.

Or worse, specifically as Professor Floding's son.

"Poor boy," one of the staff had clucked her tongue over him earlier as he'd passed the circulation desk. The slender, almost skeletal, woman had graying hair pulled up atop her head displaying ivory-colored skin above the high neckline of her white blouse.

Under most circumstances, he wouldn't have heard. His own fault that he usually maintained a spell increasing his hearing in certain ways as a matter of course, to give advance warning if certain other of his fellow high schoolers had thoughts of rolling him over or extracting homework assistance from him. They couldn't do that if they couldn't find him . . . but too often he forgot to undo it in the library.

"He's not much like his father, is he?" Another staff member, a White woman about the same age but with a round figure and her skin and hair tinted gold, leaned against the counter as she filed cards into pockets in books.

"No, and just as well." The skeletal woman raised a thin, painted eyebrow and shuddered delicately.

Neither counted as an original observation. Douglas's paternal grandmother lamented his lack of resemblance to his father every time she came to visit. His height always offered one point of disappointment, with him still standing shorter than his mother as well as his father. His grandmother also always tutted over his coloring—so similar to his mother—and his build—stocky unlike anyone else in the family that she could think of except a distant great-uncle about whom the less said the better.

Worst of all, she'd say, staring at him over her glasses, was his phlegmatic disposition. So unlike his dashing father.

In contrast, his maternal grandmother thought that one of the best things about him.

At least the college students didn't connect him with his father, even those who studied under the old man. The female students certainly paid him no mind.

Five women crowded around the table, all in sweaters and knee-length skirts. One brunette had gold highlights gleaming under the lights, her smooth complexion likewise tinged in gold and her seat accidentally placed so he had the best view of her. The others appeared as little more than arms, backs, and flowing ponytails in darker brown and black.

The librarian on duty at the reference desk didn't hush them despite their giggles. The librarians rarely did, for at least one was a sorcerer and responsible for the muffling spells circling designated tables.

Even magicless students had noticed that they could talk

louder at certain tables, although they attributed it to the odd acoustics of the atrociously designed would-be castle structure.

Douglas never fought to occupy any of the muted tables. That would attract the attention of the college students, and they might make a stink about a faculty brat taking up their space just for the heck of it, or roust him out some other way.

He came not to be noticed, but to *not* be noticed—and get his homework done, on time and as high quality as possible. Top grades might earn him ticket out of the town, a scholarship to another college or university, rather than go to Timms as Professor Floding's son, poor boy, so different from the dashing old man who was always taking off to lecture somewhere else and forgetting the children left behind with their mother.

But he'd picked the wrong table this instance. Who would've guessed one of the other town students, faculty brats, would be here this day, this time, with several of her friends?

Isabel Bullen, the town golden girl who'd sailed through high school supposedly batting her long eyelashes at any teacher who dared give her less than an A-. Cheerleader, homecoming queen, prom queen, voted most likely to be married within the year.

Yet she'd made it all the way into the start of her second year at college without a ring on her finger.

Despite the giggles, she and her friends were studying, all bent on making the most of their time in the library as the female co-eds had an early curfew on weekdays.

Back when she was in high school, other people might not have noticed—except her teachers, and he wasn't too sure about a couple of them—but Isabel did study. She'd earned her grades.

He'd lived next door to the Bullens all his life. Until she moved into a dorm, his bedroom had an excellent view of her window. Not that he'd peeped, but anyone sitting at his desk facing his window couldn't help seeing Isabel at her desk at the matching window across the way.

She'd always been worth watching. Her hair had darkened to gold-limned brown, and sometimes sadness made her face droop. Nevertheless, most of the time she sparkled. Drew attention. At least, drew *his* attention—across the yards between the houses and over the tables separating them. The other girls around her were no doubt equally attractive, but his eyes went to her whenever he glanced that way.

With little hope he'd find her gazing back. A girl might glance at a boy two years her elder and find him looking back at her, and faster than you could say Jack Robinson they'd be cooing and him giving her his pin or his jacket.

The same rarely happened with boys and older girls, though look they did. But anyone could admire anyone else, her grit and persistence, without any cost or risk of teasing from other fellows—or, worse, younger siblings—as long as he kept it discreet.

So he kept watching when he could, however surreptitiously. Didn't help getting his schoolwork done.

He tucked his head down, even when the clock ticked later and the distant tower bells tolled out three measures.

Declined to glance up while the girls exclaimed and packed up their bags as they grabbed books to check out and take with them back to the dorm.

Kept his eyes on the wretched essay due in English, drafting line after line of nonsense as soft shoes scuffed against the carpet headed away.

Then a whiff of lilac perfume and a thump across from him made him glance up and jerk so hard his book skittered halfway across the table. A couple of pages of notes flew up into the air and wafted across the table. Lurching, his midsection crunching against the hard wood top, he retrieved two of the flyaway papers.

Isabel snatched the third out of the air and laid it back on the table.

"Douglas Floding, fancy meeting you here." Her smooth, high tones rang in his ears as clear as the bells, the same words she'd used the first time they'd bumped into each other in the library all those months ago. She set two library books and a bag on the table and plopped into the chair opposite him. The pink bow in her hair matched her sweater.

"Nice to see you, too, Miss Bullen." He shuffled the papers into a pile, then stuffed his sweaty, shaky hands under the table.

"Are you going to go all formal on me just because my mother's still not speaking to your mother?" She crossed her arms over her chest and tilted her head. "Or are you not talking to me because they're still not talking?"

"I don't remember hearing a word from you all summer." He swallowed, mouth suddenly dry.

"I was living at home then. I had to follow my mother's rules, but I'm back on campus now." She sat back and pulled out a piece of paper and pen. The pen scratched and squeaked as she wrote, pausing to peep at him every few moments.

"Aren't you worried your mother will hear of this?" Douglas jerked his head, trying not to let heels of his shoes drum against the floor and betray nervousness.

"She won't hear." A decided shake of her head and twist of her lips. "And if she does, she won't care. Lois is her pride and joy."

"Lois?" With Isabel in front of him, he couldn't even bring an image of Lois to mind.

"You didn't notice how she's no longer wearing my hand-me-downs remade for her but new frocks?" Isabel finished writing and began folding the paper, eyebrows raised. "Though the change is just as well for her, for she never looked so well or comfortable in my old dresses and shirts and skirts. I'm happy for her, and happier I no longer get the full benefit of my mother's assistance in choosing what to wear."

"Ah . . ."

"You hadn't noticed? You're such a boy."

"Guilty." Douglas had actually recognized that Isabel's sister dressed more formally over the last year, even as she'd risen in the high school popularity ranks. It was hard to miss.

"Look, I'm sorry I didn't say anything all summer long. You're not going to pout over that, are you?" Isabel drummed her fingers against the table.

"Okay." He shrugged.

Isabel glanced around, most particularly at the large clock ticking down the minutes. She wrote Lois across the much-folded square and pushed it across the table. "Give this to her for me. At school, mind, not home. Please."

"Why ask me?" He wrenched his gaze upward, staring into her eyes. "Don't you talk to her?"

"Not enough now I'm back at college. Mother doesn't approve. Every time I tried calling Lois last year, Mother picked up the phone, even when I was sure she'd gone off to a committee meeting or party." Isabel shuddered, drawing back and clasping her hands around her elbows.

"So meet in person, after school. Or stop by your home, it's all of a ten-minute walk." Douglas laid his hands on the table, tilting his chair backward on two legs.

"I go home Sundays, for lunch after church, during which Mother never takes her eyes off me. She's just waiting for me to break down and agree to do what she wants instead." Isabel leaned even closer, pressing her breasts against the wood to the point they made the top of her sweater swell and gape. "All of which gives me no chance to spend time alone with Lois or even make arrangements to meet. How is she?"

"How would I know?"

"You wouldn't. No one would. Even I . . ." Lunging forward, she grabbed his hands and pressed the note into them.

Surprise sent him rocking forward with the front legs of his chair hitting the carpet hard. A whirl of color in the distance alerted him that the librarian had turned to watch them. Little though he cared, not with Isabel's fingers twining with his, skin warm and soft. Even the note burned hot as a brand against his palm.

"Give her this. And . . . keep an eye on her for me, won't you?"

"I don't—" Much as he wanted to swear he'd do anything for her, his tongue refused to work right or make such a promise.

"Just try. Be there, be a shadow, be a friend." Her hands squeezed his, her eyes big and pleading.

How could he refuse? "I'll do what I can."

Sharp claps made them both start. Douglas turned, pulling one hand from Isabel's but leaving the other entwined until she retreated. His fingers cooled without hers against them, and a shiver ran down his spine as though a bucket of cold water had emptied over him.

Three young men formed a human triangle a foot away from the table. The two at the back were incomplete mirrors of each other, both tall and broad of shoulder with brown-black hair perfectly molded, their shirts and trousers still showing vestiges of creases from pressing. Acne scars marred the beige complexion of the one on the right, while the left had a kink in his nose suggesting it'd been broken and reset at some point.

The brawny freshman in the lead wore an athletic jacket in Timms' red and gold, hanging loose at the front to show his white shirt and the tooled leather belt holding up his trousers. He'd slicked his brown hair back with a pomade. Pale, lightly tanned skin stretched over high cheekbones and a cleft chin.

"Well, if it isn't my fellow townies." Walt opened his arms wide as though delighted to see them, sharp teeth flashing through thin lips.

Isabel grabbed her books and hugged them against her chest, shoulders and jaw tight.

"Dougie Floding." Walt gave Douglas a slap on the back.

Douglas swayed, teeth clenched to keep from showing any weakness.

"And Izzy Bullen." Walt loomed over her, gaze dropping in a clear attempt to look down her sweater.

Red flashed on Isabel's cheeks, then she went pale. Nobody ever called her Izzy, especially not slurred so that it sounded more like "easy."

Coos and chuckles fell from Walt's buddies as they curved to form a half-circle around her, clearly writing off Douglas.

One to three ranked as lousy odds, no matter that Douglas was a sorcerer while Walt was not, unless things had changed since high school. Too late to cast a spell to make the others overlook Isabel.

On the other hand, he had additional means at his disposal. He'd had to come up with many tactics to avoid fights and brawls and the various ways students tormented each other when teachers weren't watching.

Some of the books on the nearby shelves started to rock, especially those with a good angle to slide off and slap Walt on the head. Douglas tightened his arms against his body. He hadn't realized he'd started exuding malicious energy.

With a flick of his fingers, power rushed from him and a spell for rescue headed off.

"Hey Izzy." Again Walt slurred the name into *Easy.* "How's old George doing? You heard from him lately?"

Head high, she glared off into the distance, refusing to acknowledge Walt. Yet she clutched the books so tight her knuckles whitened. Her jaw set, neck muscles taut.

Everyone remembered George. Son of the bank president, quarterback of the high school football team two years running, and Isabel's rightful match in all things academic and social their senior year. Such a perfect pairing, all the girls had cooed, even those with jealous eyes, right until the moment George went off to start at Yale while Isabel stayed behind and enrolled at Timms College—without an engagement ring on her finger or any sign the two remained a steady couple.

A heavy book fell off the uppermost shelf, nearly striking Walt on the head despite the distance. Walt leaped back. "What the—"

With perfect timing, an imposing figure swooped over to snatch up the book. Graying hair piled high in a bun atop a thin, pale face with deep-set eyes. Despite being a good half-foot shorter than Walt—and attired in a high-necked blouse with pink ribbons at the collar and matching threads tracing knot work embroidery on her ankle-length skirt—the librarian managed to look down her long nose at him and his companions.

"Mr. Ramble." The librarian slapped a hand against the cover of the book, a hollow sound raising an echoing vibration in the table between Douglas and Isabel. "Again. What did we talk about the last three times?"

"Hush." Walt laid a finger across his lips, not hiding his smirk.

"Since you seem bent on breaking the quiet, you can go

do that somewhere else for the night. You may return tomorrow, but only so long as you abide by the rules." She snapped her fingers.

Walt didn't like it one bit, but he went with friends in tow. She didn't even have to use sorcery.

The older woman turned to Douglas and Isabel, one eyebrow rising high. She had to know he'd cast the spell drawing her attention, but she couldn't say anything about it with magicless Isabel around.

Alas, Isabel showed no more sign of noticing sorcery than she ever had when living next door.

"Five more minutes to curfew." The librarian checked her watch and cast a warning glance at Isabel. "Have you checked out your books?"

The younger woman shook her head, shoulders loosening but skin still drawn and face turned away from Douglas.

The librarian's chest rose and fell in a heavy sigh, but a small smile softened her face. "I'll trust you this time. Bring them back first thing tomorrow morning."

Swiveling to the side, the older woman admonished Douglas with a pointed nod before continuing around the floor.

Isabel stuffed her books into her bag, not looking at him. The contents bent beneath the weight, papers crumbling, but her shaky fingers kept shoving all the same.

"Are you okay?" He stood as she lurched to her feet.

"Go anywhere else but here. That's what I should've done, but I left it too late." She grabbed his hand again—lifting her face long enough to catch and keep his gaze. "Watch over Lois for me. Carry notes for us again this year. You will, won't you?"

Before he could ask her anything more, or agree, she fled. The note she'd pressed into his hand remained as warm as when she'd held on.

# OUT AND ABOUT

The note all but burned a hole in Douglas's pocket the next morning. The ones he'd carried for Isabel last year had done the same, no matter where he tucked them in. Warmth emanated from ink on paper—Isabel's handwriting—as though a single ray of sun beamed down on his upper right thigh. His jeans stretched and shoes squeaked as he pumped away at the bike pedals, the early morning wind cooling everywhere except *there*. Puddles dotted the street and sidewalks, and the damp made his shirt and baseball jacket stick to his back. At least once every block, his glasses slipped down his sweaty nose. The dirty gray canvas bag slung over his left shoulder made things worse, weight pulling him down. He had to lean hard to stay balanced and avoid washing out.

Dipping a hand into the wide opening, he grabbed a newspaper. Slung it at a brick house with a green door. It thumped down on the lowest step, a dry spot. The crabby old White man would have one less wet paper to complain about the next time Douglas collected payments, though he likely still wouldn't ever receive a tip larger than the nickel the man's wife had shamed him into adding on.

He pedaled hard, wheels squealing as he turned a corner. A passing car kicked up grit. He blinked and rubbed his face with his arm. The leather sleeve was soft, though not so much as Isabel's hand. The distraction meant he nearly overshot his next delivery.

Left and right, up and down, he tossed papers here and there as he wove back and forth down street after street.

Further along, Douglas spotted his mother's boss—couldn't miss that orange hair—walking toward campus with one of the professors. A colleague of Douglas's father, notable only for having pretended to pull a quarter out of Douglas's ear every time they met until he reached ten, but never giving the coin to Douglas. Skinflint.

A quick pass along the square, where he got off the bike and walked up close enough to each big house to be sure the paper landed on the porch. *Little things like that'll get you big rewards*, his father had told him when Douglas first signed up for a route, one of the few pieces of decent advice he'd ever handed out. Right he was though—little things brought Douglas big returns, whether tips or wallops on the ear.

Douglas jumped back on his bike and hurried on. Only a couple more blocks. The bag of papers grew lighter with each one.

The lighter it grew, the more he itched to rub the pants pocket holding the warm note.

He'd never seen the contents of any of the couple dozen he'd carried. He could, for cousins on both sides had shown him dozens of spells to read things upside-down, inside-out, tucked into envelopes, folded into strange shapes, and what-have-you. Then again, neither had he read much more than the front of the papers he delivered, and the sports pages, above once or twice a month.

He was a messenger. Reliable day after day. Maybe it wasn't so surprising Isabel had settled on him to pass notes for her.

Angling around another corner, he skidded the wheels enough to scatter gravel. A quick spell turned him into a blur as he grabbed the last paper and tossed it in front of the Bullen house. A middling tall, middling wide, middling balding White man in a gray suit darted out of the house, waving the paper at Douglas as he retreated. Douglas knew better than to nod or wave back. Mr. Bullen hadn't canceled his place on Douglas's route, but they never met or talked. Payment for the subscription and Douglas's tips appeared in his mailbox without notice.

A blue skirt fluttering in the far corner signaled that Lois had already left for school. She hustled off at a rapid pace hand-in-hand with a taller girl, dark-haired but dressed in a similar color of blue. Familiar, but he couldn't place who at this distance. Susan? Sarah? Danielle?

He'd see Lois in homeroom soon enough and find a way to slip her the note.

Just a normal route, a usual morning. Nothing worth remembering except the note still warm in his pocket.

# AT THE DRUG STORE

$\mathcal{N}$o note heated Douglas's pockets Saturday as he settled onto the corner stool, only a couple of nickels. The cushion hissed as it compressed, but not enough to let his feet rest flat. He shifted his seat so his right heel rested on the floor, balanced by the tip of his left shoe hoping no one would particularly notice. Him or the adjustment, but definitely not the latter. On the other side of the red-and-chrome counter stood a harried young drug store clerk, a White kid only a year or two older than Douglas, sweating in a white striped shirt and a boat-like hat atop slick black hair. The clerk's florid coloring clashed with the decor as he worked pumps to build a Coca-Cola from the syrup to a squirt of lime to the carbonated water. Douglas's mouth watered and he sucked on the straw as soon as he got the curved glass.

No need to dress up, unlike certain other places in town, though he wore a newish, still-crisp blue button-down shirt, a good pair of trousers, and slip-on shoes all the same. He'd stopped by in grubbier clothing in summers, after a pickup baseball game, but this was Saturday night and something better was called for. Despite the evening hour, and the growing dark outside the big picture windows, the floor gleamed near sparkling clean. Vanilla and spicy cologne filled the air. Glass jars stocked with colorful candies lined the back wall.

This was the happening place to be. The crowd at the other end of the counter shifted and surged. Several of the counter's stools sat empty, but customers thronged the open area where the register sat, closer to the front with its round tables and wire-back chairs, and wooden booths for those desiring an illusion of privacy. Mostly high school students— a bunch of the football players huddled together, none daring to try the wire chairs—but here and there some from the college. They tended to go for the booths.

He'd nearly finished his drink, his weekly treat for getting up early day after day to deliver papers. The coins remaining in his pocket didn't heat up much. He slowed down to a sip, to make the pleasure last.

At which point she came in. Not Isabel, to his disappointment, but Lois. Pretty enough in a white top and matching sweater over a flouncy green shirt. Hair pulled back in a ponytail. Eyes bright. Just like the other half-dozen girls she came in with. All alike in a few respects: lips bright red and shirts so tight he didn't dare more than glance down. They swarmed the counter, giggling and crowding close to each other, except they stayed down at the far end. The drug store proprietor, a gray-haired man with as florid a complexion as his son, came out to help build drinks and serve customers, adding to the noise.

"Fancy seeing you here."

He jumped as Ruby dropped onto a stool at right-angles to him. She'd slicked her hair up with something smoky, golden hoops dangled from each ear, and she wore green pants instead of a skirt but otherwise had the same general curvy outline as Lois and the women at the far end. Lily-scented perfume wafted over from her. "Hey, Ruby, where'd you come from?"

"You go on, I'll catch up." She waved at a group of other Black students. Two women and four men all dressed much the same as the others, down to the football jackets on the man with the broadest shoulders. Most nodded back and drifted along the shelves, while the last parked himself at the end of an aisle, arms crossed. "I've been here near five minutes, you could've seen me nod at you in the mirror if you'd looked up."

"I was a bit busy." He tapped his glass.

"Yeah, busy staring over there." The stool squeaked as she turned it half-around, indicating the crowd of other students with her chin. "What were you looking at, or should I ask who?"

Heat flooded Douglas's face. He pulled off his glasses and cleaned them on his shirt. "I don't know what you're talking about."

"Aw, come on." Her stool squeaked again, then the drug store proprietor deposited a fresh Coca-Cola in a gleaming glass.

"Miss Warren." The gray-haired proprietor nodded, lips pressed into a thin line.

"Thank you." She gave him a wide, toothy smile and passed over coins. Her hands molded the curved sides of the glass as she pushed aside the straw and drank straight.

"How does he know your name?" Douglas blinked, but the glass was still there, complete with a pink lipstick mark at the top. "I've lived here as long as you, but I'd swear he couldn't name me out of the blue."

"That's because you don't notice hardly anything." She took a second swallow.

"I d—"

"Do not," she said. "Until a little over a year ago, anytime me or someone like me came in here to get a drink, the old man would serve us, sure. But as soon as we'd finished, he'd take the glass and throw it in the trash can so hard it broke—and make sure we knew he'd done that, because he wasn't going to serve anyone else, anyone White, from a glass we'd drunk from."

"What happened?" Douglas picked up his glass studied the decorative ridges and swirls. Even almost empty, it was heavy in his hand. Imagine breaking it just because Ruby or another Black student drank from it. He tilted the tall column back and drained it, swallowing hard on the sweet taste of Coca-Cola.

"I figured out we only ever came here in twos and threes, and not that often, so I got a whole bunch of us together. My cousins, other students, anyone I knew who he'd ever done that to. We all came in at once. Everyone ordered Coca-Cola. He stood there,"—she nodded at the empty middle of the area behind the counter, father and son staying at the far end—"and realized if he broke the glasses we used he wouldn't have any left to serve anyone else, and he'd have to pay to order all new. He's never done it again."

Douglas's jaw dropped. "Wow."

"And you missed all of that." She shook her head.

"Okay, you got me there." He shifted his weight to the other side, turning slightly away from Ruby and toward the crowds around register, tables, and booths. Lois had also moved, away from the register to the point she was at the edge of the crowd. "But that doesn't mean I don't see anything."

"I didn't say anything about seeing. It's noticing and going beyond what things look like that you don't do."

"I picked you out as,"—Douglas drew a quick spell on the

counter to keep the magicless from hearing—"a sorcerer, back when we first were in class together."

"You didn't figure that out until after your mother and mine had caught on to each other." Ruby laughed. "Your mother probably told you there was at least one sorcerer in your class, even if she didn't name me. That's the tip of what you don't ever get, no matter how much you see."

"Maybe." He hunched his shoulders, glasses slipping forward.

"I'll prove how little you notice." She pointed a finger at her throat. "Turn this way, don't look around."

He sighed and did so.

"You've been staring at Lois Bullen."

He jerked, and she waved a hand. A static charge ran through him, suggesting she, too had cast some type of privacy spell.

"Yes I guessed who, because I do notice." Her earrings glinted blue-gold as they caught the light. "Since you stared at her recently, tell me about her. What she's wearing, who she's with, what she's doing, how she's feeling."

His brain hardly worked, turned thick as mud. He ran a shaky hand through his hair and swallowed hard. "She's got on a white top with sleeves down to her elbows and a green skirt."

"A white sweater set and a green felt pencil skirt with a wide cinch belt."

"So I don't know fashions." His elbows pressed against his sides. "She's at the edge of the crowd near the register, smiling and laughing at something, or she was."

"The only thing you got close is where she is." Ruby shook her head and wrapped her hands around her glass. "She keeps turning her head, as though she's looking for someone. She might be smiling, but she's as tense as you and I'd say she's anything but happy. When she tilts her head the right way, dark shadows under her eyes show through her makeup."

Swiveling around, Douglas took a second look. And a third. Nothing much changed, so he gritted his teeth and removed his glasses. With great care, he cleaned the lenses and made the action a spell to help him see—and notice—more clearly.

The instant the wire frames settled on his nose, things snapped into focus. Lois's head tilted down and her arms pressed tight against her sides, as his had. One of the football players loomed over her, a hand on her shoulder although she'd turned her torso away from him.

"What do I do now?" He only realized he'd spoken aloud at Ruby's half-laugh.

"Why do you have to do anything? It's her life, her problem. People need to face facts and pull themselves up by their bootstraps." Ruby stood up, posture mimicking the high school principal as she parroted words he said at least once a week.

"Well, I can't just not see now." Douglas tapped his frames.

"You could ask to walk her home." Ruby rolled her eyes.

"Her family and mine don't talk. Her mother ordered them all to stop talking to us after my parents split, and everybody obeyed." Everyone except Isabel, and even she dared only on campus safely far from her mother.

"Well don't tell her mother. Pretend you're being a gentleman,"—another eye roll—"making sure she gets home safe, no interest in anything else. You've got me rooting for you, though don't ask me why, maybe just because it makes me feel all warm and cuddly seeing you so helpless, so I'll give you a bit of help." She rubbed her hands together, then extended the right. Pale amber light glowed between her fingers. "For the next fifteen minutes or so, Lois will be able to see you for who you are, if she cares to look."

"Sounds like a blessing curse." Douglas paused with his hand upright. He swayed, pulled by two competing worries. On the one hand, how had Ruby ever come up with such a spell in the first place? But equally, what kind of person would Lois see?

"Isn't everything?"

"You're not offering me the same for her." Though he'd rather be able to see Isabel for who she was, and whether she might have any warm feelings for him. Probably for the best that it wasn't an option.

"You already spelled your glasses to help you." Ruby flexed her fingers and extended her hand further. "Also, you're the only one standing here, so you're the only one who gets the choice to show or hide. I'm not in the business of helping anyone steal someone else's secrets. Now shake or don't shake, but choose."

A dare. Her teeth flashed in a grin, but her gaze was level.

He licked his lips and took her hand, letting the magic zip through his veins and reverberate in his bones.

# WALKING HOME

*D*ouglas lost sight of Lois as he forged through the crowd. Several different perfumes assailed him—rose, lavender, a mix of citrus—making him sneeze. Warm bodies, those closest to the doors in slightly damp clothes, parted just enough to let him through. The bright lights inside and dark of night outside turned the picture windows into blurry mirrors. Scanning right and left, he spotted Lois just right of the door by her reflection.

The twist of light turned her reflection's eyes to dark pits in a pale oval face, and added lines at the edges of her mouth pointing down. The white of her shirt—sweater set—and green of her—pencil—skirt brightened and appeared as though a size too big, although on her actual body they fit her fine to Douglas's admittedly inexpert eye.

More noticing. The back of his collar itched. He adjusted his shirt and pulled at the top button to make room to swallow. Easier to not pick up uneasy details, but he wasn't chicken enough to dirty up his glasses already.

Lois leaned against the glass. It must've started drizzling

outside, because a drop of water traced a path through her reflection as though she wept.

Time to stop noticing so much, as if he could stop it, and start acting.

Except, he couldn't think of anything to say that didn't sound dopey.

"Hi Lois."

"Hi." She raised a hand and wiggled her fingers in what could pass for a wave. A moment later, she jerked away from the glass and turned to stare at him. "Douglas?"

"Yeah. Remember me? From next door?" He pointed in the general direction of their homes.

"You're talking to me?"

"Who else?" His cheeks warmed as she rolled her head indicating the crowd around them. "You're the only Lois in town that I know of. I know, I know, your mother told you not to talk to anyone in my family, but she's not here. She's hardly going to know if we exchange a couple of words."

"You hope." She wrapped her arms over her chest and glanced around, so he did too, but no one paid them any attention.

Save for Ruby on the far side of the room. The Black student who'd watched her and Douglas sat next to her. She lifted her glass in salute and drained it, then the two rose and walked the other way.

"I'll do my best to make sure. But doesn't look as though you're hanging with friends much, so if you're really worried, how about I walk you home? We can talk on the way. No one's likely to spy on us, and I promise to fall behind or go ahead when we get close to home. I'll be a gentleman and stay a couple feet away at all times. Scout's honor." He raised his right hand. A cool gust of wind dampened the back of his neck as the door opened behind him.

He didn't have to look to notice Ruby slipping out, her lily perfume mixing with the drizzle drops clinging to his back.

Lois's teeth pressed against her lower lip. She moved toward the door.

Douglas backed through it, holding it open. The wet metal damped his hand, but it wasn't really raining yet. More of a thick mist that gave the streetlights amber auras while fuzzing the buildings into blurs of color. Drops condensed on his glasses but slipped away leaving him able to see clearly —better than his usual spell to reduce rain glare. Maybe the noticing spell had other benefits.

Two steps brought Lois far enough out to glance both ways down the street. She sighed, remaining in place rather than retreating into the light and warmth.

"If I walk you home, you can give me a message for your sister," he said.

"Or I can pass you a note for her on Monday, as I'd planned." The wistfulness on her face vanished, swallowed up by a flash of irritation.

"Or both." He shrugged.

"Look, I . . ." She put a hand on the door and started to turn back inside, only to pause. Her brow furrowed as she stared at him.

One breath, two, three. His collar tightened around his neck, and he stuck a finger to loosen it. More mist coalesced on his scalp. Stray hairs slicked to his forehead.

"Very well, let's go," Lois said, moving out onto the sidewalk. "Looks like it will start raining soon, anyway, and I forgot my umbrella at home."

"So did I." He waited until she'd started along the street, then fell into step close to the curb. A few feet separated them, as promised. A car shot by, kicking up dirty drops from the street to soak into his pants.

They proceeded down the street in silence. The damp

night provided noises instead. Tires squealed on wet pavement as the car sped into the distance. Laughter and the chink of glass poured out of a bar further down the street. The diner across the way looked to be doing decent business by how fogged the windows had got.

Then they turned off onto a side street that would lead to another side street and on to their homes. No one sat on the front steps this night and few lingered on porches. A house with all the lights on the first floor flooding out around it had windows open and people sitting or leaning against them, many smoking cigarettes.

Douglas waited until they were well past that house before saying, "Isabel asked me about you, last time."

"You've seen her." Lois clasped hands against her chest. Her ponytail slicked against her neck, a few strands curling over her ears. "How is she?"

"She seemed fine to me." Though . . . how would Douglas know, if Ruby were right that he didn't notice much? He stomped on as the mist slowly soaked through to his underclothes. "She was studying in the library with friends, laughing and having a good time. That's where we meet, the college library, when she has notes for you."

"I'm so glad," Lois sighed. "When you see her again, tell her I miss her. I put it in the notes, sometimes, but it sounds more real spoken."

"Don't you talk? She said she tried to call you."

"I can guess how that went." A half-laugh escaped her.

"Your mother answered." They turned a corner. Most of the houses on this block had lights shining through curtains, but windows closed. One on the far side, half-down, had the front light on. Otherwise, they walked through a dark, wet night.

"She always does. Mother won't let Isabel be alone with any of us anymore if she can arrange things otherwise." A half-laugh again, or was it a half-sob? "They had a big fight before Isabel left. I don't know what it was about, except it ended with Isabel yelling that she'd tried things Mother's way and now she was going to do what she wanted. Next thing I knew, Father arranged for Isabel to live in a dorm room that would have otherwise been left vacant, he said so we'd have peace in the house but . . . I don't know why I'm telling you this."

She stopped in her tracks, eyes big and fearful even in the heavy mix of shadows.

"I can keep secrets." He turned to face her, hand raised as before.

"It's not a secret, just nothing anyone talks about anymore."

"Same deal." Only two blocks left to reach their houses. "Look, is there anything else you want me to tell Isabel? Other than that you miss her?"

Wet, Lois looked worse than she had before. Or he was finally seeing it. Her bones looked fragile, head heavy, and the shadows in her eyes weren't just the darkness.

"Anything? Because if she asks how you look, I can't say you're any too well. I don't mean to be rude, but you look like you're sad."

"At least I'm not pregnant!"

He froze. Barely drew in a breath. Only the rumble of a car on the cross-street broke the silence.

Lois went completely pale except for red flags on her cheeks. She clapped her hands over her mouth.

"Umm." He cleared his throat. "Good?"

She lurched, torso twisting as a hacking cough escaped her, but she didn't say anything or do anything. Was she waiting on him? But what else could he say—he could either ignore what she'd said and move on or go with it.

Ruby'd spelled her to be able to see him as he was.

Douglas blamed the news-bomb on that. Might as well go with his gut in that case. "You want me to tell Isabel . . . *that?*"

At which Lois burst into tears. Soft sobs, barely audible. Drops flowing down her cheeks, shoulders hunched, and mouth working without any words coming out.

Douglas cast a quick privacy spell, careful to ensure no one would see or hear them—or bump into them in anyway. He stayed where he was, facing her and back to the street, not doing anything. He ached to run away. Drop this all in his mother's lap, or Mrs. Warren's, or someone who could really help but there was no one but him around, save the distant clop of shoes hurrying against pavement.

Lois ignored the distance, fumbling her way over to him and crying all over his already wet shirt. He patted her back, as though she were his little sister, who'd hopefully never be in the same spot.

"It's going to be all right." Such stupid words, but what else could he say? A couple more pats, and then she hiccuped, then dried her face on a handkerchief. "You said you weren't . . . right? If something's still wrong, my mom knows some . . . I mean she's a nurse, if you ever need that kind of help."

"Never if I can help it." She sniffed, voice muffled against his shirt. "I'd have to . . . with a guy . . . and I don't ever want to with him or anyone. Not ever. Unless . . . I'd kiss Sarah if she let me, but I'm not supposed to . . ."

"Uh."

She ripped away from him, tripping back a few steps with one hand pressed against her mouth. "Oh, God. I said that. Forget you heard. Please? And don't ever tell Isabel."

"Not if you don't want me to." An easy promise to make, as he pressed a finger to his lips. He should've refused Ruby's spell. He didn't want to know other people's secrets.

"Don't tell your mom, or anyone else either, especially not my parents." Lois shivered, arms wrapped across her chest.

The thud of shoes sped up, coming closer. Something about the speed triggered the noticing spell, because Douglas lifted his head and turned before the new arrival whipped around the block.

A tall young White woman came to an abrupt halt several feet away, right under a streetlamp. She wore a yellow slicker and blue skirt and looked just familiar enough for Douglas to place her as a fellow student. Her hands were raised, fingers twitching, as she squinted through the rain.

"Sarah?" The name escaped Lois as little more than an exhale.

The other girl—Sarah, who was in two of his classes—cupped a hand around an ear and glanced around.

Douglas abruptly remembered the privacy spell and broke it with a finger snap.

Just in time, for Lois darted across the empty space right into Sarah. The taller girl braced herself. She wrapped her arms around Lois, and their heads nestled next to each other. This was who Lois would be willing to kiss?

They'd probably realize where they were, but maybe not soon enough. With a wave, he reinstated the privacy spell around them. Sarah's head jerked up and she met his gaze across the distance—the spell didn't block the caster—then nodded at him before tucking her head back next to Lois.

Douglas left them to each other. Better for Lois to find consolation with her friend than him. Whether or not they did kiss was none of his business, and better so.

Though . . . Lois had never answered the question of whether or not he should share her other bombshell with Isabel. He'd promised to keep the kissing thing secret, but Isabel's questioning him suddenly had a much bigger, more serious weight than the problems with her mother. What might she suspect? That her sister *was* pregnant, in which case he should tell her Lois wasn't?

He removed his glasses and rubbed them against his sodden shirt. They remained spotless, no matter how much he tried to create smudges.

Somehow, he'd worked a more powerful noticing spell than he'd expected . . . or wanted.

# AT SORCERY LESSONS

*P*ain throbbed at Douglas's temples as he biked over to the Warrens' house. A day and a half after casting the noticing spell, the sun looked brighter, even with a red-and-white Cincinnati baseball hat shading his eyes, and the wispy clouds skittering across the sky more ethereal. Someone down the street mowed the lawn, their motor louder than before and the smell of cut grass fresher. All due to one spell that he'd cast on sight alone?

He leapt off his bike and wheeled it up the driveway. The bungalow loomed before him, appearing more solidly built than before, its wide front steps and spacious porch more inviting. Gravel crunched under his shoes, the sound soon muffled as Dr. Warren backed his big car down the driveway. Douglas quick-stepped out of the way, and let his bike fall onto the front lawn. He dusted his hands, then his pale green shirt and black pants, as the car stopped next to him. The doctor leaned over and rolled down the passenger window.

"I'm on call, so I'm off. Cora will take your lesson today." The older man adjusted his glasses on his nose as he stared at Douglas.

"I understand. See you another time, Dr. Warren," Douglas said.

"I see you cleaned your glasses." The doctor smiled. "Very nice."

Putting the car back in gear, he rolled into the street and headed off. Douglas took off his baseball cap and scratched his head. He cleaned his glasses on a regular basis. Surely the smudges weren't that bad before.

Or had the doctor noticed the noticing spell?

Mrs. Warren must've heard them, for she stood in the door. Her green blouse was almost the same color as Douglas's shirt, skirt a few shades darker. The combination brought out amber highlights in her skin—not something he'd ever paid much attention to before. Or how she'd picked a complementary shade of red for her fingernails. "Come on in."

A painting of an old, graying shack deep in an emerald-green forest hung on one wall. A bright needlework sampler faced it opposite. In the far corner stood a tall vase with lovely pink flowers he didn't recognize, their gentle smell mingling with the breeze bringing the scent of cut grass through the windows.

A pitcher of water with ample ice, sides sweating, sat on a blue ceramic tray on a corner table, with two empty glasses. The plush yellow sofa stretched to one side of the table, under the big front window, and a matching armchair on the other. Clearly, Mrs. Warren intended them to take the seats they usually did, him on the armchair facing the wall by the door and her on the sofa with a view of the rest of the house. He moseyed over to the chair, keeping an eye on her in case she wanted to swap seats, and waited to sit until she had, hanging his hat off one knee.

A sigh escaped her as she settled at the close end of the sofa. She leaned back against the cushion rather than sitting straight, and for a moment looked about to nod off. The next minute the impression melted away as she tilted her head and studied him.

"Your glasses are clean!" She clapped her hands together. "Quite a change. How long ago did you clean them?"

"Saturday." Douglas took them off. Turning them around, he squinted at the lenses. They didn't look any different than before. He held them up to the light streaming in through the windows and noticed a few pieces of dust. A quick swipe of his shirt hem took care of them, then he returned the glasses to his face. "Were they really dirty before?"

"It varied, but there's a different light to them today." She lifted her brows. "You're viewing the world a little differently, at a guess."

"It shows?"

"At this moment, looked at in good light." Mrs. Warren gestured at the bright, natural light filling the room. "The magicless wouldn't notice."

"My mother didn't notice. All I did was use cleaning my glasses to cast a spell to make me notice more. I wasn't expecting . . ." He shrugged, at a loss for words.

"What did you expect?"

Of course she'd ask. He frowned and squirmed. His hat started to fall, but he caught it and sent it home to his bedroom with a clap of his hands. Settling his feet flat on the floor, he rested his hands on his thighs. "Just . . . details. More details than before. What color clothes someone had on, how they were feeling."

"Did you think about that while you were casting the spell?" She filled both glasses halfway, ice cubes chiming as they plopped into one or the other.

"No . . . I don't think so? I was rubbing the lenses and concentrating on the action to trigger the spell, since I'd never cast anything of that kind before." He mimed his actions. "It's not as though I do a new spell every day."

"That is a truth." She cupped her glass. "So far, you've seemed to mostly cast spells you learned from other people—your family, books, my husband and myself—and only rarely adapted existing spells to new purposes or developed new ones."

The words hit a chord. He did use a lot of spells others created or shared. "Is that bad?"

"Not at all. There are many sorcerers who excel at refining existing spells." Her fingernails rapped against the glass. "Yet if you rarely experiment with new spells, you run a greater risk of leaving room for accidental magic when you do cast a new one. Which may be what happened this time. You focused on the action, and thus cast a wider spell than you'd intended."

He snatched his glasses off his nose and turned them around and around searching for whatever she saw in them that he didn't. "I can undo it." Or he could try.

"Why?" Mrs. Warren asked.

"It's so much information." His temples throbbed again, worse. He rubbed them and willed away the pain. It subsided, but only a little.

"Try it a little longer." She summoned a container of headache medicine with a snap, and passed it over.

He popped a pill in his mouth, grimacing at the sour taste, and chased it down with a long swig of ice water. "What will that do?"

"Enlarge your world?" She leaned back, eyeing him head to toe and back. "What are your five favorite spells?"

A trick question? No, she looked to really want it. But how to choose? What counted as favorite? He did so many little spells, no easy way to pick five from them.

"That doesn't seem to work. How about . . . name the first

spells you've cast recently that come to mind." She held up a finger, tapping the side of her face. "Other than the noticing spell."

That was easier. All Douglas had to do was work through the spells he cast nearly every day. "Making sure my bike tires stay inflated and don't pick up any punctures. Make sure my bike works. Adjusting traffic so that I don't get stuck halfway through my route on the wrong side of the railroad crossing when that long early morning freight train passes, just because I've got those couple houses over in the west corner. Grabbing my books from my bedroom while I'm still downstairs because I'm running late and don't want to waste time on the stairs."

"Enough." She laughed, though her gaze narrowed. "What do these have in common?"

"I don't . . ." He shrugged and guessed. "They're small spells?"

"Small, yes. Requiring little power and accomplishing little save to make your life easier. And?"

What else? An easy, if uncomfortable, insight jumped out at him. "They're all for me."

"Benefiting you and only you, do you mean?"

"Yeah."

"That's pretty common, particularly in someone your age."

Her voice was gentle, but heat flushed his face.

"Even I cast a lot of spells that help me, though I also sneak as much sorcery as I can into my workday, since most patients don't understand enough about medicine to know the difference." She drank and refilled her glass, more ice chiming this time.

Douglas did not find this particularly reassuring. A prickling sensation along his spine kept him alert, waiting for what else she might let drop.

"The spells you described, they're not just small spells, they're the kinds of things you cast daily," Mrs. Warren said. "Usually when I ask sorcerers to name their five favorite spells or spells they've cast recently, there will be a mix of small and large."

"Which means . . . what?" He braced his feet against the floor, leg muscles aching.

"Listing only small spells, mostly conventional ones, suggests you may be out of the habit of casting large spells. More, it makes me wonder if that's all you ever cast, in which case you're at risk of forgetting the first rule of magic."

How could he? "Anything is possible." Though his mother usually added that possible didn't mean probable.

"Exactly. But if you repeat the same spells with little variation, then you may forget just how many factors to keep in mind when you create new spells." She tilted her head to the side, eyebrows quirking upward. "What is the primary difference between born and turned sorcerers?"

"Born sorcerers learn magic from the get-go while turned learn later?" Douglas shrugged.

"That's a small part of it. Sorcerers born to magical families learn spells their families know and often have a harder time dreaming what else magic can do if they don't have a good imagination to start with—and may dwindle and never go beyond small, convenient stuff." She gave him a hard look. "From what I've heard, that's happening with your father, just one reason of many that your mother arranged for you to study with my husband and me. Sorcerers who discover magic later in life are more likely to question everything and anything and come up with spells no one else has ever dreamed of. There are dangers to both extremes, and I fear you may be stuck in a rut." She folded her hands in her lap. "Describe how you cast the spell, everything you remember."

"Ruby challenged me. Sort of." He repeated the actions

without the intent and power this time, though his glasses flashed in the light all the same, and felt warm when he put them back on. "Anyway, I took my glasses off and rubbed the lenses with my shirt, using the action to channel power into the spell. I focused on cleaning as a symbol for noticing more."

"Noticing more . . . what?"

"Just noticing more." He shrugged.

She shook her head and sighed. "If you do not consciously define what anything is when you cast a spell, then your unconscious—or someone or something else—will do so instead."

"So I cast a big spell by accident, because I was too busy casting it to set limits?" He swallowed hard, then grabbed his glass and drained it in a gulp, but a lump remained in his throat.

"Because you didn't set limits or, according to your description, even define exactly what you meant by noticing." She clapped her hands, leveling a stern gaze at him. "So for today, I think we should go over the basic principles of magic so that if you ever do this again—leave a variable up to fate—it's by intent, not accident."

# HERE AND THERE

*E*ach day that week got progressively worse. There never was any end to more things to be noticed. Monday morning, he prepared for his usual paper route hyper aware of all the sorcery he plowed into his bicycle. The route looked new and different, with each and every change from the day before leaping out at him. This house had a newly trimmed lawn. That customer had left his car out of the garage overnight for the first time. The White man sneaking out of one house who caught the paper as Douglas threw it was not the husband who paid for the subscription.

At first, he thought school would offer a welcome oasis of familiarity from the noticing that plagued his paper route. Even before the warning bell rang for first period, he had some idea of how wrong he was. He'd always recognized that students formed groups and claimed spots in the yard and on the steps. It was safer to avoid certain parts, not least the side of the building where the smokers hung out or the front steps where only the in-crowd gathered until the bell. Most of the Black students clustered in groups on one side of the schoolyard. The few Shawnee and one Delaware attending the school formed a knot in a corner, near the Jewish students.

He'd never before particularly appreciated the negotiations going on within the groups over who ranked where, or how these might change in moments by whim or design. Not until he watched Lois moving from the outskirts of the popular students to the inner circle and then back out as she lingered last on the steps and brushed hands with Sarah, who ranked among the bookish. Then, later, maneuvered to just the right spot to pass him a note as she entered home room.

It was cold comfort to notice how much other students missed, particularly those most like him—or who he'd been before.

Home offered no safe retreat either. That evening, for the first time he recognized that he and Scottie left the messy dinner table to his mother and sister to clean up. It only took a few spells and snaps, but he'd never thought to do them, or if he had, he'd considered it only fair because he regularly took out the trash and mowed the lawn. The trash he could sometimes do magically, in the middle of the night when no one was awake to notice, while the lawn had to be done manually because certain neighbors noticed if grass got cut overnight without the sound of mowers. Yet those chores happened less frequently than the regular tidying and cleaning up that, even with magic, required a solid chunk of time out of his mother and sister's days.

Tuesday, he had it all to do over again: the same realizations, but with more nuance. On the paper route, he appreciated for the first time the similarities between his route and the cart delivering milk. At school, he couldn't stop hearing the different ways people spoke to and about each other. Boys describing girls, egging each other on to get the deepest blush. White students using words and names that roused wariness—and resentment—in the eyes of Black, Shawnee, and Jewish students.

Not just the students, either. Teachers' voices and faces seemed different. He'd never before noticed the half-apology, half-insult in the history teacher's voice when he told Ruby that she'd written the best report but couldn't get more than an A- because the best grade in the class couldn't go to *her*. Not because she wasn't good enough, because she was. Everyone knew it—even Douglas had recognized it before he'd cleaned his glasses. Worse was the way Ruby stood straight as she listened, chin high and body tense.

In the college library that evening, he glanced once at Isabel studying with her friends, then kept his head down. He'd known, without admitting to himself, that she was only using him to pass notes. That he didn't matter, he was just the convenient individual carrying them. He didn't want see what new revelations the noticing spell would add, so he cut his time in the library short and dropped Lois's note next to Isabel as he passed by her table.

Only to feel guilty and go back Wednesday evening to get Isabel's reply for Lois. Except Isabel wasn't there. He wandered the stacks, picking up books that might work for the history paper he had to write on the American Revolution, and returned to the reading room. Still no Isabel.

But Ruby sat at a small table on the edge of the reading room with several books in front of her. She hadn't changed since school, still in a navy-blue dress with white collar and cuffs, hair pulled back in a knot, and a small gold hoop glittering in each ear.

Three other Black women clustered around one of the tables where talking was allowed, spells carefully dampening sounds to allow others to study in quiet. Occasionally one or another glanced Ruby's way and smiled, but they were clearly taking advantage of being able to talk while Ruby wanted to read.

So did he. Carrying his books and bag, he hovered over the empty seat opposite her and waited. After a few moments, she swallowed and glanced up at him, then gestured at the chair.

He started to set up a spell for privacy, only to halt because maybe he should ask her first?

Ruby's lips tightened, and she went ahead and cast the spell.

"I didn't know you came here." He kept his voice low anyway.

"You ever come here on Wednesdays?"

"No," he said.

"Then you wouldn't know." Paper rustled as she turned a page. The book open before her had long paragraphs with lots of small print. Impossible to read upside-down unless one had a spell—which he did, but decided not to cast.

"Why Wednesdays?" he asked to be sociable, not thinking there was any reason other than maybe her parents worked late mid-week.

Her shoulders stiffened and arms pressed tight against her side. "Miss Bates usually works Wednesday evenings."

Douglas turned around. A middle-aged woman in a plain gray dress sat at the desk. It took a few moments to register who she was, because he'd only seen her a few times before. The first time, his father had sneered at her, telling Douglas afterward that she was one of the librarians who wasn't a sorcerer. He hadn't realized before, but the two librarians who were sorcerers usually worked on Tuesday and Thursday evenings. "Why does that make a difference?"

"Do you really want to know?" Ruby set her book down, holding her place with a finger.

"Only if you're willing to tell me."

"How kind of you." She gave him a half-smile, with a bitter edge.

He snapped his mouth shut and opened a book at random. Scanned the table of contents, then browsed through the first chapter. Ruby re-opened her book and read as well.

A few minutes later, she broke the silence. "Miss Bates is the only one who doesn't watch me all the time while I'm here."

"She doesn't . . . because you don't need help?" He asked, but the lump forming in his belly suggested there were more nuances for him to notice.

Ruby shook her head. "The other librarians who work nights, they're sorcerers and they watch me wherever I go. Every time I take a book off the shelf, I can feel magical eyes taking down the title and call number so they can be sure I don't steal it or write in it. They don't say anything, but that's what they do."

After a moment or two of imagining being constantly watched, Douglas shuddered. "That's . . ." He couldn't think of what to say that she wouldn't have thought of already.

She leaned back in her chair, the tightness in her face and shoulders easing a little. "Your glasses are clean and you're still noticing things. Good for you. I expected you to quit within a day or two."

Douglas shifted on the flat, unyielding wooden seat, uncomfortable at her admission of low expectations. "There's so much to notice."

"So much?" She laughed. "You've been noticing things half a week at most and you think that? Let's see what you say if you make a month, or even a week."

"You don't think much of me, do you?"

"I expect you to be who you are, that's all. That way I'm not likely to be disappointed."

"Then who am I?" He sat up straight, arms crossed over his chest.

"Oldest child, oldest son." She mirrored his posture, gaze level. "A good enough sort for your kind. A bit spoiled. Book-ish. Loner. Don't care much for the town, because you're bent on escaping and shaking its dust from your shoes as soon as you can."

She ended there, but Douglas's mind added onto the last line that he was focused on escaping town and to hell with anyone who might get in his way.

"Even now?" After all, she'd practically dared him to cast a noticing spell, before her dare to let Lois see him as he was. Though Lois had trusted him further than Ruby's description would suggest.

"Ask me again in a week or a month," Ruby said. "You're noticing things, but you're still you. It's one thing to notice and another to do something about it."

"There's more than noticing?"

"You have no clue." Her mouth stretched in a tired smile —the exhaustion clearly due in part to him. She piled her books together and left. The privacy spell broke as she passed through, and her heels thudded against the carpet as she took her books to Miss Bates at the desk and left the library.

She'd left because of him, and didn't take her books. Miss Bates placed them on a cart behind her desk. A sour taste bloomed in his mouth.

Douglas picked two at random from the pile of books he'd accumulated and slung his bag over a shoulder. He made it three steps away from the table, then turned and grabbed the rest of the books. Once in front of Miss Bates, he asked to check out two but gave her the rest to be returned to the shelves. As she processed the loans and stamped the due-date cards, he studied the books Ruby had brought over: a slim volume of poetry entitled *Annie Allen,* and three thick tomes about politics and power.

"Did Miss Warren forget her library card?" He nodded at the books.

Miss Bates studied him, then leaned forward. "She doesn't have a library account."

Of course. Her parents weren't affiliated with the college. He only had borrowing privileges because his father was a professor, one of the benefits offered to family members.

"Check the books out to me, then."

"You realize you'll be responsible for them." She gave him a stern glare.

He shoved the books he'd checked out for himself into his bag, using the movement to send them directly to his bedroom. Ruby's books he left in the bag. They weighed it down more than he was used to, except when hefting a full newspaper allotment.

Getting on his bike, he headed for Ruby's house. He went slowly, expecting to catch up with her along the way—but she'd vanished. Three times he stopped to switch his bag from one shoulder to the other, both aching by the time he reached her house.

Mrs. Warren answered the door looking, if anything, more tired than Sunday.

"Sorry to trouble you, ma'am." Douglas pulled the books out. "Can you give these to Ruby for me?"

The older woman glanced over the titles, then read them a second time. Furrows appeared on her brow. "*Annie Allen* I can understand, but she wants to read . . . these?"

"Yes ma'am. They're what she had when I, er, interrupted her." He grimaced. "Can you give them to her and tell her I'm sorry about that?"

"You can tell her yourself." She nodded, expression still

tired and puzzled, as soft rustles indicated someone came up the sidewalk behind him.

Douglas turned around, holding out the books. "I . . . you would've had more time with them if I hadn't . . . I'm sorry."

Ruby looked them over, then gently lifted them from his hands. "This doesn't count as you doing instead of just noticing, but I accept your apology."

Douglas biked away, chest and back lighter and not just because he wasn't hauling her books anymore. Getting them to her, and clearing things up, had washed away the sourness. The balance left him more aware of how uneven he felt about carrying notes for Isabel and Lois.

He'd never pushed Isabel much about why. Maybe it was time.

*D*ouglas took his usual seat in the library the following night. The regular Thursday librarian sat at the desk, a sorcerer capable of casting watching spells all around the building. He only brought one book from the shelves to read. Although he brought out a notepad and pen, he barely glanced at the text as he kept his head down.

Isabel, too, was at her usual place along with her friends. She glanced his way several times. He didn't have to look her way, but twitched at the flickering feeling of being watched. It wasn't so bad now and again, but all the time would be intolerable.

He didn't have a note to deliver. If she had one for him to carry, she'd have to approach him. That was how it happened every time, all the last school year and starting again this time. Did he really want to keep on? The reward of doing her a favor, of having her notice him and seeing her smile, wasn't worth as much as it used to be. The more so with the noticing spell making him unable to forget that any other high school student who used the college library could do the same. He wasn't the only, just the most convenient. She didn't really see *him*.

Though, given how Ruby described him, maybe that was just as well.

He wasn't getting anything done this night—certainly nothing that he couldn't do at home. Two perfectly decent research books waited for him at home thanks to the night before.

The only reason he'd returned here was for those few moments with Isabel.

Who was watching him.

He rose and slipped his notepad and pen back in his bag. Soft rustles betrayed when Isabel slipped over to the table opposite him. Warmth emanated from her, and roses perfumed the air. She glanced behind, then placed a note on the surface and gave him a half-smile.

The note looked the same as all the others, folded over several times with Lois's name written on the front. He didn't reach for it. "Don't you want to hear how your sister's doing?"

"You talked to her?" Isabel sucked in a breath.

"And she talked to me, too." Fear flashed across Isabel's face, and he raised his hand in reassurance. "Nowhere your mother could see."

"Yes, but we can't talk." Again she looked behind. At least one of her friends gave her a little wave before turning back to talk to the others.

"Not here, not now?"

"Exactly."

"Then when?" he asked.

She clasped her hands together so tight her knuckles whitened. "Tomorrow afternoon? Three? At the bench behind the student center?"

"Okay." He started to leave the note behind, because he

didn't trust her to show if he had it, but reconsidered. As he turned back, he remembered Ruby's spell offering Lois a chance to see him for who he was. Ruby might not have had such a good opinion of him, but Lois had wound up trusting him—sharing more than he really wanted to know. He swept up the note, willing the action to invoke Ruby's spell for Isabel. In case it made a difference.

He even delivered the note to Lois the next morning in the schoolyard. She appeared pale and withdrawn, saying nothing to him. Several hours later, she slipped a much-folded piece of paper into his hand as she left school.

Although he arrived early, Isabel was already there. She perched on the slatted green bench in a dull beige blouse and brown skirt. Did she think the colors made her less notable? Her legs moved restlessly, right heel tapping against the packed earth. A small copse of trees shaded the area, a temperate breeze rustling through the branches, making it a contemplative spot—except for anyone as nervous as she.

He couldn't do anything about her fears that someone would notice them, but he could ensure that no one actually did. Setting the privacy spell as he walked, he settled onto the far end of the bench and held out Lois's note.

Isabel snatched it up, scratching his skin in the process. Though she didn't draw blood. Her hands shook as she unfolded the paper. Read it, then crushed the note in a clenched fist.

"What's wrong?" Douglas asked.

"She's not waiting. She might not even let Lois graduate high school." Isabel tilted her head back, eyes closed. Her fist pressed against her throat, bits of paper visible between fingers.

"Who's she?"

"My mother. Doing the same thing to Lois that she did to me, except sooner."

Drawing in a deep breath, Douglas uttered the most dangerous words he could think of. "Can I help?"

Isabel didn't look to have heard, too busy shaking and clenching her fist even tighter. "She doesn't understand!"

"Your mother?" he asked.

"No, Lois. She thinks it'll all be fine. She doesn't realize that every step is weaving a net around her until she's trapped and it's too late." Isabel turned and dropped her head against Douglas's shoulder, fists tight against his chest.

Her body was warm against him, but he suspected she'd forgotten who was with her, which made it sting. He winced.

Isabel pulled back. Eyes wide, she looked at him. He caught the moment when she registered who he was. Neighbor. Note-carrier. Would-be friend.

"How can I help?"

"You can't." Her shoulders slumped. "Just stay away from my mother."

"You're all warnings and no why." What else had changed?

"Do you really want to know?" Isabel shifted to sit sideways on the bench, calves angled demurely away from him.

As uncomfortable as the noticing spell had proven, he couldn't go back to what he was before. Ruby had challenged him to move from noticing to doing—although getting Isabel to confide in him probably wasn't what she'd been thinking of. Yet the mere thought of his prickly almost-friend brought the perfect answer to mind—make her decide. "I'd like to know only if you want to tell me."

"No one really knows what she is, except me. Even my father. He forgets so fast." She sniffed, pulling a handkerchief out of a pocket to dab at her eyes. "Might as well have you be the second. It would be nice to have someone else know."

Douglas reseated himself on the bench, legs sprawled forward and back against the slats.

"Mother always wanted to be the best and the brightest,

to marry the best and the brightest. She was born to be the wife of a president or general, someone important, but she wound up with my father instead. I never dared ask how." Her shiver rocked the bench. "This wouldn't have been so bad for her if he'd had any desire to be provost or president of the college, but he never did, and all her pushing couldn't get him anywhere but here doing what he loves."

"That's doesn't sound so bad." Douglas wouldn't mind a life of doing what he loved, once he figured out that was.

"For him, but not for her. So she turned her ambition on us instead. Charles, of course, is her pride and joy. He just *has* to rise to be a general or chief executive officer or president or the top of whatever profession he chooses. But the rest of us are girls. Our place is to marry presidents and generals. Mother spent so much time preparing me, making me beautiful and a lady capable of running a household and navigating crises without showing so much as a drop of sweat."

The golden Isabel that Douglas had looked up to when she was still in high school. But something in her voice prompted him to ask, "Was that what you wanted?

"How would I know what I wanted?" She rubbed her forehead, bits of paper still peeping between her closed fingers. "It's what she'd told me I should. I was her good girl. By the time I was in high school, she had the perfect man for me picked out and I was sure she was right."

Quarterback, valedictorian, bank president's son bound for bigger things. All that plus the kinds of looks the girls had sighed over. Even as little as Douglas had noticed back then, he couldn't miss that.

"But it soon became clear that he planned to go to college somewhere else, somewhere better and far away, and Mother worried he'd forget me. Being engaged wasn't enough. She never said, but from something my aunt let drop, I think she might've had a fiancé who threw her over for someone else when he went to college, so she wanted us married before he left. I had to force the issue. But I couldn't." Isabel hunched over and rocked back and forth, arms wrapped so tight she hugged her shoulders. "I tried, but couldn't . . . I'm her failure."

"You're a student here at Timms, that's hardly a failure." He was missing things, how much he didn't know, but he could counter that last.

"My grades are good enough, but I only survived my first semester with my roommate's help, and my second was horrid. Still, I'm Mother's failure because I'm not married or likely to be anytime soon. So she's turned to Lois, to making Lois the perfect, pretty daughter and matching her up with the perfect husband." Isabel slumped next to him and lowered her hand. Opened her fingers to reveal Lois's note.

Douglas took the paper, gingerly smoothing the creases until the smudged pencil marks were legible.

*I'm doing well. Walt Ramble is taking me to the dance Saturday. Mother's happy. It will all work out.*

"No doubt Mother has her eye on having Walt marry Lois and move into married student housing, maybe even by next semester." Isabel waved a hand at the student center and rest of campus beyond. Tears glittered in her eyes.

Memory of Lois's confession flared, making Isabel's tale all the more believable. Lois had said she didn't want to kiss any guy and now she was dating Walt Ramble of all people? He'd swanned through his high school years with his nose in the air, at least the two years Douglas had overlapped with him. Worse, Isabel's mention of marriage and married student housing brought back Lois's comment about not being pregnant. Hardly the kind of thing Douglas could drop on Isabel without warning. Before he could think how to introduce the subject, she grabbed his hands.

"I can't go anywhere near the high school. It's part of the

bargain Father made with Mother. I stay on campus, out of the town." Her warm fingers squeezed his. "Will you go in my place? Please?"

"What do you want me to do?" He could count the number of school dances he'd been to on one hand, without using most of the fingers.

"Make sure she's only going with him if she really wants to, not because Mother wants her to."

"I . . ." He'd never expected such a request, even with the spells at work—him noticing things, letting her see him if she wanted, trying to do above and beyond noticing. The way her eyes met his made it clear that she knew who she was talking to. She wasn't asking him as a warm body but as *him*, Douglas Floding.

He still might have been able to say no, or mention Lois's secret, except Isabel kissed him. Warm lips pressed against his, and every rational thought flew out of his mind.

AT A DANCE

"It's not much of a dance," a senior in a peach gown sniffed that Saturday night, as she paraded along the side of the gym in company with three other girls. "Or even a hop."

They barely glanced at Douglas as they passed. He'd picked the corner to slouch in for that exact purpose, the better to see and not be seen. His white shirt and pale blue pants and jacket were clean and freshly pressed, and uncomfortable as all get out. The tie was the worst, tight and stiff under his chin. He might look like all the other boys in the room, but he felt out of place.

Several dozen couples swung and writhed in the floor as the disc jockey spun records and played tune after tune from the speakers set up on the stage—all with big brass and saxophone sections rousing reverberation in everyone's bones, or Douglas's for one. Streamers and banners in the school colors adorned the side walls, and at the far end sat a table with a big punch bowl and glasses. Several chaperones lurked nearby, not surprising since he'd caught whiffs of alcohol when three or four boys and one girl passed by.

He hadn't tried the punch—or danced, though he liked the music. To dance, he'd have to ask a girl to partner him and what if they said no? Or didn't like the steps his mother had taught him in their living room?

Besides, he was here because Isabel asked him to look out for Lois.

Who hadn't shown up yet although members of the senior and junior classes dominated, including most of the athletes and cheerleaders and popular circles. It made for a good crowd, and the class officers appeared happy enough, though he couldn't help noticing that at least half of each class was missing—all present from the mostly wealthier and White neighborhoods in town. None of the Black students or those who lived out on farms or in the poorer areas had shown up.

A girl with brown hair tossed her head on the far side of the dance floor. Douglas shifted down the wall for a better view—not Lois.

Sarah had come, looking as uncomfortable as he. The sleeves of her violet dress fell past her elbows, although most of the girls had short sleeves or sleeveless gowns. She huddled near the door, leaning against the wall and hands tucked demurely together. Looking for Lois, probably, because her head turned back and forth.

"Looking for Lois?" He skimmed the edge of the dance floor, sidling up to her. This close, strain and worry were so clear on her face he couldn't *not* see.

"She's not here." Sarah tilted back, head pointed at the clock above the door, hands rubbing her temples. "It's too late even to be fashionably late. She said they'd be here."

"Did she say exactly that?" Douglas asked.

"She said Walt was bringing her to the dance." Sarah scuffed a saddle shoe against the floor—a far cry from the light dance slippers other girls wore.

"Is this a dance?" Doubt made for an uneasy stomach. "Another girl,"—he pointed in the general direction—"called it a hop."

"Dance, hop, potato, po-tah-to." She threw out her hands. "Where else would she be?"

"Maybe the important thing is where else would Walt take her? There could be a dance somewhere else."

"That nobody here heard of?" Sarah frowned. "He could've meant a party instead, on campus?"

"Or at the country club." All the way on the other side of town, and farther away than Douglas wanted to go, especially since he'd biked rather than borrow his mother's car.

"Well, find out." She poked his chest.

"How would I know?" He should've known better than to say yes to Isabel's request in the first place.

"You're a sorcerer, aren't you? Your mother is, so you should be."

He froze, glancing this way and that to make sure no one else had heard. Fortunately, a long trumpet solo was just winding up.

"Well?" she asked.

"Are you?"

"No." She scowled. "It's not permitted, not yet. But I believe. So you're my best hope for finding her."

"If she wants to be found."

"She's only going with Walt because it pleases her mother," Sarah said. "She'd be happy to have both of us hanging around, distracting him."

Shades of Isabel. If only Douglas had remained clueless and unnoticing, but he'd promised. He retreated to a nearby classroom, leaving the door ajar. The music continued in the distance, but the lower volume made it easier to think. Sarah followed behind, breath hot on his neck as he nabbed a barely-used piece of paper from a trash can.

A flick of his fingers crafted a quick spell to offer privacy and discourage any chaperones from investigating—he hadn't recognized any sorcerers among them.

Then he laid the paper flat on a desk and stroked it. A rough map of the town materialized, streets only with no names or marks for buildings. A trio of bright dots shone in three places: the high school, the campus near the women's dorms, and a spot roughly halfway between. "Three dances or parties with lots of people our age or close."

"They must be at this." Sarah pointed at the campus dot, shoe tapping against the tiled floor. "But what's that other one?"

"Don't know." It wasn't a street he delivered papers to. He'd biked down it on occasion—mostly small houses and a couple of apartment buildings.

"We'll check it on the way."

"We?" Douglas asked.

"I can't do magic, and it might be needed. Besides,"—Sarah wrinkled her nose— "Lois said her sister wrote in a note that she'd asked you to look after her."

He protested and complained, but somehow he ended up leading Sarah down the hall and out the door to where he'd left his bike. She'd walked. If only he'd known better back when he first carried a note for Isabel, except she'd clearly picked the right sucker. He knew she'd worry, could see Sarah's concern, and his now-noticing brain kept suggesting things that could go wrong with Lois being out with Walt on campus.

The balmy night was perfect for biking. Not too hot, not too cold, and almost no wind. A thin layer of clouds covered the sky, moonlight shining through. Romance in spades, too bad the dance or hop or whatever was inside.

A flick of his fingers extended the bike seat so that Sarah could sit behind him, but then he had to summon something for her to use to tie up her skirts so they wouldn't tangle in the chain. She wrapped her arms around his waist, fingers twitching against his belly. She weighed more than a full bag of newspapers, and having her behind him made biking heavier and pedaling harder. One by one, he adapted his usual spells for bike maintenance, balance, and speed to allow for her, but it all took time.

"We should go straight to campus," he yelled over his shoulder as they approached the non-campus party. Easy to hear, given the hands clapping and twang of guitars—not to mention the mouthwatering aroma of meat on a grill.

"Just check," she said back, right in his ear.

"They're not here." Douglas stopped a few yards from the oasis of light, music, and food. Even in the dark and at that distance, it was clear the gathering included most of the Black students who weren't at the school hop, along with parents and younger siblings, all together in the courtyard of an apartment building.

"So, go on to campus." Sarah's hands loosened and tightened around his waist, her torso swaying behind him. The unpredictable movements made it hard to kick off and go on —and her voice had gone softer or fainter, or some other change that had the hairs sticking up along the back of his neck.

A figure at the edge of the party set their hands on their hips, then strode down the street toward them.

"Douglas Floding, whatever are you doing here?" Big earrings glittered at Ruby's ears, and her blouse and skirt were bright shades of pink no one ever dared wear to school. She walked light, as though bouncing on her toes. "And who's that with you?"

"It's Sarah . . . Sarah . . . what's your last name?" He winced, having forgotten it. She didn't answer, leaning against him as though falling asleep. "We're on a wild goose chase, or something of that kind." He shrugged.

She stared at him.

"For Lois."

Ruby shook her head, a scornful laugh escaping her. "She's not here, that's for certain."

"No, we figured not. We've been at the school dance already, not much going on there. Hope you're having fun." He steadied the bike, readying to push off.

"Wonderful." Ruby's lips stretched in a huge smile. "I'm celebrating. My parents promised to stop pushing me to go into medicine! Hallelujah!"

"Great." Douglas returned her grin, then twisted around to check on Sarah who'd started to slip sideways. Her whole torso slumped as her grip loosened around his waist. "Can you help me?"

"What's the problem with her?" Ruby grabbed one side as he lurched off the bike and braced the other.

It wasn't enough. Sarah turned into a deadweight, dropping into a heap on the sidewalk. Weirdly, her eyes remained open but completely unfocused. Bit by bit, she curled in on herself. Wrapped her arms over her chest and began to chant in a low voice. "Let her go, don't touch her. Let her go."

"Did she drink too much?" Ruby summoned a cloth from somewhere to slide under Sarah's head.

"She didn't—doesn't—smell of alcohol, and she was fine earlier." Douglas dragged a wake-up spell from the depths of his memory, and adapted it. He tapped Sarah's nose. "Focus. We have to find Lois."

Sarah's head rolled up, vacant eyes staring at them. "In the clearing."

"Where?"

"Clearing?" Ruby slapped a hand against the sidewalk. An instant later, Sarah's skin glowed green.

"Hurt. Crying."

"Where?" Douglas asked.

Ruby sat back, all her earlier party energy gone as she met his gaze. "I know."

# IN A CLEARING

Oh for the day when Douglas only carried messages between Isabel and Lois, when his life was simpler. He pulled Sarah's arm over his shoulder, holding tight as Ruby took the other side. Even with sorcery lightening the load they made for an awkward, sideways progression through the woods.

The dark woods.

Lampposts were few and far between, and the moonlight diffused through the clouds where it wasn't blocked by the canopy of leaves and branches. He'd cast a spell for light, as had Ruby, but there were still too many shadows—except in the ever-shrinking distance where rays of spectral green light filtered through the trees and bushes.

Worse, the path was made of stepping stones set at regular intervals. Once upon a time they might have been even, all raised slightly above the packed earth, no longer. Several slanted, none the same direction, easy enough if they walked single file during the daylight, but they didn't. The path wasn't wide enough for three abreast. They walked at an odd angle, Douglas leading and taking the bulk of Sarah's weight as he tried to keep her from stumbling.

She kept mumbling. "Hurts." "No." "Stop." He kept on regardless, because the words weren't meant for him or Ruby, given the way her head rolled on her neck and her wide eyes never focused. By the time they entered the woods, her mumbling had dwindled to a low chant of "Lois."

His lungs worked hard, and a few feet behind he could hear Ruby breathing heavily. Their breaths, grunts, and footfalls were the only sounds. No birds, nothing else nearby making any noise whatsoever.

He half-stepped on a stone and lurched to the side, pulling Sarah with him. This rocked Ruby off-balance, and she in turn stumbled forward, pushing Sarah against him and him into a tree. The bark scratched his face until he straightened up.

"Why are we doing this?" Ruby asked.

He push-pulled Sarah back onto the path and forged ahead, Sarah's movements indicating that no matter her grousing, Ruby hadn't let go.

"Because we're here and we have to do something. You're the one who told me doing was harder." Was the green light through the trees growing stronger? Rays angled down through a break in the trees a few feet ahead.

"I sent word to my parents for help. We could have waited for them," Ruby said.

"And felt guilty if anything happened to Lois while we dawdled?" Douglas asked.

"Lois, Lois, Jean, Lois." Sarah's head rolled, but her eyes blinked. It might've been a trick of the light, still Douglas paused long enough to note a second blink.

"If we're going to help, keep on." Ruby managed to kick his shins.

"Sarah's blinking, maybe we're getting close. How much

farther?" He adjusted his hold on Sarah and moved forward, shin stinging for several moments.

"Head for the green light."

"Has to be sorcery." He didn't like the looks of it.

"This is all sorcery."

The kind of sorcery he could live without. He'd much prefer staying with nice, safe, tame bicycle spells. First thing he'd do when he got home was undo the noticing spell—he just had to survive the night.

The green light illuminated a narrow passage through the trees. No stepping stones here, only packed earth, which should make walking easier if it weren't for the uncanny light and the way each and every tree and bush reached out a branch in to touch him. The sickly emerald glow made it hard to tell what lay beyond—until he reached the halfway point.

Branches formed an arch at the end. Between them stood a figure, a silhouette rocking back and forth. Head bowed. Hair streamed down their back with the ends fluttering slightly in time with the hem on the knee-length skirt. A darker mound rose between the figure and the entrance to the clearing.

"Lois?" Douglas called.

No response, even when he called her name a second and third time.

Sarah's limp body started to slip from his hold. He grabbed for her arm. Ruby lurched on the other side.

"Let's set her down here, where she's safe." Ruby angled Sarah's body toward a soft patch of moss between two trees.

Douglas leaned down to whisper in Sarah's ear as he helped ease her onto the moss. "Sarah, Lois needs you."

Sarah jerked. Her eyes flickered open. "Lois," she croaked.

Douglas glanced at the clearing, but nothing more than a

shiver passed along Lois's statue-still body, and that could have been a trick of the eye.

He inched along the last few feet separating Sarah and the moss from the clearing. Ruby was one step behind him, her breath hot on his neck. He froze at the edge of the clearing.

The green light emanated from anywhere and everywhere, then resolved into half from a tall stump and the rest from the perimeter. Softer than daylight, it nevertheless showed the two people in the clearing down to the right shoulder strap of Lois's pale pink dress, pulled down nearly to her elbow. Fingermark shadows marred her shoulders. There was no wind and the still air felt heavy, but she rocked back forth endlessly pulling a pink ribbon through her fingers.

Closer-by, the lump resolved into a man curled into a fetal ball. One hand pressed against his groin. The other stretched toward the opening. Mud-streaked skin, shirt, pants, and brown hair.

"Lois! Walt?"

Neither moved. A wind started to circle the edge of the clearing, blowing counterclockwise. The glow from the stump increased, mixing white and green in a way that combined with the gusts to create the illusion of eyes hovering in the air. Dozens and dozens of eyes—brown, brown, blue, and green—all open and staring.

"We need to get them out of there." Ruby licked a fingertip and tested the air, flinching. "Aunt Hazel didn't think it was evil, but I don't like the looks of this."

"I'll go." Douglas stripped off his jacket and dropped it next to Sarah. A shiver rippled through him. Balmy the night might be, but it was notably cooler in only his shirt.

"You sure?" Ruby asked.

"You know more of what's going on than me." Her comments during the long walk from party to campus had made that clear. "You're the brains. I'm the muscle. For now."

A choking laugh escaped her.

He crouched, gauging distances. The grass swayed gently rather than whipping, as the circling wind centered at torso height, and was slighter lower down. "I can get Walt easier than Lois. Give me room, okay?"

A cold blast to his left and the crunch of shoes on dirt told him when she pulled back. Drawing a deep breath, he lunged. Cast a spell to lighten Walt's weight as he grabbed the other's hand and yanked.

He expected to take a couple pulls and count himself lucky if he didn't dislocate Walt's shoulder. Instead, the man's body gave little to no resistance. Douglas toppled onto his back. A moment later, Walt flopped atop him gentle as a leaf. Then the weight spell dissolved and drove Douglas's breath from his body. He rolled over, pushing the other man to the side.

Walt said nothing, just curved tighter into a ball, this time with both hands tucked over his groin.

"Now her." Ruby laid a hand against Walt's neck. "He's breathing at least."

Douglas rose to a crouch. He darted through the wind, ducking under as much as he could. Hissed at the bitter chill. His hair whipped back and forth, practically pulled out at the root, then settled in a rough mass when he was through—where the air was warm, almost hot, and smelled so strongly of roses he sneezed.

The earth below glowed with hundreds of wavy lines crisscrossing the clearing. He picked his way across, rising on tiptoe several times to try and avoid stepping on the light. The eyes glowing in the circling wind all focused on him.

Lois showed no signs of noticing. She rocked, staring at the stump and the array of flowers circling the base.

"Lois?"

Still no response.

He reached toward her arm, to get her attention, but the movement made the staring worse. The wind picked up, whirling faster. Vague outlines of heads began to form around the eyes. He recoiled, but the changes continued. Necks followed heads, then shoulders . . .

"Lois, Sarah needs you!" Her head moved slowly, turning toward him. Her eyes resembled Sarah's: unfocused and dazed.

"This way." He waved and pointed.

She didn't move.

"Let me help you. Sarah's waiting."

She started blinking at the repetition of Sarah's name, though her gaze remained diffuse.

"Hurry!" Ruby called. "Before the eyes grow full people!"

Douglas grimaced. Lois wasn't moving fast enough, wouldn't at this rate. He'd have to touch her to get her out, but where? Bruises marked her shoulders and upper arms. He went for her waist, slipping an arm around to urge her on —pull if necessary.

She arched and cried in pain.

The wind yowled, then stopped in an instant. The eyes vanished, covered by long gray veils. Human forms lined the clearing, at least two deep. Every part of the clearing, even the entrance. Behind them rose a dome of lightning. Together, forms and dome completely hid Ruby from view.

The light changed, red bleeding into the green.

One by one the figures around the perimeter raised arms, pointing at him. Lightning crackled, passing from finger to finger.

Then someone broke from the crowd. All but that one paused, power simmering, as the form stumbled forward. The veil melted away, revealing Isabel in an unfinished white gown trailing threads behind—then the dress shifted to a lace-trimmed yellow nightgown covering from neck to knee. Her bare toes dug into the grass and she spread her arms out as she rushed to stand before Douglas and Lois, shielding them. "Don't!"

With a wave of her hands, the forms blocking the entrance moved to the side and the lightning parted just wide enough for one to pass.

"Go!" Isabel yelled.

Douglas pushed Lois ahead of him into Ruby's waiting hands. Whatever held the electricity back started to collapse. Flickers began to reform in the air, sparking and crackling. Very real hands on his shoulders pushed him through.

Even as the force exploded.

# PART IV
# MARTA AND HAZEL

Saturday 22 September 1951

## DANGER

Marta's hands ached from gripping the leather steering wheel. A dark street stretched before her, the blurred edges only half due to the night, for she had trouble focusing. Buildings and stands of trees resembled each other—all big masses of shadow and the occasional flicker of light. Goosebumps pebbled her arms and legs along skin exposed by the short-sleeve shirt and shorts she'd pulled on at random. She'd stuffed her sockless feet into her gardening shoes, the soles so thin she could feel every ridge in the gas pedal as she slowed.

Each blink overlaid the street, houses, and trees with the image of a girl rocking and sobbing in front of a tree stump. The hem of a yellow nightgown fluttered under garish green light. The girl's crying echoed in Marta's ears with every rumble of the motor and squeal of tires as she took a turn.

Stretching her fingers, she grabbed the gear and down-shifted. The headlights reflected off a car parked, one tire resting up on the curb. Nearby lay a large, shadowy mass. She slowed further and gritted her teeth as she focused enough to catch the outline of trees and branches rather than walls and roofs. Rolling down the window let in a hint of pine. Surely this was the right place, or close enough.

Her hands shook as she parked and turned the car off. She opened the door and stumbled out, clutching the frame.

The other vision threatened to swamp her, sobs filling her ears to the exclusion of all else. No, she had to hold onto the physical world and keep the vision back. Had to hope that she wasn't too late to save her son. Merely thinking about the moment—him in the clearing, Lois yelping in pain, and the sudden surge of fury that had swept through and burned away the peace . . .

No. No. Leaning back into the car, she snatched the key and held it in a fist. Held onto reality.

A quick swirl of her wrist, a thrust of power, and she turned her hand into a flashlight to guide her toward the trees. An odd-shaped shadow lay nearby, metal reflecting the light.

A bike—Douglas's bike.

She was close, but someone else had arrived first. A man blocked the entrance to the path through the wood, a tall man with orange hair who swayed as though drunk, although he didn't smell of alcohol. His white, button-down collar shirt was mis-buttoned over a white undershirt, and both only half-tucked into dark slacks. The toes of fuzzy blue slippers peeped out from under his pant legs. Even so, there was no mistaking Marta's boss no matter how unusually clad.

"Dr. Thomson, whatever are you doing here?"

"Had a dream," he rubbed his forehead, eyes wide and gaze abstract. "A girl in the clearing. Another girl. Crying."

"You?" She wouldn't have guessed him to be caught in the spell, but his dishevelment and swaying, stumbling state resembled how she felt. "You should go home."

"Have to check." He shook his head.

"Marta, Doctor Thomson, have you seen Sarah? She's not home, but I can hear her crying." Esther lurched across the grass toward them. She had on sensible shoes, but her skirt and blouse were wrinkled as though snatched up from a laundry pile, and the kerchief over her hair sat further back than usual. An older man followed her, his suit tidier than the doctor's except for a gap in the middle where he'd missed a button in fastening his shirt. His face closely resembled Esther's, apart from the prodigious gray-streaked dark beard. "Help us, please."

Marta tried to urge them to go back home, with no luck —and time was wasting.

A few moments later, a large black sedan pulled to a stop by the curb and Hazel emerged. She stalked across the intervening space in blue top and pants paired with a lavender silk turban, the only person whose clothes did not appear to have been thrown on in minutes.

"Whatever—" Hazel waved at the small crowd.

"We need to go." Marta gave up on sending them home, as the spectral sobbing threatened to drag her back into the vision. Esther seemed likewise overwhelmed, sagging against her brother. "They'll have to come," she said to Hazel, then turned to the others. "Follow me."

Without waiting to see if they listened, much less cooperated, she turned and jogged down the path. Hazel's footfalls sounded directly behind, and less organized thuds farther back.

Even with Marta's makeshift flashlight, the path was dark at first save for irregular light from lampposts and a paler glow filtering down through the tree cover. Within minutes, a green-white glow formed a backdrop to the trees and bushes between them and the clearing.

Marta turned onto the short dirt path, and then halted so

fast she swayed. The pull of the vision faltered and eased, diminished by sheer surprise at the number of people crowding the narrow passage.

A young White man lay sprawled to one side, Dr. Warren kneeling nearby asking questions in a low voice. The man didn't answer, beyond minute nods and shakes of his head.

A few feet beyond, Lois and Sarah sat against a tree, clinging to each other and weeping, and brushing each other's tears from their faces. They swayed, eyes wide, clearly under the influence of the clearing. Cora, Ruby, and Douglas hovered over them.

"Sarah!" Esther called, stumbling past Marta.

Sarah lurched to her feet, bringing Lois with her. Esther blinked in surprise, but enfolded her daughter in a big hug. Her brother joined them. Sarah leaned against both, one hand reaching out from the embrace to keep hold of Lois.

The far end of the path was blocked by a thick, green-white mist sparkling with power. Even several yards away, Marta's skin prickled as though she were covered with static electricity.

None of that mattered—the important thing was Douglas was alive, standing, well. She grabbed him in a tight hug, a shock darting through both of them, until he grunted in protest.

"Not now." He squeezed back and then pushed away and pointed at the flaring wall of magic. "Isabel's still in there."

"Isabel?" Hazel had followed close on Marta's heels. Farther back, Esther and her brother clustered near Sarah, who now rested a dazed head against her mother's chest. Dr. Thomson had fallen to his knees between Dr. Warren and Lois, until the former claimed his attention for the prone man.

"Lois's sister." Marta frowned at her son as she totted up

scratches on his arm and the way he grimaced as he stretched his back. "Whom you've been carrying notes for."

"She asked as a favor." Douglas scowled at her. "Did you know her mother banned her from coming home as long as she lives on campus? Won't let her talk to Lois on the phone? All because Isabel refused to go along in trapping her old boyfriend into marrying her before he went off to college?"

"Good for her." Marta wouldn't put much past Bettina. "But what does that matter—"

"She's in there. She saved me, helped me get Lois out, but she's there and no one else—not me or Dr. or Mrs. Warren or Ruby or *anybody* can get in to help her."

"You're certain?" Hazel asked.

Before he could answer, a new arrival stumbled into a tree trying to pass them. His white undershirt shone in the odd light, straining over a beer belly. His jeans hung low on his hips, and bits of shaving cream still clung to the sides of his pale face. After a moment's surprise, Marta recognized Mr. Bullen.

He, too, had wide unfocused eyes and swayed as he mumbled, "Lois. Isabel. Lois. Isabel."

"Daddy?" Lois squeezed Sarah's hand, then pitched across the intervening space into her father's arms. He staggered under her weight, then the two rocked together.

"You say Isabel is on the other side. Anyone else?" Hazel asked, edging closer to the crackling wall.

"Just her," Douglas said.

"I'll check." Marta turned to her son. "Count to ten, then grab me and do whatever you need to make sure I answer you."

Before he could protest, she leaned back against a tree and closed her eyes. A deep breath filled her with scents of the forest and the faintest hint of roses. She clung to that as she let go of reality and let the clearing pull her in. Not the reality of the clearing, but the spectral vision.

Her hastily donned clothes vanished, replaced by the gray dress. A veil covered her face without impeding her vision. Instead of lying on the grass, or dancing, she stood tall and unmoving—one of many gray statues circling the clearing—with a single gap. A low thrum of peace and joy passed through her in two directions, coming from the figures to either side and going on. Heat zipped behind her. Across the clearing, miniature bolts of lightning flashed behind the matching statutes.

Waves of sorrow lashed at her, coming from the center of the clearing.

Isabel crouched in front of the stump, rocking back and forth. Tears streamed down her face, glittering when they caught the light. The skirt of her yellow nightdress pooled around her ankles, showing feet bare and streaked with green.

Behind her, the stump glowed the same green-white as the shield—save for thin streaks of red snaking up along its sides. Blood red. The color seeped into the lightning encircling them.

"Mother!"

Marta returned to her body as Douglas shook her. His face shone sickly green and bloody in the light of the wall. Red leached into the shields, shifting the smell to burning roses.

"Is she there? Is she okay?" Douglas asked.

Marta slumped against the rough bark, still feeling the pull of the vision. "Isabel's there, but . . . why is she in a nightgown?"

"She appeared out of nowhere and pushed me out of whatever this is." He waved at the clearing. "She saved me. There were these veiled statues all around."

"She appeared out of nowhere?" Hazel asked, gaze narrowing as she studied the wall.

"She was one of the . . . the statues."

"Us." Marta touched her chest.

"You?" Douglas stared at her.

"And others. I saw it." Marta nodded. "You grabbed Lois. She shrieked, and a wave of such anger and agony ripped through me. A desire to inflict hurt, to save her from you, until Isabel broke out . . ."

"So she managed to shift from being there in spirit to in person, whereas you,"—Hazel pointed at Marta—"and the others had to get yourselves here the hard way. Is she a sorcerer?"

"Not hardly." Douglas shrugged. "I've been carrying notes for her to her sister, and she wouldn't need that if she could do magic."

"She must be the key to the spell that binds these souls and the trees." Hazel reached toward the sparkling wall, then winced and snatched her hand back.

The red streaks grew larger, wider, and began to branch.

Marta slipped around the others and tried the wall herself. Dueling powers burned through her—peace and anger, joy and loathing, green and red. The same feelings at odds within the clearing. Instead of burning at her, the wall *pulled*. She yawned, exhaustion pressing down.

Because she was inside as well as out—and something sucked energy from her. More with every passing moment.

"I think I can get through." She shivered, rubbing her cold hands together.

"Are you certain?" Hazel asked.

"I'm there almost as much as here. I have to do something. It's drawing energy." A glance back showed Mr. Bullen cradling Lois as they rested at the base of a tree. Esther yawning as she held a sleeping Sarah.

Drawing a deep breath, Marta threw herself into the wall. Pain flooded every mote of her body. She screamed, but the words didn't belong to her.

*No! Don't! Stop!*

# SECRETS

Marta fell through into the clearing and dropped to her knees. Sweat dripped from her forehead, and she panted until she caught her breath. Sitting back, she took in the merging of the two clearings—dream and real. The surrounding wall formed a dome, trickles of red growing up along the sides as though trees taking root. Gray figures lined the edge. There were two gaps in the circle. One Marta had noted earlier, perhaps Isabel had jolted from there. The other space missing a statue might have been Marta's. The clearing no longer called to her as a place of joy and peace. It was a space in the woods filled with trees and sullen magic ready to lash out.

The remaining figures were unmoving, and yet the poses varied. Some still had a hand raised and finger pointed at the center, while others appeared to be twisting and trying to get away. A few leaned forward, both arms outstretched toward the sole living, breathing being—other than Marta.

Isabel didn't much resemble her mother at the moment. Golden-brown hair hung in thick, damp strands around an expression of agony. Tears seeped from eyes clenched closed.

No makeup, and her skin was blotchy. She pressed fists against her chest, or was she beating herself? Her nightgown might've started clean, but now was streaked with dirt and rose petals.

Rising, Marta took the few steps necessary to cross to Isabel, and dropped back down. She laid an arm along Isabel's shoulders. The younger woman jerked, then turned into Marta and burrowed her head against Marta's chest. Marta held her in a warm embrace, rocking her and murmuring sweet nothings. The phrases Marta had used when her children were little and had bad dreams fell readily from her lips, no matter how ill-suited, most notably "it's going to be all right."

The young woman shuddered, then her sobs slowed. "It's not. Never will be."

"Nothing is impossible." A variation of the first rule of magic, though the girl showed no sign of recognizing it. Marta checked her pockets for a stray handkerchief, then used the hem of her shirt—cleaner than Isabel's nightgown, to dab at the girl's face.

No protests at this treatment. Isabel barely moved and still hadn't opened her eyes, though her tears slowed. "Can you bring Jean back? Or turn back time?"

"I can't, but that doesn't mean that no one can." The red streaks in the stump and wall remained, but the color shifted to a lurid shade of pink. Marta brushed sweaty locks back from Isabel's forehead. "There is magic in the world, my dear, and you're part of the most complex spell I've ever seen. That alone should show you that anything is possible."

"Magic?" Isabel opened her eyes, and even focused on Marta without evidently recognizing her. Her head made tiny circles, suggesting she was still dazed.

"Tell me how this came to be." If Hazel was right and Isabel the key to the spell—perhaps even the one who'd cast it—then getting the girl to share truth should make a start at resolving the situation—and hopefully help her as well. The younger woman didn't seem to understand what she'd done, though surely she'd turned sorcerer . . . unless she'd somehow worked an immense spell of accidental magic without ever realizing what she'd done. The chill in Marta's bones suggested the latter, little though she wanted it to be the case.

"I don't . . ." Isabel's head turned down. She picked up a white rose from next to the stump. She stroked the browning, crinkly petals, and said nothing more.

"You knew Jean Neville, didn't you?" Marta asked.

"We were roommates."

Marta sighed. Roommates, which made Isabel the person who'd reported when Jean left and didn't return. "You miss her."

"So much. She was like a sister. The only person in the whole dorm who understood that I didn't want to go home, even though we didn't talk about it." Isabel swallowed hard. "Or why she didn't want to go home either."

"You came here after her death, putting out flowers?" So many flowers, the more recent resting atop older. Mostly white roses, with some asters and goldenrod mixed in.

"It was the least I could do." Isabel leaned back against the stump. "And it was so very peaceful here."

"But the spell didn't start until weeks after Jean's death." Marta frowned. When had Hazel said the first inklings of the spell were felt? April? Too big a gap for Jean alone to be the trigger.

"Spell." Isabel's pupils dilated for a moment and she swayed.

"You came back here in late April, didn't you?" Marta asked.

No response from Isabel, head drooping as she rested against the tree.

A soft whisper added "the tenth." Marta blinked, risking a glance around. Hazel's voice, but she didn't see the other woman anywhere.

Isabel evidently heard the words too. "The tenth. Oh, that was when . . ." The young woman paled. Her shoulders hunched and arms wrapped across her torso.

"Yes?"

"That was the only day Mother ever came to visit me." A bitter laugh escaped her. She shook all over, then sat straight, hands fisted. One crushed the white rose, petals sticking between her fingers. "She looked around and asked was I sorry yet?"

"You weren't." Marta didn't have to guess.

"She didn't care to hear me say that." Isabel said. "She'd come to tell me that George was engaged."

"George?" The name rang a bell, but Marta couldn't quite place it.

"My boyfriend in high school. My perfect match, according to Mother. He went off to Yale. Mother wanted us to be married before he left, and when he wouldn't propose, she told me to . . ." Isabel's fists shook, then the vibrations spread through her whole body to the extent the very air around her pushed Marta back. Yet the other woman's words flowed with ease, suggesting she wanted to share, to be heard. "She wanted me to get pregnant, picked the perfect night, and sent me off."

"Oh, God." Marta struggled against the pain rolling off the young woman. It roused an ache in her own breast, and memories of being young and certain that marriage to the right man would lead to a beautiful life. She'd gotten that so, so wrong.

"I'd always done everything she wanted. I was her good girl, and she promised if I did as she told me I'd have a beautiful life and be all but a princess." Isabel's face turned up, eyes wide and mouth trembling. "But then, lying under him while he was . . . it hurt, and all I could think was that if I did get pregnant this would be the rest of my life. I'd be living the life my mother wanted."

The streaks in the walls and on the stump had returned to a blazing red. The circling statues began to shade a pinkish gray as Isabel's fury filled the air.

Bettina made for a perilous friend, but a worse enemy. Marta hadn't realized how much this applied to the woman as a mother, too. Such a different case from Marta. Her husband had betrayed her when he threatened their children. She wasn't proud of her many mistakes and errors, but they were hers, not her mother's.

"I was lucky and my period came right on schedule. She was mad and wanted me to try again, but I couldn't! Even when she swore that if I didn't, she'd throw me out of the house. I went to Father." Isabel's expression softened, if only a little. "He offered me a chance to get a degree and live away from Mother, and find out *I* wanted."

A blast of satisfaction blew away the fury and pain. The red streaks turned to deep green, so that the surrounding dome bore silhouetted trees, and the stump briefly appeared to put out branches.

"You did well. Your father did well by you, as much as he could." He'd resisted his wife for Isabel's sake, something Marta would never have expected of him.

A tentative smile tugged at Isabel's lips. Her fists unclenched and she stroked the mashed rose resting on her palm.

Yet Isabel's escape from her mother still hadn't led to the clearing and the spell.

Or April tenth.

"Then she came to remind you of what you'd rejected," Marta guessed.

"As she left, she turned and told me she'd make sure it would be different with Lois." Isabel's fists came up again. "I ran after her, but she left too fast. I wound up here, instead . . ." She turned around, as though for the first time realizing her sorcerous surroundings.

"And you unwittingly cast a spell."

Again, the word roused only a dazed reaction in her. She leaned back against the stump, puzzlement on her face. "Ever since, I dream of this every night. Sometimes during the day. A place of peace and joy away from the world."

"Isabel, you're not the only one who's dreaming, who's trapped in dreams." Marta waved at the still figures surrounding them. "You need to let them go."

"Go? How?"

The air before them shivered, and Hazel appeared. She stretched out a hand to Isabel.

"Give the spell, the magic that binds souls and trees, to me."

# WARDING THE LAND

Two startled faces turned up to Hazel, so different and so alike. Despite the myriad energies whirling about the clearing, she remained still. She'd slipped in through the gap left by Marta's passage before it filled back in. The mix of magic and anguish made her teeth and bones vibrate. The air was redolent with roses and rotting vegetation. The stump and dome each were bright enough to cast shadows, doubling and tripling shadows cast by spirits frozen in a myriad of poses.

All while the younger woman, Isabel, rested on the land with pressure equal to two or three times her weight. Already her feet had begun to sink into the dirt and roots, did she not notice?

So many contradictions. So much sorcery—and danger if the tension were not released. The earth warmed beneath her, sending drafts skimming up along her body in a plea for ease.

Her stillness opened room for her mother to watch, listen, and speak. *Do not hesitate.*

*Or move in haste.* Hazel wanted least to cause the pent-up energy to explode.

*There is much good here.*

Sympathy flooded Hazel, her own and her mother's, but the hardships that prompted Isabel's unwitting creation did not justify leaving it as it was. The immense spell had captured too many others in the span of months, as moths drawn to the light. How many spirits ringed the clearing? With the overlapping shadows, Hazel couldn't easily count. Then there was the magic manifest in the stump and walls, and the flickering lights in the earth below speaking to an intricate web of power running through the roots. And all of this was the unconscious work of a woman who had yet to accept the existence of sorcery!

*If it can be saved, I will,* she promised her mother.

But Isabel clearly couldn't handle the sorcery, and didn't know how to undo it. Each time Marta had mentioned magic or spells, she'd blinked. She showed no understanding of what she'd created.

Hazel wasn't sure she grasped the whole of it yet herself. Feet firmly set on the earth, she held out her hand.

"Give it to you?" Isabel blinked. Grabbing hold of the stump, she rose but wavered as she tried to stand without assistance. A faint tremor rippled outward as the earth struggled to support stump and woman.

"You have made a wonder here. This clearing gives to humans peace and ease, receiving in return power and energy and knowledge, but it grows more complex and unwieldy with the addition of each unknowing soul bound into the exchange. Equally, it takes energy from those who don't realize what they are giving up." Hazel moved closer, stretching out a hand. "I am willing take on the burden of dismantling it and ensuring the well-being of those humans and plants caught up in it. Take my hand if you will accept this."

A rush of air alerted Hazel as Marta stood up. The other woman opened her mouth. Hazel gestured for her to remain silent and not interfere. Isabel had to choose whether or not to hand the spell over, free of influence.

The younger woman searched Hazel's face looking for something. Sorcery crawled over her body, thick as old ivy vines hugging a tree to death. Inch by inch, breath by breath, she stretched out her hand. Palm hovered over palm as the air between them heated and sparked with miniature lightning bolts.

Then Isabel laid her hand in Hazel's.

Hazel stiffened, fingers tightening on the girl's though she heard a cry of pain. Power enveloped both of them.

A blink, and the clearing was remade in her sight. Isabel and the stump sat at the center of two overlapping networks.

Of the two, Isabel's was the smaller. Each of the spirits circling the clearing had a connection to her, direct or through one, two, or three others. They fed crackling power in with every breath. Surely they had received something in return. In the past, Marta had mentioned relaxing into peace and joy, but there was little of either in the air at the moment. The draw of power flowed so heavily that every mote of Hazel's being vibrated as the connections passed to her.

Below lay a still more extensive and intricate system of roots connecting trees throughout the town, as Hazel and Ruby had mapped. Yet they were the smaller part of the network, which included bushes, shrubs, and even collectives of grass. They pulled not merely sorcery from Isabel's network but knowledge—some degree of understanding how humans hurt each other, and ways to protect them.

And the power to do so.

Did any of the people tangled up understand that they were sharing their energy as well as their knowledge with the land?

Marta showed no awareness that a measure of power—small, but steady nonetheless—flowed from her into Hazel and from there to the web, and she was one of dozens. Hundreds.

What Hazel couldn't do with the power, to ward the land and more . . .

Yet, if Marta didn't know, or the other spirits caught in the web, then the power they contributed did not belong to the grid, to roots and plants, by right.

The bushes and shrubs shivered, not wanting to give up the steady supply. She couldn't replace it alone, might provide only so much as she could spare. More would follow, as others agreed to contribute, but it would take time. This would be the slow growth of trees.

Two lines linked Marta to Isabel, one directly and the other through a shared connection. Insubstantial though they were, Hazel pinched one with her fingers and plucked it, then the second.

Marta jerked onto her toes, eyes wide and one hand going to her throat. Then she settled back down. "I didn't realize . . ."

One by one, Hazel plucked the remaining links. Some she recognized—her boarders, many of Ruby's classmates, and those waiting in the woods on the other side of the lightning shield. Others were vaguely familiar, but she couldn't put a name or face to them, and the remainder strangers. Most female, but some male and a few with the feel of both. Each corresponding statue dissolved into nothingness, leaving behind a few glowing sparkles that died away.

The flow of power dwindled, ended save for that between

Hazel and Isabel. She plucked that last, and removed the connection between the young woman and the stump.

The shield still whirled about the clearing.

Hazel walked over and stroked the glittering light. With that one touch, she drew its power and channeled it into the system of stump and roots, now linked to her alone.

Yet when she turned, magic still glowed in the clearing. Barely more than pink haze, it clung to Isabel's skin.

Shouts, the woman's name, other cries broke the silence. Someone started to run past her, at Isabel, but Hazel stopped him with a raised hand. "Wait!"

She strode back to Isabel's side. The pink haze resolved into swirls of red and white, both faint enough to be unnoticeable under normal circumstances, which this most definitely was not. The layer covered every bit of her—except for five great rents down her chest.

"You're still under a spell," Hazel leaned close, and got a whiff of decaying flowers. From the pile of roses, asters, and goldenrod near the stump or the spell?

"Spell?" Isabel's eyes went wide, pupils unfocused.

"What other magic have you cast?" Hazel asked.

"She carries a spell?" Marta squinted, then shook her head. "I don't see anything."

Hazel offered Marta her hand, sharing the vision when Marta took it.

"The magic is so faint, it's almost not there." Marta pulled away. "I have to work to see it."

"Magic?" Again the word barely registered, with Isabel's gaze going distant. Then she shook her head. "I'm sorry, what did you say?"

"Enchanted, since you didn't put it on yourself." Hazel studied the swirls and rents.

"She's not the only one." Marta said, pointing at a man

and girl who resembled Isabel. Both bore similar skin-tight coats of magic save with no tears.

"May I touch?" Hazel asked Isabel.

The young woman managed to nod, squinting and studying her arms.

A finger quickly swept across Isabel's cheek granted Hazel a sense of something invasive, constrictive, and filled with determination.

And it smelled of roses.

# PASSING JUDGMENT

Several dozen roses nodded in the light breeze. Red and white, they flowered on bushes planted along a white picket fence. How many times over the years had Hazel stood here and marveled at the long-lasting blooms? She'd talked to the gardener often, regularly walking away with a few flowers for her mother.

A cool night breeze tugged at the ties of her turban, a harbinger of autumn. The cloud cover parted enough to allow silver moonlight along the length of the street. She kept both feet on the sidewalk, several inches back from where the fence met the walk up to the house. Mr. Bullen would likely give permission for Hazel to step onto his property, but better to conduct the confrontation under the sky with the plants and land as witness. Trees nearby eagerly bent branches close to absorb every moment.

Remaining outside also allowed her to ensure full view for three human groups of witnesses. Family first: Mr. Bullen stood behind and to the side, Lois under the curve of his arm. Isabel had moved up next to Hazel. Then neighbors: Marta and Douglas, balancing on the sidewalk to the other side of the walk. Lastly Hazel's own family, to attest to her passing judgment: Cora, Luther, and Ruby were arrayed behind. All of them dusted with dirt and leaves and bedraggled after their time in the woods. The others from the clearing had gone home or to the infirmary—Sarah reluctantly following mother and uncle—though Hazel planned to check in a day to see if any had turned sorcerer and needed training—or if they'd come up with a rational explanation not to believe in sorcery and would remain magicless.

Ruby maintained a privacy spell around the area to keep anyone else from noticing magic at work. Thanks to Isabel's unwitting spell, there were already too many other magicless who might turn sorcerer. No sense contributing to still more. Perhaps sorcerers should stop using the term magicless when it wasn't true that they were without magic, just that they didn't have the conscious ability to use it.

Only unconscious.

Hazel hoped that was the explanation for the thin spells coating Mr. Bullen and his daughters. She feared not, so much that she was procrastinating.

Perhaps this was her true test: not merely warding the land but carrying through protection to the bitter end.

"Do you want to go into the house?" Mr. Bullen asked. "She might be asleep."

Such hope, likely soon to be dashed. "No, thank you. We'll do this under the open sky."

"Bettina can't be the cause, she's not a sorcerer." Marta stayed in place but turned a puzzled expression Hazel's way. "I thought once she was, but she denied it. For years."

"There's magic here." Hazel reached for the closest bush. Bending a stem, she plucked a red rose that bent and swayed atop the fence.

"She won't notice," Isabel said. "I've been stealing roses for weeks and she never noticed."

"She didn't catch you in the act, but you stole white roses. I took a red." Hazel moved to block the opening in the fence. "She'll notice."

Five breaths later, the door opened and Bettina Bullen strode out. In contrast to the dusty condition of those facing her, she was impeccably dressed in a crisp white shirt, blue slacks, and blue pumps, her makeup exquisite, and her lipstick matching the red of the rose in Hazel's hand.

Bettina's gaze flickered, no doubt taking in the numbers facing her. She strode lazily forward with each step deliberately placed, heels clicking against the walk. On reaching the end of her property, she laid her right hand on the fence, fingers curved possessively over the top, and held out her left.

"That rose belongs to me." Bettina focused on Hazel.

"You gave me flowers before." Hazel said. No doubt never again.

"I gave you them. That is still mine." Bettina's fingers curved, fingernails as red as the rose. "Return it, and we shall speak no more of this."

"Return the rose, or return them?" Hazel nodded in turn at Isabel, Lois, and Mr. Bullen, all still glimmering with magic.

"They are mine, my pride and joy. You have no rights here." Bettina raised her chin.

"We have rights." Marta offered. "I filled my half of the bargain. Lois's shoes will no longer turn muddy in her closet. Keep your word to never threaten my livelihood again."

"Done." Bettina waved her hand, then turned to stare at her oldest daughter. "And you've brought Isabel back to me."

"No. Never." But Isabel's body bowed as though resisting urge to move forward. Hazel laid a hand on the younger woman's shoulder, and tension drained from her though her chest heaved as she dragged in deep breaths. Shuffling sounds behind suggested Mr. Bullen and Lois had both started toward the house, but Luther and Cora kept them back.

"She is a grown woman and belongs only to herself." Hazel brushed the red petals against Isabel's cheek, but never took her gaze from Bettina. "Remove your spells from her."

"You have no power to censure me. Your mother scolded me once, years ago, did she tell you that? For a small spell of obedience cast on a rebellious child." Bettina cast a sharp glance at Isabel, then bared her teeth at Hazel. "But I learned from that lecture what she was, and the limits of her power, your power. You are the landwards. Your care is for the land and not people, no matter that you've fooled others over the years, driven less careful sorcerers from this place. My children are mine to cherish, mine to shape, mine to protect from the errors I made."

Hazel's mother had tried to deal with Bettina Bullen and failed? No wonder she'd worried about Hazel passing judgment on others and dwelt on the importance of understanding one's limitations. She reached for her mother in the stillness and felt her watching but keeping counsel.

*She's right that our power rests in the land. Since she didn't abuse it, I couldn't stop her.* Sorrow poured through from Hazel's mother.

*You tried. I never realized until now she was a danger,* Hazel returned.

Something in Bettina's words struck a chord. Bettina's children were her pride and joy. But so, she'd said only days earlier, were her roses. More, the spells Bettina had cast on her family smelled of the roses that she nurtured with magic. That was no sin. Many other sorcerers did likewise.

But Bettina's rose bushes had entwined roots, much as the spell Isabel had unwittingly cast entwined other roots and was fed, in some small part, with roses stolen from her mother's garden.

Hazel studied the plucked rose, the rose bushes—and the faint sorcerous connections between the plants' roots and Bettina's family.

"Come back now, and we will speak no more of this." Bettina stared in turn at her daughters and husband.

Marta, Douglas, and Ruby joined Cora and Luther in holding Bettina's family back.

"You are wrong." Hazel still blocked the way. As a test, she plucked a petal from the rose and let it drift.

Bettina stiffened, eyes wide and cheeks paling.

"Your family and your roses are your pride and joy, that's what you've told me over the years. They're what you plowed all your magic into: prize-winning roses and prize-winning children." Hazel plucked another petal and tossed it to the wind.

And another.

"They deserve the best the world has to offer. I will make sure they do well." Bettina cast a scornful glance at Isabel and her husband, though the muscles of her throat tightened and her breath came in pants, "if they will only cooperate."

"If they submit to your will." As more petals fell, Hazel risked a glance at Isabel. The magic on her skin had visibly faded.

"I know best." Bettina turned ever more pale, back bent as she crumpled in on herself. She remained upright thanks to both hands wrapped around the top of the fence. "You can't do this. I did nothing to the land!"

"You would not even let your family believe in magic, because they might realize how many other spells you'd wrapped around them." Hazel pulled off several more petals. The pistil at the center showed yellow through the remaining red. "You condemned them to ignorance, so they would do as you said. When one broke free of your will, she still carried the residue of your spells."

"I didn't hurt the land!"

"You ensorcelled your family as you did your roses, entwining humans and plants, and so your sorcery is forfeit until your children are grown and you have lived in truth as magicless as you have pretended." Perhaps pride in her early defeat of Hazel's mother had made Bettina arrogant, or she'd accidentally mingled the two. Regardless, Hazel took advantage of her weakness. She raised the almost denuded rose and tore off the remaining petals in one yank.

Bettina collapsed on the sidewalk.

Isabel and Lois hugged tight, holding each other up as tears poured down their cheeks. Mr. Bullen stared at his wife and the house, as though both had turned to ashes.

Luther and Ruby, Marta and Douglas, all gazed at Hazel in awe—Cora in awe and relief.

In the stillness of Hazel's heart, her mother's pride in her unfurled and planted seeds that sprouted. Within moments, the first buds of becoming landward grew within her.

*Welcome, Landward Hazel,* her mother said, *my baby all grown up.*

# EPILOGUE

Marta
10 November 1951

Autumn had blown into the clearing and left fallen leaves scattered everywhere. They crunched under Marta's shoes, red and orange and brown. Blades of grass poked through, marking the sward on which she'd lain weeks earlier. Seemed to be much longer since then, and also just yesterday. She pulled the collar of her winter coat closer around her neck as a wintry blast tore through. Her legs shook, hose offering little protection under her uniform.

Sunlight streamed weakly through the bare branches. Only an hour of so of daylight left, and then the temperature would drop even further. Signs of frost lingered on the northern sides of tree trunks, and most especially the stump at the center. No new flowers graced the thick roots, but the old remained even though they were now little more than lines of brown leaves, stems, and rotting buds.

Marta shouldn't have put off visiting. Nevertheless, she'd done so successfully for so long, through curious coincidences and suspicious diagnoses, but the last case had broken her ability to believe the dream spell completely over and done.

Yet nothing here spoke of sorcery still at work. It was just another woody spot following the seasons from fall to winter.

She stripped off a glove and bent to brush the soft grass surviving amidst the leaves.

So cold!

Shivering, she recoiled and fumbled donning the glove. Stuck her hand in her pocket for extra layers of protection.

"I wondered when you'd come back." Hazel stood on the far side of the stump, a solid figure warmly wrapped in a long, tan winter coat and matching hat. She crossed her arms over her chest, head tilted to one side and a smile slanting her lips.

A familiar face by now. Marta wouldn't ever mistake her for anyone else, not after regular meetings over tea or coffee. A delicate dance, for they weren't quite friends—maybe someday—nor student and teacher, but rather cordial acquaintances exploring overlapping approaches to sorcery.

"How often do you visit?" She moved closer to the stump, standing within a patch of light to catch the last hint of heat.

"Rarely." Hazel patted the stump. "I don't need to."

"But you expected me to stop by." The wind picked up. Marta hunched her shoulders, increasing the sorcerous warmth layered into her coat. It still wasn't quite a match for how the drafts cut close around her.

"Once. Others already have, for one reason or another."

"Isabel, of course." Marta had accepted the charge to give the young woman her first lessons in sorcery, although Douglas somehow always arrived home right when they were about to end, ready to help her practice spells. Ruby, too, often visited around then, sometimes bringing younger cousins to the point that Marta often had a sorcerous study group meeting in her house.

"Of course. Three times so far."

"Lois?" Who studied with Marta alongside Isabel, an extra opportunity for the sisters to connect. This had proved a mixed blessing, for all of the Bullen children had started coming over to Marta's house once or twice a week, although neither Charles nor Evelyn displayed indications of turning sorcerer. The way they played with Scottie and Janie, it might be only a matter of time.

Bettina's face often appeared in one or another window of her house as she watched her children leave or return, but she still made no sign of acknowledging Marta's existence in public. Marta would never know if Bettina realized the way her attempt to blackmail Marta had led to her own downfall. Marta had promised to find the answer to the mystery of Lois's dirty shoes. She had, and in return Bettina would never threaten Marta's livelihood again.

Unlike his wife, Mr. Bullen, stopped by often to check on his children and left with a wistful glance when they said they wanted to stay.

"Lois and Sarah." Hazel counted them off on her fingers with a gleam in her eyes.

The two were often seen together despite the disdain in Bettina's gaze, and the concern with which Esther watched them. Sarah did not study sorcery with Marta or anyone else that she knew of. *"She may someday,"* Esther had confided in a quiet moment, *"but she has agreed to honor her uncle's preferences—and mine—so long as she lives under the same roof."*

"Esther?"

"Yes."

"Douglas?"

Hazel nodded.

"Who else?"

"Ruby, Cora, my mother, and many of the magicless who were caught in the spell, though I hope their memories fade with time since none have turned sorcerer." Hazel moved closer, leaves rustling underfoot. "And now you, last of all. I'd started to doubt that you ever would. So." She clapped her hands together. "Why now?"

"I wanted to see if there was any sign of life remaining." Marta turned in a circle, noting the branches bending in the wind and the last leaves floating in the air.

"There is always life in the woods, even in winter." Hazel coughed, hiding her mouth—and possible smile—behind a tan glove.

"I meant the spell." Marta set both hands on the stump, only to feel unexpected warmth. More than the sunlight would explain. She leapt back, elbows stiff against her side as she glared at the other woman. "And you know that."

"Interesting word you chose—not merely any sign of power remaining but life." Hazel patted the stump. "The trunk, branches, and leaves are gone, but this tree lives. Its roots tangle with others, giving it a far reach."

"What about the spell?" Marta checked her gloves, but found no sign of burns or damage to the cloth.

"Why do you ask?"

Marta glared at the teasing response. "The doctor didn't turn sorcerer and managed to forget all he'd seen, but I haven't. He's had two patients since with what he diagnosed as an unusual venereal disease, causing impotence. It's magic. I could see that clearly even if I couldn't tell him that."

"The effects will wear off, as long as the patient doesn't repeat the action that caused the spell or offend trees." Hazel shrugged. "I wouldn't worry too much about them."

"But if the sorcery is still at work—"

Hazel raised a finger to her lips. "It is and it is not. Say rather, a variation on the spell now exists. One which draws power only from those who knowingly choose to contribute. A spell that shares with plants knowledge of the kinds of wrongs we would wish to prevent if we could. The trees learn fast, but they make their own decisions. It is our hope that, as time passes and more sorcerers are willing to contribute energy, the network of plants aware and willing to intervene will grow."

She held out a hand, and a brilliant red leaf dropped into the center.

"The trees protect girls who are being pursued against their will?" Marta drew in a deep breath and let it out slowly, some of the tension in her body easing.

"Those and other wrongs. When and where they can, they offer help to those in need, though there are too many places they cannot yet go or act." Hazel lifted her chin in challenge. "This is my judgment. My decision."

Tree branches curved over, blocking the last sunlight and casting both Hazel and Marta into shadow. This was the heart of a small but growing collective of living trees, with their own ideas of good and evil, able and willing to punish humans who hurt others. The stuff of nightmares by some measures—or a new source of help for those in need? The trees couldn't reach everywhere, after all.

It all depended on which way one looked at the matter— and whether Marta trusted Hazel's judgment.

Marta stretched out a hand to the nearest tree. A branch lowered, brushing a leaf against her palm. "Good."

THE END

# ORDINARY SORCERY

Read on for a sample from *Swan and Shadow*, the first installment of Ordinary Sorcery!

Viola values family and friends above anything else. After suffering abusive bullying in high school, she delights in a tight-knit group of friends at college.

Until the night she witnesses them meeting without her. The same night her younger sister calls with news their parents' marriage further disintegrated.

Running off into the forest, Viola witnesses sorcery and winds up tangled in a decades-old curse.

Lovely and poignant, *Swan and Shadow* mixes *Swan Lake* and *The Magic Flute* into to a gripping, emotional page-turner.

A swan turned into a man on the best worst day of my life. Everything sucked big lemons until that moment.

My sneakers pounded against the path around the lake, kicking up bits of gravel that skittered in my wake. Crushed pine needles scented the air and made me long for fall and cups of hot chocolate. The air lay still and warm, but I worked up a nice layer of sweat. My Arden College T-shirt and matching green shorts stuck to my skin, although my hair streamed back from my pony tail. Even my fingers pinked up where I held tight to my cell phone, making my skin rosy against the black case instead of the usual beige. Alas, every twenty steps or so my wire-framed glasses slipped down my nose no matter how many times I shoved them back up.

Varied trees grew along the path. Pine and maple, oak and sycamore. A few leaves showed signs of turning orange and gold, but most remained green. I ran through a world of deep shadows and flickering lights. Lampposts cast ovals of light on the path at regular intervals. Here and there blue lights gleamed from emergency phone towers.

Starlight reflected off the lake to my left, along with bits of moonlight from the waning crescent high in the sky. When the path moved farther from the water, the reflected light dwindled to firefly-flashes between thick foliage.

Across the lake, warmer yellow streetlights and lamps affixed to houses glimmered as though not-so remote stars flickered between branches. They grew closer and bigger as the path wound around to where the college's property ended and the suburb began.

The house at the edge of the development had a six-foot wrought-iron fence lining the path. Someone had cleared the ground between fence and lake. Or maybe it was like that to begin with: a rocky stretch with a clear view of the water and the bright lights of the college across the way.

Nothing burned so bright as an immense star blazing across the dark sky.

Pausing and panting, I backed up against the fence. My skin cooling as my sweat dried.

By then, the arcing light hove into closer view. Not a star but a swan, bright and radiant as it danced in the air. Drew near, moved far, and back and forth. It circled and sank down toward the surface. White wings widespread and neck arched in the air reduced to a blurry blob in the reflection mirroring the flight from below.

The swan landed close by and swam nearer. Ended up half-turned away from me a bare five feet from the beach.

So beautiful. The classic image of bright white plumage floating on an almost mirror-perfect surface. A few faint ripples marred the swan's reflection.

The swan reared up. Feet paddled hard, churning the waters, as it spread its wings wide. Wider. At least as broad as I stood tall. The gold-tinged beak sharpened.

A silvery aura outlined the bird against the dark waters and the distant shore.

In that moment, everything changed.

Wings shrank into human arms. The oblong body narrowed and lengthened to a broad torso. The beak dwindled into a nose, and the small white head expanded and grew brown hair. White feathers darkened to gold-tinged skin and shimmering lake waters lapped at a well-shaped backside.

The swan became a naked man.

My mouth hung open. Body swayed. Hands gripped the iron fence posts tight.

One blink, two, three. The bird didn't re-materialize. The man remained there, naked as the day he was born and in the spot I'd seen the swan a moment earlier.

Feathers floated on the water around his thighs. Another rested atop his head as he stared down at the lake surface. Part of the feather's down tangled in the man's hair, but the shaft stuck out. It bobbled. Ridiculous, yet a sudden desire to hold the feather rose within me.

An instant later, a gust of wind blew it loose to dance on the breeze, wafting my way until it hovered above me. Letting go of the fence, I stretched out a hand. The wind died away, letting the broad, white feather float down into my palm—still warm from his body.

Physical proof a swan had flown in. I swayed, then slid down against the fence poles into a heap at the bottom. Wrapped my arms around my legs and hugged them to my chest. My lungs ached with every breath, as though the air turned to liquid ice.

The swan-turned-man failed to notice the feather's flight. Instead, he slapped the water, raising a great splash. Drops arced through the air, glittering as they fell back into the lake.

A moment later, he beat the surface of the lake full throttle. Shoulders flexed and arms lashed out. He fought the water as though an enemy bent on destroying him. Smacked the surface hard, each blow resulting in great waves and gouts. A few drops reached me despite the distance.

How did he resist crying out in pain? His hands must've hurt from the blows, yet he only huffed.

After a few minutes he ended as he'd begun—staring down. Head low and shoulders heaving.

My fingers stroked the soft feather over and over.

Then he turned and trudged out of the water.

Fine muscled legs, strong chest with a dusting of dark hairs, and . . . oh . . . even in the sharp contrast between light and shadow, he had an unmistakable face. An oval dominated by deep-set eyes and thick eyebrows. Angled cheekbones and stubble on his cheeks and upper lip. Starlight leached color from his skin, turning it silver-white against dark hair cut short.

Evan Roth.

Twice a week since the semester started—and all of last year before that—I had an excellent view of his face bent over a violin during orchestra rehearsal. One of the heart throbs of the orchestra, after the lead percussionist and the concert mistress.

Evan—a swan.

My fingers tightened around the feather.

Standing on dry land, he clapped his hands and a towel—white with red stripes—appeared out of nowhere.

He dried himself off with efficient snaps of the cloth against arms, legs, and torso.

Another clap, and the towel vanished.

More claps summoned clothes piece by piece. Dark brown shorts. Battered sneakers which he slipped on without socks. An Arden T-shirt matching mine only his had the Tree of Knowledge sprouting from a scroll of music instead of a book. Then a comb to run through his hair. He bent over the water once to check his reflection before he sent it back from wherever he'd summoned it.

Each spell made my hair stand on end as though I'd taken a too-big bite of mint ice cream.

Magic, magic, magic.

He still hadn't seen me.

I couldn't let him run off without talking to him, asking about it all, no matter that I'd meet up with him at the next rehearsal.

A fog seemed to have settled in around us. Not seen but felt. Certainty thrummed in my bones that I had this moment, this chance—if he went off, I'd forget.

I set my jaw and vowed it wouldn't happen.

"Hey, Evan!" Springing to my feet, I grabbed hold of the fence for steadiness.

He startled, arms pulling tight against his sides and hands

rising in fists. Then he got a look at me and relaxed. He gave me a polite smile, the kind meant to keep people at a distance.

"Hi, uh, Viola, right? Clarinet."

In other words, he found me familiar but not memorable. I gave him points for getting my name right—*Vi*-ola, like violet, because no way am I a stringed instrument. But while he got the general category of instrument I played right, he guessed the actual one wrong. Unsurprising because he ranked as one of the orchestra's good lookers with instrument or without. Not me, in part because no one looks good close up when blowing through an oboe, or other wind or brass instrument for that matter. Indeed, oboists often joked the instrument was an ill wind that nobody blows good.

He nodded, then turned to walk off.

I lunged after him and grabbed his arm.

"How'd you turn into a swan? From a swan into a man, I mean, but you must've turned into a swan first to turn back."

He stiffened, eyes staring right into on me—close enough to show thin, spiky yellow rings spread through the green.

"Are you a sorcerer?"

"What?" My turn to draw back. "A sorcerer? Is that what you call yourself?"

"You are, aren't you?" His hand wrapped around my wrist, holding tight enough the sinews made a crackling sound. He stopped the instant I winced. "Tell me you are."

I shook my head, glasses slipping down my nose until I pushed them up with my free hand.

He grimaced and cursed. Not magical curses, or even creative. A lot of f-bombs. After which he stared right at me again—still holding my wrist, though not so tight.

"There's still time. Forget. You saw a swan. Fine. You saw me. Fine. You didn't see me change shape, or anything else sorcerous. Forget before it's too late. You're only safe if you don't believe."

He pulled free, waved a hand, and ran off.

I gaped, then snapped my jaw shut and pelted after him . . . but everything that could go wrong did. I tripped on the second step and lost seconds righting myself. A sudden wind whooshed up fallen leaves from the underbrush and blew them across the path ahead of me, making me slow and bring up my hands to shield my face. Somehow I knocked off my glasses off. They fell into the bushes with a clatter.

After several minutes of searching, I found them—without a scratch.

Too late to catch him, so I gave up.

He told me to forget sorcery, but he shouldn't have used it to slow me down and keep me from following him. That made me believe all the more, though his warning rang in my ears as I headed back to campus.

*You're only safe if you don't believe.*

Be among the first to learn of new releases: sign-up for her newsletter at https://BookHip.com/PCSWMCK. Book recommendations, updates on stories, and snippets from works-in-progress—plus a free Dancing Princesses story for signing up!

# ABOUT THE AUTHOR

Alea Henle writes non-fiction by day and fiction by night. Contemporary and historical fantasy, fantasy romance—and more! Check out her website www.aleahenle.com.

www.ingramcontent.com/pod-product-compliance
Lightning Source LLC
Chambersburg PA
CBHW061526210726
48287CB00006B/1842